Praise for the writing of Sedonia Guillone:

It's always a pleasure to read something new from **Sedonia Guillone**. *Aki's Love Song* is a sweet and sexy little read that encapsulates a lifetime's desire in a single night. Tamotsu is a thoughtful, likeable character and it's satisfying to see his love for Aki finally come to fruition. Though I prefer **Ms Guillone's** longer and more complex stories, *Aki's Love Song* would be a great taster story for those new to her work. ~ Fallen Angel Reviews

Sedonia Guillone has a very special love story in Aki's Love Song that blends friendship and love into a seamless thread that kept me wanting more. I was so touched I found myself teary- eyed in a few places in this short but touching story. ~ Two Lips Reviews

Ai Press books from Sedonia Guillone

Aki's Love Song

Taming Kate

Fallon's Jewel

Dedication

For Mitch, always

Acknowledgements

A million thanks to Ruth Axtell Morren for so much time spent editing this book. And to Les for the great cover. You two are awesome.

Trademark Acknowledgement

The author acknowledges the trademarked status and trademark owners of the following wordmarks mentioned in this work of fiction:

Manchester United: Manchester United Limited Corp.

Fallon's Jewel

Sedonia Guillone

Chapter One

Terran Outpost A, Earth year 2586

Falling, falling, surrounded by blue. Fluffy white clouds race heavenward as Kenji shoots down, and brown parched earth rushes up to meet him. A woman screams from above him, others scream below. He screws his eyes shut and gives rise to his mantra in preparation of death, for the moment his spirit departs from its physical encasement. Though only in his twelfth year of life, he's been preparing for death a long time now.

Closer and closer the hard-packed earth comes. Then stops. He is suddenly suspended, his sandaled feet mere inches above the ground. Something large and strong holds him back from death.

"I've got you," a voice says close to his ear. "You're safe now."

He gasps. A human being is holding him. A man in military uniform, wearing a jet pack.

Kenji looks up at him, but heavy goggles, black and shiny like a bug's eyes and a helmet obscure his features —

"Hey, Kenji, how about a kiss?"

The voice dispelled the vision. Kenji blinked and collected himself then looked around to see if Spike was nearby and would reprimand him. The vision came regularly, even during the middle of a busy shift and as always, immobilized him.

"Kenji! You ignoring me?"

Still savoring the ghostly feel of those strong arms

around him, Kenji yanked his bar towel from where it rested on his shoulder, wiped the bar surface and hung the towel on its hook, the signal his shift was over. Grabbing his jacket, he lifted the small hinged door that would let him out from behind the bar. *I've got you. You're safe now* the man's voice teased his brain, made his body tingle—

"Kenji!"

Now he turned.

Bud, one of the roughneck patrons just back from Earth leaned over the bar, waggling his eyebrows. Apparently, booze hit a man harder when he was changing atmospheres. The man's shaved head gleamed with sweat under the lights. In the background, someone hooted loudly at the live erotic show going on in the next room.

The whispery remnants of the vision receded into the heavy feeling which plagued him so often. Bud was a nice enough guy but he wasn't…never mind. That was a fantasy. He worked a smile onto his lips so as not to hurt Bud's feelings. "Just on the forehead, Bud, remember?"

Disappointment shifted through the other man's stubbled, sweaty face. He gave an exaggerated sigh, causing the acrid smell of gin to puff between them. "Well, all right. If that's the only way I'll get one."

"Yeah, sorry." He retrieved his bar towel and wiped the man's forehead.

"Damn, Kenji, am I that bad?"

"Do I have to answer?"

Bud grinned. "No. Just give me that kiss."

Smiling, Kenji leaned forward and planted a small kiss

10

on the lines across the man's forehead. Some day with the right guy, he'd give in to temptation and do it on the lips. But not until then. That is, if he didn't already have someone out there…

Bud's face darkened and his bleary eyes got a bit of a dreamy look. "Shit, Kenji, you're hot. And that eye patch, that really does it for me."

Kenji's cheeks heated and he was glad for the dim light. Bud wasn't the first guy to want favors from him. Many of them wished he was a hustler instead of a bartender so they could sample more of him for a fee. Spike would let him switch over if he wanted to, but it didn't feel right. If only he could remember. Did he already have a…lover out there, somewhere? Maybe on Earth? So, instead, he poured drinks, Stellar Beer and Stellar Gin, and sometimes the more expensive stuff imported from Earth. There weren't many choices this far away from the mother planet.

But the men who came to Spike's didn't care about choices. They were mostly space cowboys, off-duty Intergalactic Space Patrol agents and bounty hunters coming to cut loose, get drunk and get some action with a hustler in one of the small back rooms reserved for the purpose. Bud, a regular, was one of them, coming in every couple of weeks after one of his treasure-hunting stints around the galaxies.

"Kenji." Bud was, practically hanging over the edge of the bar, his eyes hungry and dreamy, as if Kenji's lips had delivered a spell.

Kenji chuckled though he took a step back. "What is it, Bud?"

"When are you going to give in to my charms? I could show you a really good time." In spite of his inebriation, Bud sounded mostly sincere. But as badly as Kenji wanted sex, Bud wasn't the one, even with a shower and a shave and some breath improvement. He sighed. "Sorry, Bud. You're a good guy. It's just—"

"I know, I know. You must be saving yourself for Mr. Right."

"Yeah, I guess so."

Bud grinned. "I hope you find him."

Relieved he hadn't hurt Bud's feeling too badly, Kenji smiled at him. "Thanks."

Just then, one of the hustlers, James, a good-looking blond in a fancy suit, came up and seated himself next to Bud. Within moments, the two were headed to the back rooms.

Shaking his head with a smile, he grabbed his jacket and lifted the bar door again. His pockets were weighed down with tips, enough to pay this month's rent for the little room across from the marketplace. It wasn't much, but it was close to Mr. Matsuoto and his wife, the kind folks who'd looked after him when he'd shown up, naked and wandering in a daze, not even knowing where he'd come from or remembering how he'd gotten there. All he'd known was his first name and all he still remembered after three months. The Matsuotos were his only family, his only link to any kind of belonging.

Working his way through the maze of leather-clad bodies, he made it halfway to the door and stopped. The vision came again, the blue sky, the falling. It felt so real, he couldn't move. The sensation of strong arms holding him, the voice telling him he was safe, held him rooted. Bumped and jostled, assaulted by the stench of sweat, smoke and stale beer, he stood, unmoving. The screech of music and the guffaws of carousing guys thundered around him, yet all he felt was the ghostly arms, a warm safe touch that contrasted starkly with the lonely quiet of the rented room waiting for him.

When this vision first started, it had been weak enough to ignore. But each night at the end of his shift, it got stronger and stronger, rousing an ache deep within him, making him toss and turn on his thin mattress. Tonight, the thought of going back to his apartment, alone, to sleep, was unbearable.

Retracing his steps, he worked his way back toward the bar and seated himself on a stool.

Dan, the other bartender whose shift was only half over, came up to him. "You're sticking around tonight, Kenji?" he shouted over the raucous laughter and jeers at the erotic show. Kenji recognized the nature of the shouting. At this point, the performers were getting to the penetration of bodily orifices on both ends.

He nodded and accepted a glass of fizzy water with some kind of fruity flavor in it. Dan knew he didn't drink spirits. "Yeah. I thought I'd hang around here...you know, unwind a little."

"I know how it is." Dan winked at him and rushed off to serve someone waving a handful of credits at him.

Kenji sipped his fizzy water and listened to the sounds around him.

"Yeah, give it to him!" came a shout from the other room. Kenji forced himself not to lean from his stool in such a way as to be able to see the stage. If it was the same show he'd caught sight of a few times already, one muscular man had been on his knees in front of another, a gracefully slim guy, hands on his hips, sucking his cock while a third man knelt behind the sucking man and was having intercourse with him, pumping in and out of his ass. Kenji had stared, shock keeping him glued, then something else. His body came to life. Blood pumped straight to his groin, causing an erection that had been painful. Since then, he'd avoided the show.

That night he'd done something he hadn't done since waking up with no memory. He'd relieved the ache in his groin with his hand, feeling as if he tasted some forbidden act yet helpless to stop. The memory of those three men had been driving him to madness. He didn't know why the physical act seemed so illicit, but the feeling had persisted.

Seeking to distract himself, he took another sip, surveying the patrons over the rim of his glass. He allowed himself that little game, the fantasy search for the man he was looking for. The one Bud called Mr. Right.

But most of the guys were ones he saw all the time. Dirty and unshaven, clad in black leather, heavy boots and holsters for weapons, which Spike strictly demanded were checked in at the door. Some of the guys were good-looking, Kenji could see underneath the dirt and stubble, while others were too rough for his taste. Once in a while he found himself imagining one or another of them in bed with him, kissing, stroking each other's cocks, sucking, licking...

A gust of cooler air breezed through, pulling Kenji from a burgeoning fantasy. He looked in the direction of the door, closing in the wake of yet another brawny patron.

Kenji's heart beat a little harder.

The man — a stranger to him--checked his weapon.

Tall. Broad shoulders. Muscular chest straining against a white T-shirt. Dark, close-cropped hair, nice sideburns.

This one was different. Kenji's mouth went dry.

This one was hot.

By his clean-cut appearance Kenji guessed he was a cop. That was nothing unusual in this place. But there was something about the way he moved — deliberate — smooth, relaxed yet tightly wound, like he could spring in a second, that kept Kenji's attention riveted.

At that second, the guy looked up. His eyes made a brief yet slow survey of the crowded room. And then they landed on Kenji.

Kenji couldn't tell what color they were from this distance, but he could feel them. They seemed to burn down into his very soul. They seemed to know who he was even when Kenji himself didn't know.

Everything in the roomful of rowdy tattooed, leather-clad space junkies, space cowboys and bounty hunters receded. He was more captured than he was during one of his visions.

And then he began to walk toward Kenji, his eyes never leaving Kenji's, his brawny torso flexing with each step.

Was it a few seconds or minutes before the guy stood before him, so close to his barstool that Kenji could see the dark stubble covering the strong line of his chin and jaw? So close that he caught a whiff of something spicy? Cologne that made Kenji's groin tingle.

The man pointed to the empty stool. "Is this seat taken?" He had a nice smile and incredible eyes, the color of the blue through which Kenji was falling in his recurring

15

vision. Yet in those eyes was a touch of sadness the grin didn't dispel.

Kenji blinked, only just noticing the stool next to him had been vacated within the last few seconds by the hustler sitting there. He must have gotten a hit and taken his customer to the back rooms. "I was saving it for you," he heard himself say. And froze. What had possessed him? He'd never spoken like that to anyone.

A throaty chuckle. "That so "Well, this *is* my lucky night, isn't it?" He seated himself and held out a hand. "Jake Fallon, Intergalactic Space Patrol."

So he *was* a cop. Kenji accepted the offer of handshake. Warm. Strong. Nice. "Kenji."

"Pleased to meet you, Kenji," Jake Fallon said. "What are you drinking?"

Nice accent too. From England. On Earth. A bunch of the guys who came here were from England. Though they had a variety of accents, Kenji had heard this one before with its lightly rolled "r's."

"Just fizzy water," he answered finally. He raised his glass, now wishing he'd gotten something stronger. Fizzy water was so...not cool. "It's not...loaded."

Jake Fallon looked at him a moment. A tiny grin flashed across his nicely curved lips. "I see. Well, I'll have that too then." He signaled the bartender, causing the muscles in his back to strain against his T-shirt. Dan came and took his order, leaving Fallon free to turn back to him.

Kenji swallowed hard and stared down into the clear, bubbling water in his glass. His heart pounded and he wiped his palms off on his pants. "I've...never seen you here before," he said. And almost slapped his forehead. How lame was that?

Sadness flitted through the other man's blue eyes. "I haven't been here in a long time." He sighed just as Dan placed his order in front of him. Fallon lifted his glass, his sad look replaced with a grin. "As we say back in Manchester, cheers," he said, and clinked it against Kenji's glass.

He watched Fallon take a drink, his head tilted back enough that Kenji could watch the muscles in his throat work as he swallowed. Shifting on his barstool, he hoped the other man couldn't see the tightening in his cock, which started to push against his trousers. "You're from Manchester?"

"Yeah, originally. But I've been flying through space for so long now I feel more alien than anything else." He chuckled. "What about you?"

Kenji stiffened. Good question. Where was he from? He shrugged. "Around here."

Fallon paused. Then a look slipped into his face, something that said, *I understand, you can't tell me.* Lots of fugitives stalked the Terran outposts, secretive about their origins. They provided much lucrative fodder for the bounty hunters who'd proliferated with humankind's reach into space. "No worries, Kenji. It doesn't matter."

He remained silent and filled the moment with sipping his drink.

"In answer to your comment about not having seen me here before," Fallon said, "I lost my partner a couple of years ago. A fire at ISP headquarters. This was a place we used to come on our nights off when we were in this sector." He sighed and took another large sip. "I figured it's about time to be getting on with things."

That must be the sadness he'd seen in Fallon's eyes. Whoever the dead man was, Fallon must have really loved him to have stayed away for so long. His fingers tightened on his own glass. "I'm sorry," he said finally.

Fallon nodded. "Thanks, Kenji." He sipped his drink, eyeing Kenji with a thoughtful expression. "May I ask you a personal question?"

Kenji's heart thumped, but he shrugged, trying to appear casual. He didn't know what else to do in his first real conversation with someone he was attracted to. "Sure."

The other man tilted his head. "You seem...different from the usual patrons here. You're more, um, refined. Are you..." he gestured toward one of the hustlers on the other side of the bar, a guy named Pieter.

Kenji blinked. "You mean a...hustler?"

Fallon grimaced. "Sorry. That was rude of me. I'm so out of practice."

Kenji smiled. No insult there. The hustlers *were* more refined looking for the most part. It was the contrast between them and their roughneck clients that got them paid. "No. I'm a bartender here. For the last few months." He glanced down into his drink before continuing. "I usually leave after my shift, but I tonight I...was in the mood to hang around."

Fallon leaned a bit closer, bringing that great scent with him. The energy of his maleness so close sent shivers through Kenji's body, all the way to his toes. "I'm glad you waited, Kenji. I wouldn't have met you, had you left."

Kenji looked up. Again, Fallon was so close, their lips were mere inches away. Kenji caught himself tilting in closer.

"Jake Fallon, hey!"

Kenji jerked away. Bud had returned from the back room and now stood right behind Fallon, thumping him on the back in a rough greeting.

"Hi, Bud. Long time." Fallon swiveled on his stool and offered the other man his hand.

Bud pumped Fallon's hand and gripped his shoulder with his other hand. "Good to see you, man! Where ya been?" Before Fallon could answer, Bud turned a bemused look to Kenji then back. "You lucky fuckin' dog, Fallon! Kenji here doesn't let anyone within three feet of his fine little body." He winked in Kenji's direction. "I should know. I been trying to get him into bed ever since he showed up in this place. He resists me like the plague."

Kenji frowned at him, his cheeks burning. "Behave, Bud."

Bud grinned. "No hard feelings, Kenji. I know you been waiting for the right guy to come along." He winked at Fallon. "He doesn't come out and say that. It's just obvious." With a final shake of his head, he added, "You are in for a treat. Mm…mmm."

How humiliating. Unbearably so. What would Fallon think of him now? He didn't want to know. Best to get away. With a quick glance at Fallon, he mumbled, "Well, I gotta go."

Without giving Fallon a chance to react, Kenji slid off the barstool and started to jostle his way through the press of smelly male bodies. But before he got more than two steps away, a large hand closed gently on his shoulder, ushering him around. Until he was pressed lightly up against Fallon's broad front.

The corner of Fallon's lips turned up in a sexy way. "Slow down, mate." His blue eyes searched Kenji's, as if trying to read his thoughts. "You bothered by what Bud said?" A large hand squeezed his shoulder. "The guy is a bit of a wanker but he means well."

Kenji swallowed, finding it hard to speak for a second. He shook his head, trying to convey his agreement.

"Hey, don't be embarrassed. I can't think of any bloke who'd want to take him to bed."

Kenji had to chuckle and Fallon's answering grin made the remaining tension in Kenji's body relax.

The next second Fallon's grin evaporated and his eyes took on a serious look. "But, uh, if there's any truth in what Bud said, then I'm flattered." He squeezed Kenji's shoulder again, the touch like a warm brand passing right through his thin white shirt and onto his skin.

Kenji's good eyelid fluttered a bit as heat invaded his body.

Fallon's hand moved from Kenji's shoulder to his chin, chucking it. "So, do you like me enough to get out of here together?"

Yes. Had anyone else asked the question, it would have been an automatic *no.* Kenji nodded before he could lose his nerve. Something about Fallon made him feel...safe.

Fallon smiled. "Great. I know a place we can go." His hand moved down the length of Kenji's arm and grasped his hand. Before Kenji could second guess his assent, Fallon was leading him through the crowd, his brawn pushing through the bodies more easily than Kenji ever could have. A few moments for Fallon to retrieve his weapon from the check by the door, then, "I know where we can—uh--get a room." He led Kenji out the door, into the still Terran air. But then he hesitated. "I know it's...fast." For a moment he seemed almost shy. "That is, if you still want to."

Kenji gave his hand a small squeeze. "I want to."

Fallon nodded, seeming relieved. "Good." He gestured with the hand that still held Kenji's. "It's just a couple blocks away in that direction."

For several moments they walked in silence, their joined hands just swinging slightly. "Strange as it may sound, Kenji, I don't make a habit of picking blokes up and taking them to a room." Fallon grinned across at him. "I don't expect you to believe me, either. You probably hear that kind of line all the time."

Kenji's heart flipped over. "No—I don't. I mean, I *do,* but I—I believe you." Not that it mattered. ISP agents came and went. They had a few hours' leisure time and were gone again, working in the deep reaches of space.

Fallon stared hard at him a second then gave a quick nod. "I'm glad." A moment later he stopped in front of a decrepit brick building. Kenji recognized the kind of three-story structure used for one-night flops in this sector. A flashing neon sign lit Fallon's skin on and off blue, like his eyes. "This is it," Fallon said and pushed open a creaky door, still without letting go of Kenji's hand, which Kenji found oddly comforting. "Not a fancy place, I regret, but affordable with a hot shower."

"It's fine." Kenji smiled at him though his heart continued to pound. So many times he'd imagined doing this with someone and never had. Now he really was…

At Fallon's insistence, Kenji waited for him in the vestibule while Fallon went to rent the room and get the key from a tired-looking desk clerk with a tobacco stick hanging from between his lips. The man handed him a pile of towels. When Fallon returned, Kenji offered to carry them then followed Fallon up a flight of dimly lit stairs. The place didn't seem any different really than his apartment house.

Except for the various moans and groans emanating from behind some of the closed doors they passed. Kenji stared at them, thinking of what was transpiring behind them. Things he and Fallon would probably be doing in just a few minutes —

"Here we are, Kenji." Fallon stopped in front of one door which unlocked and held open, gesturing with a flourish and a smile. "Not the Terran Towers, but the sheets should be clean."

With a swallow, Kenji stepped over the threshold into the dark room. Fallon closed the door behind them and flipped on a light switch. "Let me take those," he said, retrieving the towels from Kenji and setting them on a nearby table. He slipped off his weapons holster and set it on the table next to the towels. "You want a drink?" He opened the door to a small cooler. "Well stocked, I see."

Kenji figured they charged for the drinks, and he wasn't thirsty anyway. Just nervous. "No, thanks."

Fallon closed the small door and came over to him. Those large hands covered his shoulders and began gently massaging them. Kenji felt himself tremble at the warm

22

contact. As far as he knew, no one had touched him even this much. Fallon's blue eyes simmered down into his. "Seems we both have our reasons for the rush," he said softly.

Kenji couldn't answer. His heart pounded so hard and his mind was so muddled, he could only stare into the other man's rugged face. Without thinking, he reached up and placed his hand, palm down, on the left side of Fallon's chest. Rock hard muscle quivered under his touch. Just underneath, he felt the beat of Fallon's heart.

"May I ask you another personal question, Kenji?" Fallon's voice was lower now, huskier. Yet uncertainty tainted the blue of his eyes.

"Sure." His voice came out sounding anything but sure.

"If what Bud said was true, then why me? Why now?" Fallon's large hands continued their sensuous kneading, causing Kenji to relax and become almost drowsy.

Kenji didn't answer right away. He couldn't. No words formed in his mind. For several moments, he let his hand roam across Fallon's chest, over the furrow between his pectoral muscles to the other side, even as he felt himself mesmerized by the motion of Fallon's fingertips on his shoulders. His breathing deepened and slowed.

There was just something about Fallon, something...good. Something that reminded him of his recurring vision. The falling and being caught. The steady sure voice telling him he was safe. He couldn't quite identify what it was or how he knew. He just did. His body knew it, too, felt it deep down. "It's just you," he said finally. "It's just—" he shrugged helplessly.

Fallon's fingertips tilted his chin up a bit. His eyes were

dark now, hungry, yet the hint of sadness remained. "I understand. I feel it too." He leaned in and closed his lips over Kenji's.

Wow. Nothing had prepared him for something this incredible. And this was only a soft touching of lips. What else was in store for him tonight?

Fallon's lips took their time exploring his. Back and forth they went, rubbing against Kenji's until they parted and a soft moan escaped. Kenji's eyelids fluttered closed. His body leaned into Fallon's as his legs found it harder to support him.

Or was Fallon pulling him closer? Fallon's hands tightened on his shoulders. Their chests pressed together, Fallon's a bit higher because he was taller. Fallon groaned and slipped his tongue between Kenji's lips.

The sensation was strange, raw, hot and wet. Flavors and textures Kenji couldn't have imagined before now flooded him. Another human being's lips against his. Fallon's tongue dancing with his. Fallon's scent filling his nostrils, seeping inside of him they were standing so close.

Fallon's hands slid around to his back, rubbing in wider, more feverish rounds. Their kiss became a wild chafing of lips and tongues until Fallon pulled away, eyelids low, back heaving. "Kenji, you are luscious," he breathed, then moved in again and closed his lips against the side of Kenji's neck.

The warm feathering of Fallon's tongue sent jolts of heat right to Kenji's cock. He tilted his head to the side, receiving a more fervent tongue massage in response. Indeed, Fallon seemed to be devouring him, as if the mere feel and taste of his skin drove him wild. Kenji felt his shirt

24

being lifted from his trousers, followed by bare hands against his back muscles.

Wow, he thought again, his body swept up in a possessive tide. One of Fallon's hands slid around to his chest. Fingertips brushed his nipple, sending zings of heat down to his groin. Fallon kissed every inch of his neck, over and over, returning to the places he'd just moistened with hot kisses as if he couldn't get enough, even as his thumb and forefinger rubbed and pinched Kenji's nipple, until Kenji stood on his tiptoes, wanting more.

When Fallon pulled back again, he yanked Kenji's t-shirt all the way over his head, forcing his arms to lift. The next second, he was bare-chested, the t-shirt tossed on the floor. Kenji shivered slightly, his instinct causing him to wrap his arms about his torso.

"Cold?"

Kenji shook his head.

Fallon grinned at him. "I see. Your first time, eh?"

I don't know. But it sure felt like the first. At least the first in his memory. That counted, right? Slowly he nodded.

"Ah. Don't worry then, I know well enough what to do." Fallon pulled off his own shirt, threw it aside and reached out for Kenji's arms again.

Kenji stared at Fallon's bare chest, his mind melting into a warm mush, his vision blurring. The guy's chest was broad, hard, and dusted in the upper portion between his nipples with soft black hair. And oh, those nipples. Tawny, flat disks that made Kenji want to pinch and play with them. Was that what he should do, though?

"I know you're new at this." Fallon wrapped his

brawny arms around him and whispered in his ear. "Don't worry, I'll guide you."

Kenji jumped. His hands tightened on Fallon's back muscles.

Fallon stilled then pulled slightly away. "Kenji, what is it? Did I do something bad?"

Kenji stared up at him, captured by the blue of Fallon's eyes. So much like the sky. "No," he murmured finally. "It's all right."

Fallon smoothed back Kenji's hair, his face relieved. "Good. I wouldn't want to frighten you."

"You didn't." Fallon's caress on Kenji's hair made him melt again. He became aware of Fallon's hard back muscles under his hands. The awareness grew, spread through his body, into his cock.

Fallon's lids lowered. He leaned in and nuzzled the side of Kenji's neck again.

Kenji sighed and tilted his head back. The sensation of falling took him over again and he sagged in Fallon's arms, held firmly in place.

Then they were moving. Kenji felt as if his world were tilting this way and that. Something soft met his back then he found himself lying on the bed, Fallon's body over his, pushing him down into the mattress.

Fallon gulped at Kenji's lips and tongue greedily, one hand smoothing back his hair, a caress that contrasted strangely with the hunger of their kisses. Fallon's hips moved against his in a short, rhythmic pulse that made Kenji's whole body weak. The hard bulge of Fallon's cock against his...oh, another sensation he couldn't ever have imagined. He'd thought of it so many times, dreamed of it while rubbing himself to release these past months, discovering what his body could do. But the reality? Beyond words. All he could was clutch Fallon's back and hold on.

Fallon's hand slipped between them and worked open his own belt, then Kenji's. Kenji grew aware that they both still wore their boots, but Fallon didn't seem to notice. His lips still over Kenji's, Fallon was working his pants and underwear down, then working Kenji's down.

The space around them grew hot, the air filled with the scent of two bodies having sex, a musky, feral scent that evaporated all thought. Something in Kenji slipped away. He answered Fallon's kisses with equal fervor, then lifted his ass off the bed as much as he could so that Fallon could work his underwear down far enough that their bare cocks could rub together.

"Oh, Kenji." Fallon breathed against his skin. "I'll try to go slow."

Bending one knee and bracing it on the mattress, Fallon ground their cocks together, a slow even rhythm that pulled a deep breath from Kenji each time. Heaven, he thought, eyes closed, this was absolute heaven. And moved against Fallon, instinctively.

"Ahhh." Fallon groaned and moved faster. "You're making me crazy, Kenji." He thrust his hips, over and over, harder and faster, sliding their cocks against one another while his kisses licked deep into Kenji's mouth. Kenji clutched the other man's ass cheeks, gripping hard, round globes of muscle that flexed with each thrust.

Fallon pulled from their kiss, panting and groaning. "I won't last…much longer."

Kenji answered by clutching harder, pulling Fallon tighter against him. The absolute bliss his body had wanted all this time flooded him. He couldn't think, couldn't speak. Only rub. And then it happened. The unspeakably hot explosion. He saw his climax spurt, felt the spasms grip his body.

Fallon saw it too, his eyes darkening yet more, as if the sight made him hungrier. He rubbed against Kenji, several hard, quick strokes before his body stiffened. He groaned, head tilted back, eyes screwed shut. Hot cum splashed between them, coating Kenji's chest, splattering his face and neck. Then he collapsed, one hand laced into Kenji's hair.

Kenji lay pressed beneath Fallon's largeness, unable to move, but not caring. He stared up at the cracks in the ceiling, feeling a smile on his lips, his body drained in the most pleasant way. He slid his hands up to Fallon's back and rested them there, following the rhythm of Fallon's breathing.

As the moments passed, the rise and fall of the larger man's breath slowed and grew more regular. The heart beating against his calmed.

Finally, Fallon levered himself up onto one elbow, taking off most of his weight from Kenji's body, though still half-covering it. "Sorry, hope I didn't crush you."

Kenji smiled lazily. "It's a good kind of crushed," he murmured.

Fallon's eyes grew serious. "Kenji, that was incredible."

He nodded. "It was."

"I'm sorry it didn't last longer. I…it's been a long time. I was pent up."

28

"Me, too."

Fallon's gaze on his, he kissed Kenji softly, his eyes gradually closing. Their lips lingered together, Fallon brushing his lips over Kenji in tiny back and forth movements then lazily slipping his tongue in and tasting him. Finally he lifted away and gazed back down at Kenji. One hand toyed with Kenji's hair. "You made my first time back great, Kenji. Better than I could ever have imagined." He touched Kenji's cheek. "I'll always be grateful for that."

The look in Fallon's eyes made Kenji's heart flip over again. The only word he could use to describe it was…tender. He had to say something in return. It wasn't right to let Fallon open up that way and not respond. "You, too," he murmured. "You made it…perfect." He wanted to say it was his first time, but he didn't really know and didn't want to lie. But it had felt like it. If it *was* his first time, he was glad it had happened with Fallon.

A tiny smile played over Fallon's lips. "That's good to hear." He was quiet a few moments, just sifting Kenji's hair through his fingers and looking down at him. "Will you be here in a month? That's when I can come back."

Kenji let his hand slide up and touched Fallon's dark hair. It was soft. So soft. He pushed his fingers through it, burrowing as much as he could into the shortness. "I plan to be here. I'll save your spot at the bar."

Fallon smiled. He had an incredible smile, and sexy dimples that made a tiny crinkle in each cheek. "Can I call you before that? Do you have a telescreen?"

He could use the telescreen at the Matsuotos. It was the one luxury they'd been able to afford and had offered to let him use it if he needed. "I have one I can use."

"I'll call you if you give me the access number."

"It's in my pocket."

Fallon's grin widened. "Good. That's wonderful. I'll get it later." He leaned down and brushed a hot kiss over Kenji's lips. "In the meantime, I have a few more hours. There's more we can do, if you want to."

Kenji slid his fingers into Fallon's hair again, smiled and pulled him down for a kiss. If he was going to wait another whole month for Fallon, he was going to get in as much as possible. "Yeah, I want to."

Chapter Two

One month later…

No! No! I beg you! Kenji thrashed around, flailing his arms, clawing at the hands holding him down. To no avail. There were so many of them, their combined strength overwhelmed him, forcing him onto his back. One large hand clamped on his forehead, immobilizing him. A loud buzz thundered in his ears. Something whirred in the air above his face. Lower and lower it came. Shiny, Sharp. Glinting steel, heading right for his eye…

Kenji sat bolt upright, panting. Cold heat prickled along the bare skin of his back and shoulders, coursing down into his abdomen and groin. He sweated so hard, the sheet stuck to his heaving chest. He covered his face with his hands, as if to protect it from the ghastly tool that always went for his left eye.

The nightmare. Again.

Breathe, Kenji, breathe. He inhaled deeply while his own subconscious screams still rang in his ears. No matter how many times he realized it was not really happening, relief always shuddered through him to find his ankles and wrists unshackled and to find his own thin yet soft mattress and sheets under his body.

The *drip drip* of the sink in the corner began to replace the hideous images. He sighed. Grady, that poor excuse for a landlord, had promised to fix the thing. *Last month.* If it hadn't been for the regulated atmosphere of Terran A, the place would probably also be crawling with roaches and other vermin, the way he heard was the case in some places back on Earth.

Uncovering his face, he peered around. The haven of his rented room hadn't disappeared during his sleep. Not today. The dingy walls with their network of cracks in the plaster still surrounded him. Ratty but comfortable, with the red velvet reclining chair—the one he'd dragged up from the dumpster in the alleyway—in the opposite corner, and the table with his golden statue on it still there, the one possible clue to his existence and an object which, inexplicably, gave him great solace.

He pushed back the covers and lifted himself from the bed. The statue drew him, the way it always did, making him want to kneel before it and just sit there, hands on his thighs, head bowed, his good eye closed. Those moments in front of the statue before getting ready for work were an absolute must, as if the statue itself gave him the strength to get through each day.

The thing had always been in his possession even though he couldn't remember how he'd gotten it in the first place. Somehow, though, it anchored him, a possible connection to his parents—whoever they might have been. And he *must* have had parents. No one came into existence without them. No one was just plunked down onto a planet of any kind, fully grown, to work as a bartender in a club for roughnecks who liked other men. He prayed the answers would come eventually and give him back whatever existence he had before forgetting. Even if it was worse than this, at least he'd know who he was.

Raising his face, he opened his eye and looked at it—the perfect likeness of a round, plump man seated cross-legged, one hand on his thigh, from which dangled what appeared to be a chain of beads. Seemingly nondescript at first glance, something in the man's expression held him whenever he looked at it. Lips curved upward into a smile that seemed to be for nothing in particular. Perhaps a satisfaction in existence itself, the look of a person with nothing at all to worry about. Not life, death, survival, or even loneliness. As if somehow he'd understood it all and it could no longer cause him suffering.

"Who am I?" he whispered to the statue. Of course, the statue didn't answer, but somehow, it made him feel better simply to voice his question to it. How he longed to know, especially now, since he'd met Fallon. It was so frustrating not to be able to have a normal conversation with the man. After a month of telescreen conversations, Fallon still thought him a refugee unable to reveal his true identity, as he'd come to believe during their very first exchange.

Tonight, however, if all went well, they'd be speaking in person. During their most recent telescreen call the night before last, Fallon had promised to be there on his bar stool when Kenji got to Spike's. He didn't even mind that he'd have to wait for Kenji to finish his shift before they got to be alone.

Aside from the solace he took from his statue, nothing had helped him pass the month better than seeing Fallon's face on the telescreen, his blue eyes, the way their soft color contrasted with his dark, short-cropped hair and offset the rugged look of his cheeks and jaw. And then there were the memories — those few hours they'd spent together in the love hotel, their naked bodies crowded onto that little bed together, licking and sucking and tasting every inch of each other until it was time to leave. Fallon had shown Kenji things he'd never dreamed of. Glimpsing those erotic acts on the stage was one thing. *Experiencing* them? A different universe!

Even now, thinking about it, he shivered. A frisson of heated energy travelled through his whole body, right down into his cock.

After bringing each other to climax with their mouths three times that night, dawn had lightened that hotel room, forcing them to get out of the bed even though neither of them had slept five minutes. Reluctantly, they'd risen then showered together—another first for Kenji. Before stepping into the hot water, Fallon had chuckled. "Kenji, don't you want to take the eye patch off first?"

His insides had clenched. The last thing he wanted was for Fallon to see the damaged eye, get grossed out and not want to be with him again. He'd shaken his head. "No. It stays on."

Fallon had shrugged his broad shoulders, grinning, yet compassion slipped into his gaze. "Very well, then, keep it on," he's said and held the curtain aside for Kenji to get in before him. Fallon had soaped Kenji's body and then Kenji had done the same, loving the slide of his soapy hands over Fallon's broad muscles. Of course, that had gotten them going enough for another quickie under the hot spray before they got out, dried each other off and dressed. Parting had truly been sad.

His body already tingling with anticipation, Kenji turned the sink on and splashed tepid water on his face. He wanted to go back to the same room in that place. That hot shower was nice, a luxury he didn't have in this room, and Fallon deserved better than this dingy little room. He dried his face and looked at himself in the cracked mirror. Time to get ready. He'd even bought a new suit especially to wear for Fallon.

Setting the bowl of warm water on the table, he dipped

the washrag in and wrung it out. Catching a glimpse of his reflection in the dressing mirror, he paused. Normally the question, who *am I?* usually rose. Usually he wondered what his parents looked like and which Asian country did they originate from. His only possible clue was his name which Mr. Matsuoto said was Japanese, but without a last name, he couldn't begin to find his family. They could be anywhere, on Earth or one of the Terran outposts.

Tonight, however, he wondered what Fallon had seen in him that had attracted him so powerfully. He certainly wasn't any better looking than the hustlers at Spike's, was he? He smoothed the wet cloth over his chest. Instead, he remembered the feel of Fallon's hands and mouth on the smooth tanned gold of his skin. The other man had seemed to like his texture and flavor. He remembered the contrast of their bodies together, Fallon's brawn entwined with his slim, willowy musculature. Maybe Fallon had never been with a guy who looked like he did. Kenji was insanely curious. Maybe Fallon had only ever been with that man he'd loved. The one who'd been killed.

Fallon didn't even seem to care about his eye. And hadn't pressed about it when Kenji hadn't wanted to take off the patch to go in the shower. He couldn't imagine letting anyone see it and kept the patch on at all times except when he was home alone. Though he couldn't help but wonder.

What *would* Fallon think? Would he be repulsed? Accepting? Kenji looked at his eye now. So strange. Sightless, staring, a cloudy grayish-blue, the skin around it damaged, with a scar that ran up onto his brow and slightly down onto his cheek, a scar the patch never quite covered. Which only led to more questions. What had happened? Had he been born with his eye like this? So far, no one had asked him what had happened to his eye that he had to wear a patch, and even if they did, what could he say? '*I don't know,*' was the only answer he had for almost everything except how to pour a drink.

* * * * *

Fallon grinned as the edge of the Raidon Asteroid Belt came into view. He leaned back, setting the patrol pod into auto-cruise, and sipped his beer. Another hour and he'd be on Terran A. A few minutes after that he'd hopefully be seated on his stool at Spike's, waiting for Kenji to finish his shift. Maybe they could get a room in that place again, ratty as it was. He'd barely noticed. Kenji was intoxicating with his sleek ebony hair, tan skin and eye shaped like a perfect almond. In a word, the bloke was *hot*.

And Kenji gave just about the best blowjob Fallon had ever experienced. Once Fallon had shown him what to do. Hard to believe Kenji was that innocent. But he was. No one could fake that. Or the sweet depths in Kenji's eye that rocked him to his toes each time he looked into it.

Just thinking of Kenji made Fallon's cock stir in his pants. That one night together had done wonders for him. After Nicky, he'd felt dead even though his body kept going. For a little while, in Kenji's arms, he'd felt...*alive*.

Kenji's face appeared in Fallon's mind. Again. For the last month, the bloke had occupied an unusually large percentage of his thoughts.

Fallon took another sip of beer. The greenish gold light of an asteroid, reflecting the distant sun, glinted off his windshield. He glanced over at his companion in the co-pilot's seat. "What do you think, Mike? Spending too much time alone out here in this pod, aren't I? I'm starting to obsess."

Mike barked and then whined.

Fallon chuckled. "Sorry, pooch. Didn't mean to offend you. By *alone* I meant without another human." He reached out and ruffled the mutt's furry ears, then reached into the sack on the console and pulled out a piece of soy jerky, which he fed to the dog. "There," he said as Mike snapped up the fake meat, "I made it up to you." He ruffled Mike's ears again but the dog was oblivious to anything but his feast. A part of Mike would always be that emaciated stray who'd adopted Fallon on last year's stint to Earth on the trail of a perp. All Fallon had done was toss Mike a piece of the sandwich he'd been carrying. He couldn't stand to see the skinny mutt picking through garbage for a piece of rotting vegetable matter. Impressive the animal was even alive, considering most dogs had gone the way of other extinct species once there were insufficient meat sources in the world.

But the creature had followed him back to his pod and gone right up the ramp, hopping into the co-pilot's seat and refusing to leave. No matter, the chair was always empty anyway since Fallon hadn't ever replaced Nichols. It wasn't so easy to replace a partner you worked well with, in and out of bed. Which was why he'd transferred to the Patrol Division. Special Ops was no longer an option since…

A pang squeezed Fallon's chest. It was coming up on two years since Nicky had died in that fire. The report said that a faulty power core in ISP headquarters had shorted on Terran B, destroying a whole wing of the building. And Nicky happened to be in that wing at that moment.

He shook himself and crushed his now empty can, tossing it into the compactor. "I'm getting maudlin," he said out loud. Probably explained why his thoughts seemed so attached to Kenji after only one night and a few brief telescreen calls.

He started imagining what the coming night together might bring. Maybe Kenji would start by sitting him down and straddling him so they could kiss. Kenji had beautiful soft lips and had learned quickly just how to lick and nibble his lips and tongue while he stroked Fallon's hardening cock.

He'd definitely pull Kenji's shirt off as soon as possible out so he could run his hands over Kenji's sleekly muscled torso. He'd caressed Kenji's sleek narrow hips, causing Kenji to pant into his mouth. Maybe, if he was lucky, Kenji would slide down to his knees and suck his cock until his head felt it would spin into the asteroid belt outside Terran A's atmosphere—

Fallon pulled his attention back to piloting. There'd be time enough for the real thing once he got to Spike's. Since Nicky was gone, it was all he could handle. In the meantime, he did his job and spent a great deal of his traveling time talking out loud to Mike.

It really was time to get to Terran A.

Just then his telescreen crackled to life. "Headquarters to Fallon. Come in. Are you there?" The chief's fleshy face came into focus on the screen.

Fallon flicked the switch to open communication. "I'm here, Chief. Almost to Terran A."

"Can you give me your exact location?"

Fallon frowned. He checked his coordinates and repeated them to the chief. "Is there a problem?"

38

"Well, not enough of a problem to cut into your R and R. But I thought you should know. McCray is wandering around on Terran A. He's probably on the hunt but as long as you're there, I'd like you to keep tabs on him."

Fallon heaved a sigh. Figured that one of the universe's most troublesome bounty hunters would cross paths with him on a rare weekend of leisure. "Sure thing, Chief. Do you have any details on his activity?"

"I hadn't checked Channel X yet. I was going to have you do that while you're en route. I contacted you as soon as I'd heard of his whereabouts."

"All right, Chief. I'll take a look and then keep an eye out for him."

His superior nodded. "I knew I could depend on you. Over and out."

Fallon saluted the chief and switched to Channel X, a continuous newscast of all the bounty hunters working the occupied galaxies under jurisdiction of the Intergalactic Council. The actual surface area this covered wasn't terribly large yet, since space habitation was only a couple of centuries old, but it was growing all the time and with that growth came the proliferation of bounty hunters. Most of them were legit enough, but there was the occasional complete scumbag like McCray who had no regard for civilian safety when it came to catching his bounty.

Sitting back, Fallon watched the twinkling of distant stars through his windshield while the report droned on in the background.

After several minutes, Mike whined for another piece of jerky. Fallon leaned over to fish around in the bag.

"Next bounty hunter profile," the female announcer said, "Jethro McCray."

Fallon froze and focused his attention on the telecast. Absently handing the dried treat to Mike, he felt it being snapped up from his hand as he listened to the report.

A picture flashed onto the telescreen. Yeah. That was McCray all right. Typical bounty hunter with his stringy black hair, menacing scowl and ever-present growth of scrubby beard.

Another bit of time passed with a rundown of McCray's activities for the past couple of years.

"Come on, come on," Fallon muttered. "Get to it already. Am I going to be able to relax, or not?"

"Jethro McCray is currently on Terran A, having arrived there at oh-eight hundred hours Earth time," the voice reported. "The source of his employment for this bounty remains undisclosed."

"You mean *unknown*," Fallon said though Mike was the only one to hear him. They always used the word *undisclosed* when the hiring party was as scummy as the bounty hunter, *or* when the bounty wasn't a criminal. ISP were only obligated to regulate the hunters, not the hirers. Better that way. Fallon and the rest of ISP had their hands full enforcing the laws which regulated the activities of space-traveling bounty hunters. His ears pricked up as the report continued.

"A series of attacks across all space outposts are suspected to have a connection to McCray's current pursuit. Victims are males roughly in their mid-twenties, of Asian race."

Fallon's fingers tensed on the steering column. That

described Kenji. He focused on the next words.

"The attacks have been brutal, leaving each victim blinded in the left eye. The cause for this pattern is as yet unknown, but All ISP personnel are instructed to bring McCray into custody."

Fallon's heartbeat increased by the thrum of tension through his body. *The left eye*. The report switched to the next bounty hunter, but Fallon was no longer listening. Switching off auto-cruise, he increased acceleration to maximum drive, his course set for the nearest landing station on Terran A, his eyes straining through the windshield, as if he could see straight to Terran if he looked hard enough. *Shite*. Kenji fit the exact description of the attack victims. Only, Kenji was already missing an eye. Or was he? The skin around it was scarred but that didn't mean the eye itself was missing. It explained why Kenji was so secretive about his identity. He was probably in hiding all this time.

He had to get to Terran A as soon as possible. He'd have gone directly to Kenji's home, if he'd known where it was. His back muscles tightened. The prospect that the seemingly harmless man could be in danger would have been distressing enough had Fallon never even met him. But he kind of knew Kenji and just didn't want anything bad to happen to him.

In minutes, the glowing orange-pink atmosphere of Terran A came into view. It wouldn't be much longer now and he'd be at Spike's.

Hopefully Kenji would be there too, unharmed and working his shift. Fallon flicked the controls furiously. Damn this shitbox for not having warp speed. Only the largest cruisers had such a device. He and Nicky had spent much time grumbling about the lack of power.

God knows, right now he needed it badly. Praying for Kenji's safety, Fallon set his course for Terran A.

Chapter Three

After a quick meal of steamed dumplings, Kenji opened the door to his tiny closet and lingered in front of his new suit, which hung alone on the rod. Had he bought the right color? It had looked good on him in the shop, but now he wasn't sure. His heartbeat sped up a bit. Why did it matter so much anyway? Fallon probably couldn't care less what he wore. Besides, Fallon was a cop in uniform. He probably wore the same thing all the time, a tight white t-shirt that strained against his beefiness and baggy olive drab pants tucked into heavy boots. There probably wasn't much room to store clothing in those tiny space pods the ISP guys flew around in.

He sighed and lifted his suit off the hanger. The coat of purple velvet, a bit longer than usual, made him look like a figure from a royal court from ancient Earth history. The shirt came next, a light lavender with ruffled cuffs and matching neck cloth that lay down the front, hiding the shirt buttons. Then close-fitting slacks, color to match the jacket, then his ankle boots with large shiny buckles. Those had cost him more credits than he cared to admit he'd ever spent.

In the mirror, he smoothed back his hair with enough gel to keep it off his face, except for one razor-thin lock he let fall over his forehead. He put on his eye patch and then checked his entire reflection, pleased with the effect of having taken extra pains with his appearance.

He turned to the side, knee bent in a dignified pose, then exhaled and moved away from the mirror. Why was he bothering? As if somehow Fallon was more than someone he'd spend a few hours with. He'd gotten used to the fact he was *alone*, except for the time he spent working at Spike's or sitting with the Matsuotos. That's the way it was. Not by a rational choice but from something visceral, a voice inside him that yelled, 'Alone! You must be alone!'

Not that it was terrible to be alone. Many hours of his time he spent just sitting quietly, eyes closed, the sounds of the traffic and marketplace nearby filtering through his window. He felt centered then, as if his body expanded to embrace all of existence.

Sometimes though, something was missing...something important.

One last look at his outfit and hair and he was ready.

Kenji pulled his door shut. It locked automatically with a click that echoed off the chipped plaster walls of the stairwell. As did his boot steps down the five flights of stairs. Out on the sidewalk, dusk had settled, though the marketplace was still in full swing, as most kiosks and restaurants stayed open pretty much around the clock to accommodate the swelling population of Terran City.

His building occupied the entire block on one side of the street, while the other side was taken up by the marketplace. Awnings with letters of every culture from Earth marked what was available in each stall. Vegetables crowded wagons while simulated meat formed into the shapes of animal carcasses hung in rows from the eaves of storefronts or roasted over flames; flowers exploded in blooms of colors, crowded into buckets of water; clocks crammed rickety shelves while dresses and hats, their racks stuffed beyond capacity, protruded into the narrow aisles. The air smelled of spices and baking bread from the large ovens constantly in use while music in various languages and sinuous foreign notes mixed with the shouts of sellers hawking their wares. Many of the people were directly from Earth while others came from generations of Terran A natives.

Halfway through the marketplace, Kenji stopped at a flower cart, drawn by the intoxicating scent of a ruffly pink bloom. Closing his eyes, he breathed in the aroma, an image in his mind of handing the flower to Fallon. His eyes popped open when the sound of a scream cut through the swirl of regular sounds. Jerking up from the flower, he listened, the hairs on the back of his neck standing up. The screaming escalated, coming from Asia Town, just at the end of the marketplace.

Kenji's heart flipped. The Matsuotos! He had to make sure they were okay. They weren't so young and if something was happening, he wasn't sure they could get away. He pushed his way in the direction of the sounds. The screams seemed to have multiplied, a chorus of terrified voices, accompanied by yelling and crashing, as if a kiosk were being destroyed.

Kenji's breath pumped hard with the quick acceleration of his sprint. In seconds he'd reached the Matsuotos. To Kenji's relief they were fine, both standing at the opening of their tiny restaurant, peering anxiously at the gathered crowd which hid the melee. "What's going on?" he asked them.

The elderly man shook his head, his eyes large. "I'm not sure. The crowd assembled so quickly, I've not been able to see anything."

Ignoring their cries of "Be careful," Kenji worked his way through the press of horrified people until he reached the center. He felt sick at the sight that greeted him.

A man lay on the ground, beaten and bleeding. His screams had died down to mere whimpers, his arms covering his face from his attacker.

Kenji lifted his gaze. Tables and chairs lay toppled and smashed. A huge, brutish man stood in the space, staring down at the battered man at his feet.

"He's looking for *you*," a female voice said behind him.

Kenji turned. The woman who'd spoken stood a mere breath away, her eyes fixed on him from beneath a dark hood. "Kenji, get away from here. You're in danger."

"You know my name. How —"

"There's no time to explain now. You must get away!"

He blinked, but when he opened his eye again, she was gone.

An icy shiver ripped through him. The part of him that wanted to know who she was pushed the concern away. Her message had been clear. Get away. He wanted to flee but horror kept his vision rooted to the man bleeding on the ground. Nausea vaulted upward in his gut. The brute had torn out the man's left eye, leaving a blooding socket with —

Rage and horror mingled in a storm inside him. Why had no one stopped this brute? How could he flee and leave this poor victim to his fate? The brute lifted his boot to kick the fallen man yet again.

"Get away from him!" Kenji yelled. Anger thrummed through his temples, making him ignore the woman's warning. He lunged forward just as the man's thick-soled boot connected with the victim's ribcage.

The attacker's eyes snapped to Kenji. Black stringy hair

surrounded a scarred, scowling, dirty face. His muscles bulged their way through his ripped shirt and pushed out the cross straps of magazine artillery over his chest.

A bounty hunter. A mean vicious one. Kenji recognized the type at once. Then he saw the hunter's gaze zoom in on his eye patch.

"You!" He jabbed a thick finger straight at Kenji. "What's behind that patch o' yours?"

Heart pounding, Kenji took a step back. If he was expecting the people around him to surround him and protect him, he was dead already. They were receding in a collective huddle, leaving him alone in the space they'd occupied.

"Kenji, come back here." Mr. Matsuoto materialized by his side. Kenji gently but firmly pushed him into the crowd. "Stay back, Matsuoto-san," he ordered and turned to his assailant.

"*You're* the one I want." The bounty hunter lunged at him.

Kenji bolted. The crowd parted for him and he raced through, his breath pumping through his chest. Dipping between two stalls, the tiny alleyway brought him to the street.

"Come back here!" he heard the bounty hunter shout just as Kenji reached the corner.

He leaped off the curb, missing a giant hover bus by an inch. The vehicle's driver slammed on the horn and a yell behind Kenji told him the bounty hunter had gotten trapped on the other side.

It bought Kenji a few seconds. He veered off into the

nearest alleyway. A fire escape ladder hung down and he grabbed it, scrambling up. The soles of his boots were too slippery but the adrenalin pumping through him drove him to the roof of the building. Once he'd climbed over onto the gravel top, he peered over.

The bounty hunter skidded to a halt below. Their gazes met. The hunter leaped onto the ladder.

Kenji's blood went icy hot. He raced across the roof, halted at the other side and looked over his shoulder. A large thick arm was reaching over. He gasped and crouched on the edge. It wasn't *too* terribly far to the next roof. He took the deepest breath he could, closed his eyes briefly, then leaped.

"Huh!" The impact of landing forced the breath from him. He took a second to regain his focus then took off again. Another fire escape on the side of this building allowed him to climb down and drop only a few feet to the ground. Catching his jacket on the ladder, a loud tear accompanied his landing. Kenji could feel the air circulate through the tear down the side seam.

He took off again without a look back. Spike's wasn't too far away but he didn't want the hunter to see him go inside. An idea came to him as he ran. Not stopping, he yanked off his jacket and worked open the buttons of his shirt. When both articles were off, he tossed them into an alleyway he passed. Maybe, if he was lucky, the bounty hunter would think he'd gone in that direction. A quick look over his shoulder told him he was enough ahead of the hunter not to —

Bam. Kenji ran into a something and bounced back. He blinked and the bounty hunter came into focus. His gaze met the hunter's glittering eyes.

The giant took a step toward him, a phazer brandished toward Kenji's chest. "Now," he muttered, "Show me what's behind your patch."

From the corner of his good eye, Kenji saw another giant hover bus turn the corner. "No," he panted, taking a step in the direction he needed to go.

The hunter lunged for him. Kenji wheeled around and leaped away, avoiding the large grasping hands by mere inches, and ran for the nearby curb. The approaching hover bus honked a warning but Kenji dove and lunged forward, missing the front of the bus by even less than he'd missed the hunter's grasp. The bus's blaring horn echoed in his mind, and blended with the hunter's curses. Kenji dove down and hid behind a parked taxi. He pulled open the door and climbed in, crouching down.

"Where to?" The cab driver didn't even look over his shoulder.

"Spike's."

Now the cabbie peered over the seat, brow furrowed. He was a heavy set older man with thick black brows. "What are you talkin' 'bout? Spike's ain't but two blocks from here."

Kenji pulled out all the credits he had in his pocket. A healthy enough wad that made the cabbie's expression change. "All of this is yours if you get me there safely."

"Sure, pal. Whatever you say." He turned back around and shifted gears. The cab lifted off the ground and took off. Seconds later it stopped. "Here you are."

Kenji handed over the money, probably enough to have gotten the cab to take him to the other side of Terran A and back. But Kenji didn't know anyone on the other side of Terran A. He only knew one other person who might be able to help him, and that one person was, he prayed, at Spike's right now. "Do you see a huge man with stringy black hair, covered with ammunition belts?" Kenji asked, "Because if you do, I'm not getting out of this cab until he's gone."

The driver studied the street around them and glanced in the rearview mirror. "You got a bounty hunter on your ass?"

"I think so."

"Shit. Sorry about that. For what you paid me, you could stay here the rest of the night. Your own private cab. But no, I don't see no one with that description."

"Thanks."

"No problem, pal. Good luck. Them bounty hunters are some rough bastards."

Don't I know it. The image of that poor guy in Asia Town, lying on the ground, blood pouring from his face surged in Kenji's mind as he opened the taxi door. And the way all those people stood there, frozen, letting the man get pummeled.

Kenji got out and pushed the cab door closed. He dashed into Spike's, his heart still pounding fiercely.

Spike's was nearly in full swing. The usual electric guitar-laden music blared through the air, mixing with rowdy male laughter, the clack of pool cues against balls and the catcalls from the audience watching the live nude show.

Kenji scanned the place, ignoring the sudden attention of many pairs of eyes on him, some curious, others openly leering at his bare torso. They probably thought the semi-naked thing indicated he was switching from bartender to hustler. His chest heaved and his hands opened and closed in panicked fists. He had to find Fallon and get into one of the cubicles as soon as possible. What if the bounty hunter came in here, looking for him?

"Hey, Kenji!" Fallon was at the bar on a corner stool, waving him over. A mug of something golden and frothy already sat on the bar in front of him. Fallon had been waiting just like he'd promised.

Relief flooded him, propelling him toward the bar. He halted less than a foot from Fallon, his chest still heaving. Images collided in his mind—the terror he'd felt, the frightening flight across rooftops and in front of giant buses, the horrifying glitter in the bounty hunter's eyes…he stepped up to Fallon, so close, the man's scent met his nostrils.

Fallon stood, taking hold of his arms, his blue eyes scanning him. "Kenji, where's your shirt? I saw a report on the…nnnhh—"

Kenji surged forward, cutting Fallon's words off with his lips.

Blimey! Fallon tried to pull back but Kenji grasped his upper arms, holding him in place with strength that belied his narrow, wiry frame. Kenji's lips pressed insistently to his and his fingertips dug into Fallon's triceps as if the smaller man were hanging onto him for dear life.

Oh hell. Kenji invaded Fallon's senses. The world shrank down to the dig of Kenji's fingers in his muscles and the velvety heat of Kenji's lips to his. The rowdy music and catcalls cheering on their kiss faded to the background. The

51

fervent chafing of Kenji's lips against his told Fallon everything, as if Kenji were speaking in a language made up only of kissing. Terror, relief, passion all mingled in Kenji's kiss. Fallon's inner cop understood even as his body came alive with erotic heat.

Fallon understood something else. If McCray had been chasing Kenji, they needed to cut out of here. *Fast.*

Reality yanked Fallon from his lustful haze. He pulled back and looked into Kenji's good eye. Kenji's chest rose and fell as if he'd been long distance running and his one iris was dilated nearly to full capacity. This *had* to do with the report on Channel X. He grasped Kenji's hand and yanked him through the crowds, amidst a tumult of whistles and catcalls from patrons believing they were heading toward the backrooms for a lay or blowjob. Fallon plowed through the walls of muscular sweating bodies, scanning for McCray among them. That damned tosser wouldn't hesitate to open fire into a crowd.

The back of Spike's came into view. The rear entrance with its red exit light above marked Fallon's goal. Reaching the back, he pushed it open and he and Kenji plunged out of Spike's into the night air. The door floated shut behind them, muting the bar's raucous music and patrons' rowdy jeers.

A quick scan of the dark back alley showed Fallon they were safe. For the moment. He grasped Kenji's upper arms. "Kenji, we need to get out of here. *Now.* My pod is parked at headquarters. I've got to get you on it."

Kenji's stared up at him, his bare chest heaving. "You know?"

He squeezed Kenji's arms as an affirmation. "Even if you hadn't come in shirtless and breathless, grabbing me for dear life the way you had, yes, I knew. Channel X. His name's McCray. He's the most dangerous of the lot."

Kenji nodded. "He attacked me. But not before…" He looked down again.

Fallon's heart lurched. "Before what?"

Kenji's shoulders trembled. "He attacked another guy. A guy who looked like me. Tore his eye right out of his skull. No one was helping him! I yelled at him to leave the poor guy alone. That's when he went for me."

Fallon grasped Kenji's arms and pulled. "You're coming with me now. Back to my pod. I'll get you to safety."

Kenji didn't move.

"What is it?" Fallon narrowed his eyes at Kenji. The other man looked stricken.

"I n-need to get something — at my flat.

Fallon reined in his impatience. "We don't have time. He's probably already in there. Come." He tugged Kenji in the direction of headquarters.

But Kenji stood firm. "I can't leave without it, Fallon. My statue. We've got to go back for it."

Icy heat rippled down Fallon's arms. Was the guy barmy? "We're not going anywhere except back to the pod. Don't you know what these hunters are like? You want to lose your other eye? Over a bloody statue? No!"

Kenji visibly flinched, his hand going to his eye patch. "You don't understand. I can't leave it. Please."

"Dammit, no. Come on." Fallon squeezed Kenji's hand and unholstered his phazer with the other. Pulling Kenji with him against the wall, he began to inch slowly toward the corner. Kenji moved closer and bumped into Fallon from behind. Kenji's arm slipped from his grasp. He looked over his shoulder. "Kenji, stay close to—"

Shite! Was he seeing what he thought he saw?

Kenji was right behind him, holding up a wallet. "You lost this," he said.

Fallon recognized that wallet. It was his. With all the credits he had to his name stuffed inside it. "Thanks." He went to take it but Kenji yanked it out of reach. "What the—?" He reached again, and Kenji yanked again, maneuvering out of reach.

"What the hell? You little tosser! Give me that!" He lunged forward, but again, Kenji slipped just out of reach.

He backed up, step by step, the wallet outstretched, as if teasing an animal with a piece of meat. "Catch me, and you'll get it back," Kenji said, then wheeled around and disappeared into the night.

Chapter Four

Fallon took off after Kenji. Keeping Kenji's bare, slimly-muscled back in sight was a monumental task, the little tosser ran so fast.

Kenji disappeared round a corner. Into the worst neighborhood of Terran A. Barely a soul on the street but junkies high on Space Dust.

"Bloody hell," he muttered, increasing his sprint. Losing his balance, he skidded on the same turn and knocked into a bald, leather-clad space junkie loitering there, probably waiting for a pick-up of Dust. In preventing his fall, Fallon's elbow connected with the guy's ribcage.

"Watch it, asshole!" A pair of large hands shoved him against a brick wall and a meaty, bulbously featured face pressed in close to his.

Fallon lifted his phazer. "ISP," he "Detain me and pay for it."

The junkie, his eyes wild from sniffing Dust, remained reasonable enough to drop his hands and back away. Fallon was immediately back on the move, but—dammit! Kenji was nowhere in sight. He peered up the dark street. And saw him. Peeking from a storefront a short ways up the sidewalk, waving the wallet.

"Shite." Fallon sprinted forward.

But like a vision of a mind on Dust, Kenji kept just beyond his reach. It had rained while they were in Spike's and wetness glowed off the pavement wherever signs or streetlights shone. Water splashed up with each thud of

Fallon's boots.

Kenji disappeared around another corner, but when Fallon reached it, the little bastard seemed to have vanished into thin air.

"Looking for me?"

Fallon whipped around. Kenji, half-visible around the far corner of another building, dangled the wallet. Fallon raced toward him but Kenji's lean frame gave him the agility to stay ahead. "You're in danger, Kenji! There's no time to fuck around!"

"I'm not effing around," came Kenji's voice, panting from their run. "This is important." For several more blocks, Fallon kept his eye on Kenji's sleekly muscled torso as it came into the glow of streetlights and then back out. Fallon's temper grew with each stride. McCray could be lurking in any of these alleyways or dark storefronts. Kenji was skirting the marketplace, keeping to the cluster of rundown brick apartment buildings that housed many of Terran City's Asian immigrant population.

Fallon turned the corner between two buildings and there was Kenji at the far end of the alley, waving the wallet at him in the light of one bare bulb above a door. "What the hell! Are you completely mad?" he hissed through his teeth.

"No." Kenji spun around and dashed through the door. Fallon followed, breath pumping. Damn Kenji for risking both their lives over a bloody statue. That's what this chase was about. *The little prick*. He'd help Kenji, but damned if he wasn't also going to throttle him, given half a chance. Fallon yanked open the door and lunged into the dimly lit stairwell.

Kenji was already up two flights. Fallon heard Kenji's

boots echoing on the stairs and caught a glimpse of him ascending. They both took the stairs two at a time. Kenji didn't stop till he reached the fifth floor. Fallon reached the top, his chest on fire and leaned against the rickety stair rail, panting. Kenji was already fiddling with a key in the lock. Yanking the door open, he rushed in. Taking a lungful of air, Fallon followed.

He pushed the door shut behind him then grabbed Kenji by the arm, trapping him against the door. The sound of their combined panting filled the dark room. Fallon pressed in close to Kenji, their noses almost touching. "Are you bloody kidding me, Kenji? You led me here for that goddamn statue, didn't you?"

Kenji sagged against the door, his warm breath pulsing onto Fallon's chin. "I'm…sorry…Fallon," he panted, offering up the wallet. "I couldn't…leave it…here."

Fallon exhaled. He plucked his wallet from Kenji's hand and stuffed it into his pocket. "If you weren't being chased by a bloodthirsty bounty hunter, I'd drag you in to Central for this stunt."

Kenji flicked on a light and Fallon regretted his threat. Kenji's good eye was wide and frantic.

The look wiped away Fallon's anger and his desire to throttle Kenji evaporated. The scent of Kenji's musk, mingled with sweat off his bare torso pulsed into the air between them. "All right," he muttered, "Get your statue and let's go,"

"Thanks, Fallon." Kenji swallowed, his eye taking on a sheepish look. "It's all I have. My only connection to…" He looked down.

He gave a clipped nod. "Get whatever else you need

while you're here. We've got to get you off Terran A."

Kenji blinked at the mention of leaving. "All right." He crossed the little, shabby room and stop in front of a small table on which sat a golden statue.

Immediately Fallon recognized the shape, a male robed figure seated in what appeared a cross-legged position, a serene air about his features. He'd seen statues like that before. An Indian family who ran a fish and chips shop near his parents' flat in Manchester used to keep one on a shelf behind the counter. That is, until the Religious Wars when the government cracked down on such things. In any case, the statue appeared quite valuable and could be what McCray was after. Many religious artifacts were floating about the galaxies, some sought by treasure hunters, others dealt in like art by incredibly rich business moguls who could afford to scour Earth and all its outposts for whatever hadn't been hidden away by priests and monks of the various world religions. Hiding a piece so valuable would certainly explain why Kenji was squirrely about his origins.

"Hurry, Kenji." He was already at the door, listening to any movement beyond it, every sense alert.

Kenji wrapped the statue lovingly in a towel and stuffed it into a knapsack. "Just another second." He crossed to a rickety chest of drawers from which he yanked out its contents. Kenji didn't have much. Some underwear, a few shirts, one of which he put on, a black t-shirt that hugged his slimly muscled torso. "I tore my jacket and left it in an alley when McCray was chasing me," Kenji said and went to the closet to pull out a couple of pairs of trousers. "I took off my shirt and threw that in too to make him think I'd gone somewhere else. It didn't work." He threw some toiletries into the knapsack and shouldered it. "I'm ready." Then he perused the room. "Guess I won't be coming back here any time soon."

"You guessed correctly. Let's go."

Kenji shook his head, his expression sad. He looked over the tiny, dingy flat. "I know it sounds crazy, but this is my home. The only one I've known."

Fallon grasped Kenji's arm and tugged him to the door. "I'm sorry this is happening, but we'll find you a new home somewhere. I promise." First they had to get to safety. "Let's go." He put his ear to the door again. The hall was still silent and his trained ear picked up no sound of someone breathing out there, laying in wait for them. He'd cocked the safety of his phazer and held it up. With a brief finger to his lips, he then opened the door, silently, slowly. After another moment's listening for breathing or footsteps, he signaled to Kenji to follow him into the hallway.

The solitary bulb hanging from the ceiling was bright enough and the space small enough that no one could hide in shadows and jump out at them. The downstairs was another matter. "Be as quiet as you can," he whispered over his shoulder and saw Kenji nod.

Phazer still brandished, he led Kenji down each flight, his ears trained toward the silent shadows. Even a bombastic oaf like McCray could hide like a cat if he needed to.

But McCray wasn't there and they made it to the entryway without incident. The next step was to get to a main thoroughfare and catch an airbus to the ISP station where his space pod was waiting.

Fallon peeked around the door and scanned the dimly lit sidewalk in either direction. The night sky of Terran A had a strangely purplish glow, not as dark as night on Earth, and so it was a mite easier to see that the way was clear. So far. He signaled to Kenji to follow and stepped out onto the sidewalk. Kenji's street was quiet since this area housed mostly working folk who were already tucked in for the night.

Taking Kenji's arm, Fallon ushered him along, still scanning the sidewalk up ahead and aware of alleyways from which McCray could jump out at them. He cut across the street, heading for the outskirts of the marketplace, the spot where, he knew, Kenji's lookalike had been brutally attacked. They had to get to the main street where the air buses went along their routes. Unlike hover buses that only went a few feet above the ground, airbuses could circle buildings and coast above the traffic, unimpeded. That would be the quickest, safest way to get back to the pod. It had probably been half an hour since they left Spike's. Only a matter of time before McCray tracked them down.

The traffic noise grew louder with their return to a busier area. On the corner, a small collection of people waited at an air bus stop. Fallon looked them over, making certain McCray wasn't among them. No concern here. These people were mostly well-dressed, probably on their way to the more expensive nightclubs and late-night restaurants of Terran A.

Fallon ushered Kenji into the middle of the group of people and pressed close to him. That's when he heard it. The beeping. A blaring sound that grew louder, accompanied by the grinding roar of a motorbike, a rarity on the outposts. He felt a glimmer of relief. Only cops used the tool that made that noise, a DNA lock. With that gadget and a person's genetic code, you could find anyone just about anywhere without even seeing them. Yet he hadn't called for police assistance. Which meant. *Shite!* When had McCray gotten his hands on one of those? Not even the best bounty hunters had access to DNA locks. There was nowhere to run now. He clicked the lock of his phazer setting it deep stun. Only one way out of the situation now.

The bike was rounding the corner and the beeping pulsed loudly through the air, nearly as loud as a siren. The people around them were murmuring, shuffling in growing alarm. Drawing Kenji closer to him, Fallon tapped the button on his communicator. "Request backup. Sector A, airbus route, main street." Assistance would be here within seconds.

Just then, an airbus came into view at the other end of the street. But no cops.

The motorbike screeched to a halt a few feet away, the engine idling loudly.

People in the crowd cried out and moved apart like a set of curtains, leaving Fallon and Kenji exposed. Where were those bloody cops? He jerked his gaze quickly in either direction. Nothing.

Fallon stepped in front of Kenji, just as the red light of the DNA lock glared on them like a spotlight. He squinted and saw the beefy outline of the bounty hunter on his bike. Somehow McCray had gotten a sample of Kenji's DNA and matched it. Right there in the middle of Terran City. And there was to be no help from law enforcement. He pointed his phazer at McCray.

"Give him to me," McCray yelled over the noise. "He's mine!" In McCray's other hand was a mega-phazer.

"Bullshit!" Fallon aimed fired and *smack!* The laser hit McCray in the center of the forehead and he keeled over, bike and all.

Just as the air bus pulled to a hovering stop.

Fallon yanked Kenji toward it and shoved him up the lowered steps. He showed his badge to the driver. "ISP station for Sector A," he said. The driver nodded and let them in without paying and he herded Kenji immediately to the back, keeping watch out the window over McCray's unconscious form.

"Is he dead?" Kenji's voice quavered and his hand clutched Fallon's arm.

Fallon holstered his weapon. "No. But he'll be out for a while. My phazer is set on level three. Delivers quite a shock. He'll have a scar where I hit him."

"Oh." Kenji sat back in his seat as the airbus door whooshed closed and the bus lifted high into the air. The sterile light of the overhead light track showed the paleness of Kenji's usually tanned gold skin.

Ignoring the frightened stares they were receiving from their fellow passengers, Fallon put a hand on Kenji's arm and chided himself. The poor guy was shaken. When a bloke was used to dealing with bounty hunters, it was one thing, but Kenji was an innocent. And incredibly harmless. At least he seemed to be.

A dark feeling coiled in Fallon's chest. Had he become so immune to such violence himself? "You're safe now, Kenji," he said softly, as the bus moved silently through the air, passing the lighted buildings. "I'll make sure of it." Especially since they couldn't rely on help from the Terran police.

Kenji looked at him, his right eye sad. But he nodded. "Thanks."

Fallon sat back, relaxing for the moment. Then a question formed in his mind, something he hadn't had time to consider before. He looked at Kenji again, remembering the feel of his lips when Kenji had first burst into Spike's that evening. Kenji was a great kisser. "Can I ask you something?"

"Sure."

"When you came running into Spike's earlier, why didn't you just tell me what was going on? Not that I minded what you *did* do. I'm just...curious."

Kenji sighed. For several moments he appeared to reflect on the question. Finally he shook his head. "Honestly, I'm not sure. I wasn't...thinking, really. Just acting." A look of pain tightened his features. "When I saw what the bounty hunter did to that poor guy and then went after me, I couldn't think of anything else except that you were supposed to be there, waiting for me. I was so relieved when I saw you. It all just came out...that way. You were my...hope." He fell silent and looked down.

Kenji waited for Fallon's response. When none came, he dared to peek at the large man's face. Truly, he hadn't meant to grab Fallon and kiss him that way. Even during their entire night at the love hotel, Kenji had not been the aggressor, but when he'd seen the man there at the bar, waiting, his entire being, body and soul, had responded.

Fallon wore a strange expression and seemed to be studying his hands as if they were the most interesting things he could possibly be looking at.

"Fallon?" Kenji's stomach flipped over. Bad enough he'd just admitted needing him so much, but having gotten

Fallon involved in this crazy, horrid mess…

A deep sigh. "Sorry, Kenji. I…it's just, I don't know what to say."

"Just say you don't hate me for getting you into this. I'm sorry."

Fallon's blue eyes clouded. "I could never hate you. I'm just…not used to thinking of myself as someone's hope. That's all."

"Oh." Kenji glanced back at Fallon who was now looking out the window, in the direction of the place he'd left McCray lying. Maybe Fallon's response had something to do with Nicky, the guy who'd been his partner, but he remained silent, not wanting to pry into Fallon's privacy.

"As for you getting me into this mess, I already knew something was wrong before I got to Terran A. I waited for you at Spike's only because I felt that was the surest place to find you." Then Fallon whipped around to face him. "Kenji, weren't there cops coming 'round at the marketplace? Wasn't there someone from law enforcement you could turn to?"

The scene surged through Kenji's memory. The poor guy on the ground, screaming and bleeding, clutching his face, the crowd of terrified onlookers, and McCray's scowling face as he turned, saw Kenji, and lunged for him. Kenji searched the images, realizing only then, there hadn't been one cop on the scene. Usually, there were regular patrols just about everywhere and distress calls were answered within a minute or so. He shook his head slowly. "Actually, no. There was no one there. Not even a siren to say a cop was coming."

Fallon sat back in his seat. "And no cop now when I

64

called for back-up." He ran a hand through his hair and sighed deeply.

Kenji couldn't help but notice how it made his broad chest heave under the snug t-shirt.

"No one except for me," Fallon went on, as if to himself. "I'm Intergalactic. The outposts aren't my jurisdiction. Even when I'm pursuing a bounty hunter, once he or she enters land space, I'm required to call for Terran patrols to assist me. They never take more than a few seconds to show up." His eyes narrowed, his rugged face drawn in concentration. "Something's wrong."

Kenji's blood chilled. "Why wouldn't the cops come?"

"I don't know."

"That's bad, isn't it?"

"Yes."

"I just don't understand why this bounty hunter came after me."

Fallon looked at him. "I beg your pardon? Don't you know?"

He shook his head.

"Have you fought with anyone, someone who might want revenge?"

"I don't know." His drive to remain alone indicated to him he *might* have enemies, but really, how could he know for sure?

"What do you mean you don't know? If you've had a fight with someone, I'd think you remember. Listen Kenji, you really need to tell me what's going on. I know you're in

65

hiding, but I can't help you unless you tell me the truth."

"Hiding?" Kenji shook his head. "I don't know if I'm in hiding, I swear it. I'm not lying, I promise."

Fallon's brow furrowed. "What do you mean? You're not a fugitive?"

"I mean, I don't remember anything. I just woke up one day a few months ago on the outskirts of the city with my statue near me. I was in a crash of some sort, I guess. There were pieces of a space pod not far away all charred, but I don't know anything else."

Fallon nodded. "Those happen quite regularly. Some of the pod manufacturers have atmospheric entry reactors that overheat. You have amnesia. Probably you suffered a head injury in the crash."

"I was bruised up pretty badly. I guess you're right." Kenji remembered stumbling to his feet, the statue in his arms, the remains of his charred clothing on the ground nearby, and surveying the dry, rocky terrain surrounding him. In the distance, the skyline of a city had loomed up, providing the beacon toward which he made his way before passing out and waking up in the Matsuotos' home. "So, that means the bounty hunter is coming after who I was. Not who I am now. Do you think I may have killed someone?" The mere thought made him nauseous.

"I doubt you killed anyone. You're not the type. I've seen others suffer from amnesia and they never became a completely different person. They retained their basic nature. You're gentle. You couldn't even use the "f" word earlier, for God's sake."

Kenji remembered that exchange and smiled, feeling sheepish. "Yeah. You think I'd use those words after working in Spike's all that time, but…" He shrugged. "I just can't."

Fallon pinned him with a firm look. "That aside, you're not safe anywhere. We need to get to the pod and fly out into ISP territory. Then we need to learn where you came from. If we can catch the trail, we can find who hired McCray and who prevented law enforcement from coming around."

"ISP." The bus driver's voice sounded over the loudspeaker. The airbus lowered to street level and the door opened.

Fallon rose from his seat, keeping a hand around Kenji's arm. Kenji kept close to Fallon, sensing all the other passengers' eyes on them as they went down the aisle. Kenji's nerves crackled. Any second he expected one of the other people in the bus to jump out and grab him. Only the sensation of Fallon's strong hand on his arm gave him any sense of safety at all. The entire world felt like a threatening, dangerous place of deadly shadows.

Down on the sidewalk, Fallon kept moving, pulling him firmly along. "Dammit," he muttered, again sounding as if he were having in an inner conversation "I can't believe law enforcement would be in on this. It can't be."

Kenji's heart raced as Fallon led him around the huge, squarish concrete block building toward the back. A high fence topped with a buzzing force field loomed up in the purplish night. "I'm sorry, Fallon. I shouldn't have involved—"

"You've nothing to be sorry for. It's not your fault the universe is full of corrupt bastards. Must be McCray had a scrambling device that prevented law enforcement from

67

reaching the scene. There are just a few of those illegal buggers being bought and sold through the galaxies."

"That must be it."

They'd reached the gate and Fallon showed his badge to the guard who pressed a button and stood aside. Laser beams of light across the entrance ceased to flow long enough to let them through and Fallon once again tugged Kenji along with him. "We're getting on board and out of here." Fallon strode through a wide open space filled only with police vehicles.

A dog barked and charged out of the shadows. Kenji jumped but relaxed as soon as he saw the shaggy, floppy-eared mutt. This had to be Mike, the traveling companion Fallon had told him about in one of their telescreen conversations.

"C'mon Mike." Fallon snapped his fingers at the dog. "We're out of here." He pulled a small mechanism from his pocket, pressed a button and a door on the last space pod in the line of parked vehicles lowered down. Mike ran ahead and bounded up the small ramp.

Fallon let Kenji precede him. "Welcome to my home," he said.

Kenji paused on the ramp. It was no small thing for him to be invited into someone's home. "Thanks, Fallon."

Fallon nodded to the interior. "No problem. Get in there."

Kenji stepped in, Fallon right behind him. In the next second, the door went up, sealing them inside. Letting out a breath, Kenji hugged his knapsack to him while Mike circled around his heels, sniffing at him, furry tail wagging.

"Mike, this is Kenji, our new traveling mate. Kenji, Mike."

"Nice to meet you," he said to the dog and held out one hand. "I've heard all about you." Immediately a warm wet tongue licked across his palm and then Mike pushed his shaggy head against Kenji's hand.

Kenji chuckled at the ticklish feeling of fur against his skin. "I think he likes me."

"He does. Feel praised. Mike doesn't usually take to people so quickly."

"I do feel praised then." Kenji scratched Mike behind the ears and petted his head while watching Fallon power up the controls.

"Make yourself comfortable," Fallon said, pressing buttons and flicking switches. "Once we're underway, we can begin to unravel this mystery." The control panel with all its tiny lights and screens lit up, beeped and flickered.

Kenji marveled at Fallon's ease. He'd been right to trust Fallon, For a moment he relived his terror when the bounty hunter had demanded him. So heroic, how Fallon had stepped between them. And the way he'd taken McCray down with one shot of his phazer. Wow.

Fallon gestured to the seat beside him. "Strap yourself in, Kenji. Just for take-off."

"Okay." Slowly, he sat down, his knapsack on his lap. At least the seat belts weren't difficult to figure out. He clicked the buckle shut around himself and the knapsack holding the precious statue. Mike whined once more and then retreated to a corner where he curled up.

"This buggy is a bit older model," Fallon said, still

69

pushing buttons and sliding levers up and down, "But she gives a smooth ride and is new enough to have a cloaking feature."

"Cloaking? Meaning it can be invisible?"

"Yes." The look of purpose still shone from his blue eyes. "I guess I don't need to tell you how important that feature is for us now."

Kenji shook his head. "No."

The motors vibrated under Kenji's boots and the pressure in the air changed slightly.

"Lifting off." Fallon pulled back on the largest throttle and Kenji was suddenly pushed hard into his seat. The air above seemed to press down on his head and through the windshield, the purple night sky drew closer. And closer. Fallon pushed some more controls and a whirring sound started up, echoing so loudly, Kenji felt as if it shimmered right through his brain.

The space pod surged. There was a flare of heat and outside, the air seemed to burn bright orange.

"We're going through Terran A's atmosphere," Fallon shouted over the din.

"I see!" Kenji clutched his knapsack to keep the statue from flying out of his arms.

"Just a bit more!" Fallon reached for yet more controls and Kenji glimpsed the bulge of the man's biceps and triceps with his movements.

Then, suddenly, the pressure was gone. The whirring sound ceased and silence filled the space pod. The craft felt as if it were floating. Outside the pod, the darkness of space surrounded them. Terran A was gone.

Kenji stared through the windshield. Ahead of them was endless blackness, dotted only by a distant light here and there.

Fallon gestured out the window. "You can unstrap yourself and have a closer look."

Wordlessly, he flipped open the buckle and slid off the seat, one arm still around the statue. He stood as close as he dared to the control panel and stared out the windshield. There was only one word to describe what he saw. "Incredible," he breathed.

Close by he heard Fallon chuckle. "Yes, it is. A miracle." He pushed a few more buttons and levers then undid his own safety belt. When he rose from the seat, the space pod continued as if someone were at the helm. "I have a safe place for your statue. Follow me." He took a few steps, hit a control on the wall and a door slid aside, revealing a living space with a bed, a bedside table and a chair beside some bookshelves. It looked almost cozy but for the walls of the same gray spaceship steel as the control room.

Crouching down, Fallon slid open a small hatch. "It'll be safe here, Kenji," he said. "And there's an extra drawer for your other things."

Kenji knelt by him and opened the knapsack. He lifted the statue, still wrapped in its towel and tucked it into the compartment, which Fallon slid shut again and turned a lock.

"It'll be there when you want it," Fallon said. He rose to his feet and Kenji did the same.

They stood, face to face, Kenji tilting his head to look

into Fallon's eyes. "Thanks, Fallon. I'll never be able to repay you for this."

"There's nothing to repay." Fallon cupped his cheek and brushed Kenji's cheekbone with the pad of his thumb. "I want you to be safe." His blue eyes darkened slightly and he leaned in a bit closer. The hum and vibration of the pod's engines filled the silence. Fallon's hand slid down a tiny bit and he ran the pad of his thumb along Kenji's bottom lip. "You're a great looking man, Kenji," he murmured.

Kenji's cheeks heated. Guys like Bud at Spike's used to compliment him all the time on his looks. It was flattering but none of them made him tremble the way Fallon did. "Thanks. So are you."

Fallon gave a tiny sideways grin. "I'm an overgrown space cowboy, really," he said, "but if you think I look good, so be it." He stared down into Kenji's face a few seconds more. His thumb slid across Kenji's lip again and then he pulled away. "I just realized something. You could be married."

Kenji frowned. "Married? To a woman?"

Fallon shrugged. "Or a man. Same sex marriages have been legal for a couple of centuries now." He leaned against the doorway connecting the sleeping room to the main area of the pod. "In any case, if you are married, I don't want to be a home-wrecker, hot as you are."

"I never thought of that." The idea of staying away from Fallon left Kenji bereft. Much as he'd gotten used to his solitude, his taste of being in Fallon's strong embrace had proven intoxicating. He sighed. "How will I ever know?"

"We'll have to unravel the mystery." Fallon squeezed his shoulder. "Look up at me please."

Fallon's voice compelled him to obey. For a hopeful moment, the way Fallon leaned into him, he dared to hope for a kiss. But instead, Fallon reached up and traced the edge of Kenji's eye patch with the pad of his index finger. "Now, I need to ask you for something important. Something that could provide a valuable clue to who you are."

Kenji's heart lurched. "What is it?"

"I need you to show me this eye."

Chapter Five

Kenji's throat went dry. "Is that really necessary?" One look and Fallon would probably vomit.

Fallon's fingers traced the contour of his jaw until reaching his chin and tipped it upward. "Don't be embarrassed," he said gently. "I promise it's not just morbid curiosity on my part. You said that bloke in the marketplace had his eye torn out by McCray?"

"Mm-hm." Kenji winced. The memory alone made a ghostly pain shoot through his covered eye.

Fallon's gaze took on a speculative look. "The report on Channel X was that McCray had done the same thing to several other victims."

"You mean he tore out a bunch of people's eyes?"

Fallon's blue eyes met his steadily. "That's right."

Nausea churned in Kenji's gut. "How could someone be so brutal?"

Fallon covered his shoulder with a large hand and squeezed. "Believe me, I've asked myself that question a million times. For all our technology and advancement into space, we're still quite primitive."

Kenji looked down. "That's so true. It makes my heart ache."

"Mm. Yes." Fallon's fingertips touched the elastic holding the eye patch in place.

Kenji grasped his wrist. "It's so awful, Fallon, my eye, I

mean. You'll…I don't want you to—

"Hey—" Fallon brushed a tender thumb along his cheekbone. "You're afraid I'll be disgusted, aren't you?"

He nodded.

"First of all, Kenji, you wouldn't believe what I've seen in my line of work. I won't even say it out loud. Things that haunt my dreams. Secondly, I give you my word that no matter how your eye looks, I won't be disgusted." He touched Kenji's cheek again. "I can't imagine being disgusted by anything about you."

Kenji's heart thumped at the look in Fallon's gaze. That feeling of trust came over him again. "Okay," he murmured, though he didn't release Fallon's wrist.

Fallon's intense gaze hadn't wavered. "So, what'd'ya say?"

Kenji swallowed. Of course it was necessary to show Fallon his eye. It was all they had to go on at this point. If anyone was going to see his naked face, it should be Fallon. "All right, you asked for it." Slowly he released the other man's wrist, lifted the patch and slipped the whole thing off, his gaze never leaving Fallon's face.

As the seconds passed and Fallon showed no disgust or horror and, Kenji's tension subsided into curiosity. What answer could possibly come from this deformity?

Fallon cupped Kenji's cheek. The warmth against his skin sent a pleasant shiver through him. Fallon's thumb brushed across his cheekbone almost absentmindedly as he continued studying Kenji's eye. "Mm." he nodded, tracing the scar above and below the eye with the pad of his index finger.

Kenji melted inside. Did Fallon know how gentle his touch was? Such a strange contrast to the buff, rugged guy he was. The same man who'd shot a giant down with bull's eye perfection.

"I've seen this kind of thing before," Fallon said, "from smallpox. It can scar an eye that way."

Kenji's insides jumped. "Really? I had...smallpox?" He frowned. "What is that?"

Fallon continued to observe Kenji's eye, all the while continuing to touch the area around it. "It's an illness that spread on Earth. Centuries ago, it had basically been eradicated by breakthroughs in medicine. But when the Religious Wars caused chaos in various parts of the planet, many diseases came back with the widespread devastation and famine."

A shadow crossed Fallon's features. "Corpses were rotting everywhere from those who didn't survive the disease. I'd just finished training at Intergalactic. My first assignment with Nicky was a series of large scale rescue missions on the borders of the People's Empire. We ended up transporting refugees to Terran A and B. That was about fifteen years ago."

Kenji grasped Fallon's hand. "So that means I came from Earth?"

"I would say yes. And you're probably from the Asian continent where the most outbreaks occurred." Fallon closed his large fingers around Kenji's hand. "Small pox didn't exist anywhere else. Thankfully, things are stabilized now and the smallpox virus is once again under control."

"That's good."

Fallon drew a deep breath and stepped back a fraction, signaling his inspection of Kenji's eye was over. "So, we know you've lived on Earth, at least as a child when you had the smallpox and that you're probably from somewhere on the Asian continent where the outbreaks occurred."

"Why was I on Terran A?"

Fallon scratched his head. "I don't know." He grew thoughtful. "You say you woke up and found the burnt space pod nearby?"

"Yes. My clothing was burnt too."

Fallon nodded. "Special anti-pyretic material. Protects the skin, eating the flames until it's extinguished. Saves the life."

"Oh. Well, the pod wasn't made of that stuff. There was nothing left. I peeked inside but there were no other survivors. Just a couple of…charred remains."

"You were the only one wearing the safety suit. Hmm. And then you must have been thrown from the craft." He rubbed his chin. "There were no ISP agents or emergency rescue teams present?"

"No. I was alone. Just me and the statue."

Fallon shook his head. "It doesn't make sense you'd have been on a transport that crashed and was never located. The transports are all logged in. Your ship would have been tracked and found immediately. You'd have been rescued by Terran authorities. Which means—" Fallon began to pace, an intent look on his face. Kenji watched him stride back and forth in the small space.

"Which means what?" Kenji's heart pounded.

Fallon stopped. "Which means you were on a private pod and that your presence wasn't logged into the system. You were wearing the safety suit, not the others. You were meant to be protected." He faced Kenji squarely. "Every individual who comes and goes off an outpost is recorded. If you'd been on record, your absence would have been reported to ISP who would then have conducted a search using your DNA code. No way you'd have been missing for months otherwise. And then, it wouldn't have taken a bounty hunter to find an individual from an emergency transport crash."

Kenji looked at him. "It sounds like I'm some kind of important person. Who travels privately that I wouldn't have been on record?"

"Well, that's the mystery, isn't it?" Fallon came to stand in front of him again. "Those who travel privately without being logged into the system for identification have a lot of money. It's costly to bypass the system and not have to register your DNA code with the authorities. Owners and CEOs of large companies, heads of state, people like that. They're really the only ones left who can afford a privately chartered pod authorized to enter Terran air space, with the exception of ISP. The rest of those who have their own pods, bounty hunters, and the assorted lot of hackers, space junkies and garbage scows flying around are also highly regulated and need special permission to enter Terran air space. Every individual who flies one is DNA-registered. One of those particular pods would also have been located immediately after a crash.

"So I'm a rich person?"

"Could be. Or a statesman. Which is why a bounty hunter had your DNA rather than the authorities." Fallon gestured in the air. "That also explains why whoever hired McCray to find you was undisclosed on Channel X."

"What does that mean?"

"Suffice it to say that only such people can bypass the regulations when it comes to hiring a bounty hunter."

"Oh." Kenji sagged against the wall and held up a hand. "So, we know I'm from Earth. I've had smallpox…" he ticked off the statements on his fingers… "and that I am rich or important."

"Right."

Kenji let his shoulders slump. "And we still have no idea why I'd be travelling to Terran A with a gold statue."

"Precisely. Is there anything else you can remember when you came to that might help?"

Kenji sighed and raked a hand through his hair. What he wouldn't have given to be holed up in that love hotel right now with Fallon, not having to worry about any of this. "No. I gathered up the statue and went toward the city. I ended up at the marketplace, just at the spot where the Matsuotos have their little restaurant. They took me in."

"So, this Mr. Matsuoto is the first person who saw you on Terran A?"

"As far as I know, yes."

"And he saw the statue?"

Kenji looked up into Fallon's blue eyes. "Yes. Why?"

"Well, if he was from Earth, I was just surprised he didn't tell you what it was."

Kenji thought back to those first days. He'd woken up

ill at first, his skin dreadfully hot. The Matsuotos had kept him in bed and nursed him. They'd wrapped the statue up in a sheet, keeping it tucked away under his bedding. They hadn't taken it away from him or told him he should get rid of it. "No. It's from them that I learned about the Religious Wars and the importance of hiding religious artifacts. He told me that when I got my own place, to keep the statue safe and not to show it to anyone because it was my private keepsake."

"Good for him. A friend. Did they comment about your eye?"

"No. I had a patch over my eye that didn't come off in the crash. Neither Mr. Matsuoto nor his wife ever lifted it, out of respect to me. Fallon, I need to contact the Matsuotos. What if they're hurt? They might be worried about me."

"I'll contact their telecom." Fallon went to a control panel in the cockpit area with a telescreen surrounded by other buttons and dials. It was probably the one Fallon had used to talk to him in the last month…Kenji imagined him sitting there, right as he was doing at the moment, his wide shoulders straining against his tee-shirt, his muscular arms manipulating the dials.

After punching in a complicated series of numbers, the screen lit to life. In a few more seconds the image on the screen gave way to the small shabby room in which Matsuoto-san kept his telecom. Bare cracked walls surrounded a sink with a shelf for pots and pans and a small table with two rickety chairs. Recognizing the place, Kenji jumped to Fallon's side. "Matsuoto-san?" He looked at Fallon. "Can he hear me?"

"If he's there he'll hear you."

"Matsuoto-san, it's Kenji. Are you there?"

More time passed and no one answered. The room remained empty, quiet, as if abandoned.

Kenji clenched his hands into fists. McCray had seen Matsuoto-san speak to him in the marketplace. The elderly man had tried to save him when no one else would. "What if McCray did something to them? I need to go back!"

"You can't go back." Fallon turned from the screen to face him. "It's absolutely not safe for you, and your safety comes first. I don't even want the ISP to know you're with me."

Kenji's chest tightened. His vision blurred and he struggled for breath. "Matsuoto-san...oh...no..."

Large hands closed over his shoulders and guided him toward a seat, pressing him down onto it. "Calm down." One of Fallon's hands smoothed his hair back in a tender way. Another caress followed the first one, and then another until Kenji's breathing calmed. "Does McCray have any reason to connect you with them?"

Kenji exhaled. He was making a jerk of himself now. After everything Fallon had done for him. He shook his head. "No. I...didn't think of that."

"I promise you, Kenji, if the Matsuotos don't answer our calls within a reasonable amount of time, I'll get someone there to look in on them. All right?"

He nodded, suppressing his need to pursue the issue. Fallon was the cop here.

A bit of relief penetrated the tension pulling his back tight. Fallon's hands still rested on his shoulders, as if the source of comfort emanated from Fallon and seeped in through his touch.

"There, Kenji." Fallon rubbed his shoulders, his touch firm, giving just the right amount of pressure to ease tension from his taut muscles.

And damn, he needed it. As if Fallon's touch were magic, months of guarding himself seemed to fall away. Like a mirror reflected back at him, he saw his life in stark relief, the endless days and hours spent wondering who he was, his lonely existence punctuated by meals at the Matsuotos' little restaurant and his shifts at Spike's, lit up only by the colorful goings on there and the roughnecks who flirted with him.

For the first time, he wasn't...alone. Fallon was giving him a chance to rely on someone else, rather than solely on his own wits. "I'm sorry. I'm acting like such a...I don't know."

The rubbing stopped and a warm hand cupped his cheek. "You've had trauma." He lifted Kenji's hand, the one that held the eye patch. "You want to put this back on?"

Fallon's voice was gentle. Comforting. How good it felt not to worry anymore that Fallon would be repulsed by his eye. It made him want to stay exposed. He shook his head. "No, it's all right."

Fallon brushed a thumb across his cheek. "Okay. Time for a shower then and some rest. We'll worry about the details when you're sorted out." Fallon picked up his hand and ushered him toward the back of the space pod.

Kenji let Fallon lead him. His body felt suddenly drained of its life force, as if someone had put a tube somewhere inside of him and siphoned out every drop of energy.

Back in the sleeping quarters, Fallon pressed a button on the side wall. Another small panel opened, revealing a shower cubicle. Sliding open the glass entrance to the shower, Fallon pointed to two more buttons. "Press these when you're ready. Here's soap in this dispenser." A rack outside the shower held white towels. "See what luxurious quarters I have." Fallon grinned. "Like the Terran Grand Hotel. You'll be relaxed and refreshed in no time." He gestured to the open shower. "I'll—uh—leave you your privacy."

Without thinking, Kenji grasped his arm. *Don't leave.* The words flared in his mind yet his mouth was unable to speak.

"What is it?" Fallon's brow furrowed. "Are you all right?"

Instead of answering, he reached up and placed his hands on Fallon's broad chest, acting on pure instinct the way he had when he'd run into Spike's. He lay his palms flat on each hard, round pectoral muscle, needing to feel the warm, solid flesh that was Fallon. Hard. Real. Alive.

Fallon's breath caught. The hitch made his chest rise the smallest bit. Kenji followed the movement. He couldn't lift away. Didn't want to. As if breaking the contact would cause him to spin off into deep space, into the clutches of the mad bounty hunter.

Fallon grasped Kenji's wrists and lifted. "Kenji…no. You could be—"

"I know, married." Kenji's voice slipped out, as if released by the way he touched Fallon. "I don't think I am. I don't…feel like I've done it before." He ventured upwards toward Fallon's broad shoulders.

"You don't know that. This is...a bad idea."

"Don't you think I'd have *some* memory of it?"

"Like you do of the rest of your life?"

Kenji's chest squeezed. Maybe it was something else. "Fallon, don't you want...me?"

"Oh, Kenji, if you only knew how much. I just don't want to...hurt you."

He shook his head. "You won't. The way I trusted...you...back at Spike's. I just know." He slid his hands back down over Fallon's chest, over Fallon's nipples. Of course he couldn't know for sure, but the tide of need gripped him. He couldn't imagine trusting anyone...or wanting anyone, the way he did now. So how could he possibly be married to someone else?

Fallon groaned softly. His eyelids lowered, his skin flushed, even under the emerging dark stubble on his cheeks. "Kenji..." Fallon's voice was a gravelly whisper.

Kenji slid his hands over the man's hard stomach, which caved and rose again under his seeking touch. Just below Fallon's heavy belt, the bulge of his cock swelled, pure evidence he was succumbing to Kenji's exploration. Encouraged, he tugged on Fallon's t-shirt, pulling it up, out of his waistband, just enough to get his hands under there, to meet with Fallon's warm skin, hard muscles, soft chest hair, erect nipples. Kenji raked the fingers of both hands through the mat of hair over Fallon's broad pecs. Fallon's breathing was heavier now, his velvety lips slightly parted, lids lowered.

I can't help it.

Kenji meant to say the words out loud but they were

trapped inside him. Trapped by the lump in his throat and the heat pounding through his body. Instead, he followed the silky trail of hair down Fallon's abdomen to his belly button.

Fallon pulled in another breath. "Oh shite," he breathed. His hands shot out, grasped Kenji's upper arms and pulled them chest to chest.

The room tilted. Kenji squeezed Fallon's broad torso. The man filled his arms like nothing he could ever have imagined. Fallon's musky aroma filled his nostrils, his dark eyes simmered into his. "You make me so damn hot, Kenji, I can't see straight."

"Then do something abou —"

"Nnnhh." Fallon's kiss shut him up.

Kenji tasted so damned good. Too damn good. No way Kenji didn't have a spouse or lover somewhere out there in the universe. Fallon had always made a point of keeping his hands off another man's man. But the moist warmth of Kenji's tongue dancing with his left him powerless. Slowly, he eased Kenji back down, never breaking contact with their lips. Instead, he lowered his head and slid his hands over Kenji's back. The wiry muscles shifted under his hands and Kenji sank against his front, making their hard cocks press together through their clothing.

Fallon almost lost it there. Instead, he rubbed his throbbing cock against Kenji's, prolonging the agony. Probing deep into Kenji's mouth with his tongue, he yanked Kenji's shirt from the waist of his trousers and off, then began to undo his belt. The rise and fall of their fevered breathing filled the space.

Kenji pulled from their kiss only far enough to whisper, "Fallon."

Unable to decipher whether Kenji wanted him to stop or go on, Fallon slid his mouth downward, pressing his lips to the curve of Kenji's throat. In tiny kisses, he moistened the skin.

"I want you so much," Kenji whispered, hands grabbing at Fallon shirt, lifting it the rest of the way off and tossing it aside. "All the way."

The words took a moment to sift into Fallon's consciousness. When they did, his body stilled. Now was the moment to stop. Before he created further disaster. Bad enough Kenji's life was in danger. If he survived and had a partner, Kenji's relationship would be in danger too.

"Please, Fallon." Kenji pressed in close and wound his hips.

Pleasure flared in Fallon's cock. He hitched a breath and grasped Kenji's hips, over his pants. *Push him away* he ordered himself silently.

His body disobeyed. It had been a hell of a long month away from Kenji after getting his first taste of him. He pulled.

His cock was engorged. His sac felt heavy, his ass tensed. How he longed to feel Kenji's sweet bare ass in his hands while his hard cock slathered with ointment, thrust into it.

He barely managed to lift away from Kenji's delicious neck and look into his face.

Kenji's good eye was large, the lid heavy with that inky fringe of sexy lashes, his golden skin flushed. Those perfect, voluptuous lips were swollen from their kisses. "Kenji," he breathed. He couldn't finish for the need thundering through his body. The mere thought of having his cock up Kenji's ass made his brain feel it would melt. The one thing they *hadn't* done that first night in the hotel.

Kenji nodded, his hands chafing feverishly over Fallon's chest. "In case…something happens. I want to have had that. I mean…I don't *think* I've ever been with anyone else. I'd want you to be the first. And here you are."

The thought of something happening to Kenji sobered him. "I won't let anything happen to you, Kenji," he breathed, "whether we do it or not." He tried once more to pull away.

And pulled closer instead.

If Kenji really was a virgin, part of him was selfishly glad he'd be the first to penetrate him. He would be gentle with him, treating him like the most delicate virgin. Fallon cupped his cheek and dropped a soft kiss on Kenji's parted lips, letting his own lips linger over them without exerting any pressure. Instead, he began a sensuous rubbing against them. Kenji's head fell back and a moan escaped his mouth.

The prospect of taking Kenji's virginity was hot as hell and the greatest honor Fallon could imagine. He hadn't felt that way since Nicky. Of course Nicky hadn't been a virgin. He'd slept with dozens of guys before they'd met. But once they'd gotten together, neither one had ever looked at another man.

Fallon glanced at his bed. The bed he'd spent so much time in with Nicky. A spike of guilt sliced through him and for several seconds he hovered, suspended between the sheer thrill of being Kenji's first and the feeling that he was cheating.

Kenji's large brown eye filled with understanding. "It's all right, Fallon. Maybe it's not what you want. I know the eye is kind of gross." Sadness weighed his finely sculpted features.

Fallon's heart lurched. Shite! "That's nonsense." He laced a hand into Kenji's hair. "You could never be gross, Kenji." To prove his point he took the eye patch from Kenji's hand and tossed it away. Then he tilted Kenji's chin up and pressed his lips to the damaged eyelid.

A sigh escaped Kenji's throat and Kenji's slim, wiry torso relaxed against his chest. Inch by inch, Fallon kissed his way back to Kenji's lips and covered them. Kenji answered his seeking kiss with a soft lick of his tongue. As if they'd never kissed before, Kenji plundered his mouth, tasting Fallon's tongue and teeth in delicate sweeps of moisture.

Fallon groaned and pulled away. "Come here, Kenji." He tugged Kenji toward the bed and yanked the covers down. A thin sheet and rough woolen blanket were all that covered the bed, an embarrassingly meager bed for Kenji's first real poke. If it was, indeed, Kenji's first time. But Kenji didn't seem to care. He'd already toed out of his boots and was shucking his trousers.

Naked, he stood at the edge of the bed, hands at his sides, as if to wait for Fallon's approval.

Nothing to worry about there. Fallon's hungry gaze took him all in. The lower part of Kenji's body had the same sleek, hard lines as the top. Sloping thighs and calves sprinkled with dark hair, and a delicious-looking cock, hard and ready, jutting in a graceful arc from his athletic body.

"Kenji."

Kenji looked at him doubtfully. "I look okay?"

Fallon grinned. "Shut up and get in." He pointed to the mattress then got his own trousers and boots off. By the time he'd finished, Kenji had climbed into the bed and lay on his back, his arms at his sides. Fallon smiled. With a sleekly muscular body and a cock standing like a flagstaff, Kenji wasn't exactly the image of a vestal virgin.

He approached the bed and lowered himself over Kenji. Their cocks brushed together, sending a tremor through him. Passing a hand over Kenji's smooth hair, he took the other man's mouth in a deep kiss.

Kenji sighed and lifted his arms around Fallon's broadness. His cock rubbed against Fallon's with each tiny movement, increasing the melt in Fallon's brain. He licked and nipped at Kenji's lips, as if marking his territory. The innocent look on Kenji's face, the sweet way he surrendered to Fallon's weight on top of him caused a protective surge to fill every cell of his body. Fallon kissed him, savoring his lips, feeling Kenji's hands press into his back. Oh yeah, on his life, he'd do whatever he could to make sure Kenji would be safe and well.

Kenji's inner thighs pressed into his hips, squeezing him with an eagerness that made his already hot blood go to a boil. On sheer instinct now, he pulled away from Kenji's lips and kissed a trail down the slim man's throat, down the center of his chest and abdomen, licking and teasing that smooth creamy skin as he made his way toward his goal. He'd never been with a man with such little body hair. It was almost like being with a woman, except for all the hard, flat planes and gorgeous, luscious cock.

89

"Ohhh." Kenji sighed and moaned with each press of Fallon's lips.

Fallon reached the ultimate destination and Kenji's hard cock bumped his cheek. He palmed the curving stalk and licked the length of it, base to head.

"Fallon, oh!" Kenji's hips surged upward and his hands gripped the bedding.

Fallon smiled against the silky skin of Kenji's cock and pushed the tip of his tongue into the tiny opening. When Kenji gasped, Fallon wiggled his tongue a bit more until Kenji let out a strange howl. Lifting his head, Fallon peered at him. "Something the matter?"

Kenji was panting, chest rising and falling. His eyelids were heavy and his skin flushed. The finely etched muscles in his torso flexed with the effort of breathing. "No-oh," he gasped.

Fallon grinned. "Good. Should I continue?" He gave a quick lick for good measure.

Kenji nodded wordlessly and his hands gripped the bedding.

Fallon licked Kenji's cock again. Mmm, the man tasted better than the finest Earth ale. Sweet and clean and musky all at once. He followed the path of his tongue with his hand, licking and stroking, loving the sounds of Kenji's appreciative moans and the barely contained writhing of his hips. With his other hand, Fallon caressed the inner skin of one of his thighs, teasing light circles over the sensitive area.

Time seemed to slow, their earlier fears melting away. Eyes closed, Fallon's initial carnal urgency calmed and he savored the textures, tastes and aromas of Kenji. He felt grateful to Kenji for his innocent beauty and wanted the man to feel as good as he could make him feel. He ran his tongue along the underside of Kenji's balls, appreciating the crinkly firm skin. Kenji yelped again. "Wow, Fallon."

Fallon paused, grinning. "That okay for you?" he asked, keeping his lips against Kenji's balls as he formed the words.

Kenji only grunted and thrust his balls closer to Fallon's face.

Keeping his hand lightly clasped around Kenji's cock, Fallon continued sucking and caressing his balls, feathering licks that made Kenji moan each time. Judging him almost relaxed enough for entry, Fallon wet an index finger for a quick foray. He eased Kenji's legs apart some more and angled his finger into his widened butt crack. For a moment, he only caressed the tight rosy flesh of Kenji's hole causing him it to tighten spasmodically.

Yeah, he was just about ready. Fallon pushed the finger into the relaxed hole and let it rest there. The muscles immediately contracted, squeezing Fallon's finger, as if eagerly trying to draw him in deeper. He pushed his finger in and out in a rocking motion. The massage caused the muscles to relax. Kenji's legs fell open even more and he moved his rear toward Fallon, silently asking for more. It couldn't be clearer. Kenji was in ecstasy.

This is only the beginning Fallon promised him silently and pushed a second finger in, stretching Kenji's ass a bit wider. Though he wasn't hung like a horse, Fallon didn't want his thickness to give Kenji any pain or discomfort, only pleasure. "How is that, Kenji?"

"So…good." Kenji's voice came out a whisper. Difficulty speaking. Good sign.

Kenji was ready.

Fallon reached for the bedside table, sliding open the small drawer. Of course, the lube he and Nicky always used would still be in there, untouched since Nicky was gone. Another pinch of guilt got Fallon as he lifted out the tube and popped the small cap. *Please understand, Nicky*, he begged silently.

Squeezing out some of the gel, he dropped the tube onto the table and sat up. Kenji had lifted his head and was watching Fallon's hand, the way Fallon smoothed the glistening gel onto the length of his cock. Nicky and he had always taken turns topping each other. Kenji, Fallon sensed, was different. The way he lay there, legs spread, expression begging for Fallon's body on top of his, between his legs said everything. Kenji was a natural bottom.

The thought made Fallon's blood surge hot once again. Reaching down, he wiped the remaining gel over Kenji's hole. Kenji's good eye rolled toward the back of his head and he tilted his chin up, his body sagging into the mattress. He clearly loved to have his ass played with. Pushing his fingers in, Fallon anointed the inside of Kenji's passage an inch or two in with the lube, just to make sure. In spite of Kenji's enthusiasm, his ass was still a bit tight. Kenji certainly *felt* like a virgin, even though it was always possible he'd had sex in the life he no longer remembered.

Ignoring that depressing possibility, Fallon stretched out on top of Kenji and dipped his mouth to Kenji's for another deep kiss. "Ready, Kenji?" he breathed, then realized as he pushed the head of his cock against Kenji's opening, that the question was as much for himself as for the man underneath him.

Kenji's little gasp and the rapid flutter of his eyelids in

response said more than yes. So different, a vast world away from the easy, fun sex it had been with Nicky and yet, somehow, the same. He and Nicky had been best mates, floating about space together, getting each other off. That's how he'd had seen it until Nicky was no longer there and his heart wouldn't stop aching.

Fallon gave a small firm push and the head of his cock penetrated the tight ring of muscle. Kenji gasped. Kenji's hands gripped his hips. Suppressing a groan, Fallon stopped. Pleasurable heat streaked up his cock, down into his balls. This little taste of Kenji's inner passage made him hungry to push. He remained careful. "That all right?" he whispered down to Kenji.

The slimmer man's full lips were parted. His ragged breath escaped in tiny pants. His good eye stared up at Fallon with glazed delight. "Yes."

Fallon caught himself staring, captured. Kenji was...beautiful. The soles of Kenji's feet rested on his ass cheeks. Even that light touch was sweetly erotic and urged him in deeper. The gel made his cock slide halfway in and the hunger gripped him.

Kenji pulled him in with his feet. The surprising strength embedded his cock all the way to the hilt.

He gasped at the unexpected speed of it then chuckled. The shy virgin was not holding back. Kenji laced one hand into his hair and squeezed a hip with the other, all the while staring up at him with undisguised hunger. That carnal beast in Kenji was taking over, the one who'd lunged at him in Spike's, who kissed him with maddening passion.

Fallon's thoughts whipped away. He captured Kenji's lips in a kiss and pulled back, thrusting in deep. Kenji's answering groan vibrated between their lips. Kenji was a natural at this. The passion in his depths pulled Fallon like an invisible vapor, driving him to thrust faster, harder, all thoughts of caution for a virgin passage abandoned.

He pulled away from their kiss and braced his elbows into the mattress on either side of Kenji in order to drive harder, faster, deeper. As deep as he could possibly go. He could never go as deeply as Kenji seemed to want him to, was pulling him to, hips lifting with each thrust to make their bodies meet each time.

Their syncopated breaths filled the air, as did the soft slap of their sweating bodies together, constant sounds against the hum of the pod's engines. Kenji still stared up at him, a tiny, satisfied smile on his lips, his body pliant, accepting, loving Fallon's cock inside him. Kenji's hand squeezed his hip again and the small sensation sent Fallon over the edge. His climax built and exploded with a driving force it only had when his cock was inside his partner's. His body stiffened, the waves passing in ecstatic bursts until there was nothing left.

Only then did he become aware of the warm splash against his chest and Kenji's small groans of delight. Fallon collapsed on top of him, still breathing heavily. In his haze, he felt Kenji's arms close around him. *Wow.*

"Thank you, Fallon," Kenji whispered by his ear.

Fallon closed his eyes, breathing in Kenji's sweat-laced scent. Damn, how he'd missed this! The musky smell of sex, two sweating bodies pressed together in the aftermath. "Don't thank *me*," he murmured. "You're incredible."

Several moments passed and their breathing grew quieter. Kenji's hand lay flat in the center of his back. "I

94

meant for everything," Kenji said, "not just…this. I'll never be able to repay you."

Fallon lifted up onto an elbow. The sweet, troubled look in Kenji's face rocked him. "Hey, there's nothing to repay me for. That's what friends do. They care for each other without expecting to be paid back. You'd do the same for me, I'm sure."

Kenji nodded. "Yes," he said softly, "I would."

Without thinking, he reached up and smoothed back Kenji's hair. The man's skin was warm and damp. Delicious. "Let's get some rest, eh? Then I need to check our coordinates."

"Yes. And I want to call the Matsuotos again."

"Absolutely." Fallon rolled off of Kenji and cleaned them up before settling in close again and pulling Kenji against him. Spooning Kenji from behind, he rested his lips against Kenji's back. Kenji's hand covered his and he sighed deeply. It had been forever since he'd had held someone. Nicky, that is. Kenji's smaller frame fit so well with his larger one. The comfort brought with it a sense of rest, a relaxation through his body he'd not had either since Nicky's death. Closing his eyes, he drifted off.

Then his recurring dream came.

The boy was screaming, falling, his slim body hurtling toward the ground. His mother, already in the hovering space pod, screamed frantically through the open door and practically fell out after him in her attempt to reach for him.

Fallon jacked up the power on his thrusters. Shooting up from the ground he held his arms out to catch the boy as soon as their airborne paths met.

He couldn't see the boy's face, only a flash of blue robe fluttering as the air whipped it like a windblown flag. The boy's arms and legs sprawled out as if to brace him for the impact with Earth. Instead, he fell into Fallon's arms. Fallon squeezed him close. "I've got you," he said near the boy's ear. "You're safe now."

The boy gripped his arms. His young back heaved against Fallon's chest the entire way back up to the space pod. At the opening of the hovering craft, Fallon delivered the boy into his frantic mother's arms. She gripped the boy to her, sobbing.

The boy turned his face. His gaze met Fallon's. "Thank you," he called over the loud hum of the space pod.

Fallon's jet pack allowed him to hover at the opening, long enough to see the boy's face. One large brown eye stared back at him. The other eye, scarred, the eyeball a cloudy grayish white, gaped sightlessly.

"You're welcome," he said to the boy and shot back down to Earth where a crowd still waited for his aid in removing them from the bombing...

Fallon's eyelids snapped open. "Oh my God," he whispered. He grasped at what he'd been dreaming before it evanesced.

Kenji stirred and turned over. His sleepy gaze met Fallon's then sharpened. "What is it? Are you all right?"

Fallon's heart raced. His blood pumped with heat. "You," he whispered. "It's you."

Chapter Six

Kenji froze. "What is it?"

Fallon raked a large hand through his hair. Different emotions shifted in his blue eyes. "It can't be. It was so long ago."

Oh no. This couldn't be good. Kenji sat up, heart pounding. "Please tell me. What can't be?"

The larger man shook his head. "I'm sorry. I didn't mean to frighten you. It's this dream I keep having. Remember I told you about Nicky's and my first assignment doing rescue missions?

"Yes." Tension clawed Kenji's back again.

"The People's Empire was attacking a series of city-states clustered along its Asian borders. Nicky and I were sent there. There was one particular place, a very small city-state, population of roughly a few thousand people. They were sitting ducks for the Empire. We got one pod loaded and it went to take off. Something happened and a boy, about twelve years old, fell out. He would have died but I had on a jet pack and was able to reach him in time. I caught him and flew him back up to the space pod. The thing is, I never saw his face. I deposited him and flew right back down to continue working. I still dream about it even after all these years and each time, I head back to Earth before he can turn around. Only this time…" he paused, his gaze suddenly intent on Kenji "I didn't just leave the way I usually do." More emotions churned in Fallon's rugged face.

Kenji didn't breathe. "And?"

"The boy turned to me and thanked me. He was...you," he ended in a whisper.

Kenji's heart flipped. He expelled the breath he'd been holding in one whoosh. "Impossible," he breathed.

Fallon sighed, large hand still on his hair. "I know. No doubt it was my subconscious mind putting your face in his—"

"No!" He grasped Fallon's arm. Prickles of excitement skittered along every nerve ending in his body. "I didn't mean it that way. I meant..." He trailed off, studying Fallon's face. It made sense. Why he felt so safe with Fallon. Didn't it? "I have a strange vision," he said softly, "nearly every day. In it I'm falling through the sky and then this man catches me and tells me I'm safe. I can't see his face because of the heavy goggles and helmet he's wearing. It's not a dream. I don't see it when I'm asleep. Only when I'm awake."

"Holy shite."

He and Fallon stared at each other. Was Fallon's heart racing like his? His mind reeled. Logic made him want to deny it. After all, he had no other memories, so why this one? Was he reading into it? Yet something deeper told him no, he wasn't. It was real. His body had remembered the man even though his mind had forgotten.

Fallon reached out and passed a large hand over Kenji's hair. "I felt something when I approached you in Spike's. I thought it was that you were hot. Which you are. But it was...that day."

"I was waiting for you," Kenji said, his voice near a whisper. "I just didn't know it."

98

A smile teased at Fallon's lips, surrounded by sexy dark stubble. "I guess you weren't just giving me a line about saving that bar stool for me."

Kenji's cheeks warmed. His body sparked to life. His cock tightened. Gingerly he traced Fallon's jaw line. The stubble rasped the tender skin of his fingertip, sending sparks through his whole body. Fallon grasped his wrist and pressed his lips into Kenji's palm. Closing his eyes, he nuzzled the soft flesh. His dark eyelashes rested on his cheeks. The gesture was so tender, contrasting with the man's rugged appearance. Kenji's heart fluttered.

Fallon's lids lifted and the look underneath them simmered. "We have another clue now," he said, his voice husky.

Kenji inched closer. His mind was still dazed from the revelation. "Where was I? Where did it happen?"

"The city-state of Sunyata." Fallon's thumb brushed his palm now, back and forth. "It was under attack. Everything was in chaos. Troops from the People's Empire were closing in. There was gunfire in the distance. You were among the many people we were lifting into the mountains, into neutral territory controlled by India." He shook his head. "I don't know what happened to make you fall. Perhaps you were reaching out to someone you saw on the ground and slipped."

"In my visions, there's a woman screaming. I hear her but can't see her." Kenji squeezed Fallon's hand. "Is she my mother?"

"I believe so."

His heart jumped. This was the closest to knowing his identity he'd been! So many times he'd felt that tug of warmth toward Mrs. Matsuoto, wishing she were his mother and knowing she wasn't. He dreaded the possibility that one of the charred corpses in the crash could have been...his real mother. Yet, that woman, the ghostly image in the marketplace...he looked so much like her. A new fire lit his insides. He pulled his hand from Fallon's and gripped the man's beefy arm. "Fallon, you asked me before if there's anything I remember that could help."

"Yes."

"That day in the marketplace when McCray was..." he couldn't even finish the sentence, as if saying the words would cause the image of McCray's mutilated, beaten victim to assault his mind. He told Fallon about the ghostly woman.

"A DNA lock for sure. Someone whose genetic code you share."

"Do you think she could be my mother?"

Fallon sat up straighter, as if Kenji's revelation had lit a similar fire within him. He nodded. "Yes. Unlike McCray who had a sample of your DNA from whoever hired him, she could have locked onto you if she shares your genetic code. If she's your mother, she would have the DNA necessary to track you."

Icy heat invaded Kenji's skin. He couldn't stop staring at Fallon. "Is it possible to find her? I want to see her. I want to know." Not even the shock of being pursued by McCray had as powerful an impact as this possibility. The woman's face rose in his mind, surprisingly accurate in all details considering how quickly her image had appeared and then vanished. He closed his eyes, holding the picture, studying it. "I looked like her," he whispered, still grasping at his memory. The shape of her eyes, the high cheekbones, full

100

lips, black hair pulled back—what he could see of it beneath the hood she wore. The concern in her face, an urgent look, as if his life were of utter importance to her.

Fallon's hand closed warmly over his shoulder. "I have a DNA machine here. Let's have a go. Maybe we'll find her." He pressed a kiss into Kenji's hand again, then leaned in and touched their lips together.

Kenji's eyes closed as he accepted the kiss. He brushed Fallon's stubbled jaw with his fingertips, letting his lips linger against Fallon's.

When Fallon pulled back, his eyes had that velvety look in them. "I guess we can have another go…at this…later," he said in that husky voice he had when aroused.

Kenji nodded. They'd both been ready for more, but the urgency of finding the woman who could be his mother pulled them away. He watched Fallon rise from the bed and slip on his trousers. Fallon was already through the door into the main control room by the time Kenji found his own pants on the floor and got them on.

When he joined Fallon, the other man was already powering up a machine with the usual pushing and flicking of buttons and controls. "Here," he said, "hold out your wrist." Kenji obeyed and Fallon strapped a cuff around it, fastening it gently. Turning back to the machine, he pressed a red button and watched the screen. After several seconds, the screen remained blank. "This will read your genetic code and locate the primary person with that same code." He pressed several more buttons and waited. "Hmm." He worked with the controls a bit and pressed the red button. Again, nothing. "Shite." The tone of the curse word conveyed more than just annoyance.

Kenji tensed. "What's wrong?"

Fallon's look darkened again. He unfastened the wrist cuff. "It's offline. As if it's been remotely disconnected."

Fallon didn't need to say more. The same person or people who'd made sure not to have law enforcement on the scenes back on Terran A had probably messed with Fallon's equipment. He pulled in a shuddery breath as the bloody vision from the marketplace assaulted his mind.

"Dammit!" Fallon checked the other controls on the panel. "The cloaking stopped working too." He exhaled and raked a hand through his hair again. "Think, Fallon. Think." He stared down at the controls, hands braced on the edge of the panel.

"Is there another way to get the DNA lock?"

Fallon's gaze whipped to his. "Not without being online." He bolted upright and pressed a button on the panel. "However, there is a friend of mine…" In seconds, the screen above their heads belched out lines and squiggles, then opened onto a scene.

A young man's face materialized. Blond hair pulled back off his chubby face gave him the appearance of a cherub crossed with a space junkie. "Hey Fallon!" He grinned and popped something into his mouth. The sound of his chewing crackled loudly over the speaker.

"Hey there, Pete. Long time "

"Too long, you overgrown space monkey." The angle of vision widened and Pete's torso, as chubby as his face, was visible, lounging back in a captain's chair at his control panel. Crumbs from whatever he was eating littered his black t-shirt. "Fallon, where the hell are you?" His eyes

102

rounded. "And why are you topless?"

"We're just outside the atmosphere of Terran A."

"And the bare chest?"

"Long story."

Just then, Mike lifted his head from where he'd been sleeping and whined then barked.

"Hey, Mike! Poochie-pooch, good to see you, old boy." Pete grinned in Fallon's direction. "Your dog likes me better than you do, Fallon."

"No accounting for taste. Pete, I want to introduce you to someone." Fallon gently tugged Kenji into view. "Kenji, this is Pete. Pete is the best hacker in the universe. If anyone can find the source of the DNA locks on you, he can. Pete, this is Kenji."

"Hi." Kenji suddenly remembered his naked eye. Oh no! He'd forgotten to put the patch back on. He fought the urge to cover his eye.

Pete's eyes suddenly widened and he sat up, out of his slouched posture. "Oh my God. It's you! Fallon, he's the talk of the hacking world right now. McCray is after him. How the hell? Do you realize who he is?" The wide look returned to Kenji.

Kenji's blood froze. His naked eye didn't seem so important now. "What? What do you mean? You're looking at me as if…" He whipped his gaze to Fallon. "Fallon—"

Fallon's hand landed on Kenji's shoulder again, remaining firm, as if to protect him. "Pete, what the hell are you talking about? Please, tell us everything you know."

"It's all over the hacking airwaves," Pete went on.

"We're not supposed to know about it." He leaned forward. On the screen it appeared as if he were about to poke his nose through the camera. "A few months ago, the leader of Sunyata, the Sunyatan Jewel, also known as *the one who sees*, disappeared off the face of the Earth. This, while the Sunyatan governing council made an arrangement with the government of Japan to take them in on refugee status. There are rumors that Ken—I mean...His Holiness, was sent into space. Others believe he's dead. Anyway, McCray, the idiot he is, thinks the jewel is hidden behind the eye because he's been attacking people's eyes."

"We know about that last bit, Pete. But are you sure of what you're saying? Kenji is the missing leader?"

Pete's gaze went to Kenji's face and studied him. Then he nodded. "When I looked up Sunyata in the universal database, there were photographs of you...Your Holiness, illegal ones, since *the one who sees* isn't supposed to be photographed. That was him. Unless he has a double."

"I suppose it's possible. But a woman we believe is his mother did a DNA lock on him. She called him by name."

"Ah, I see." A reverent look came over the man's chubby face. "Welcome to our humble—wherever we are—Your Holiness."

"Whoa." Kenji held out a hand. "Please stop calling me that. I'm a bartender. There's no way I can be a holy man or a leader, no matter what. I wouldn't have ended up as a bartender in Spike's."

"Look, Pete," Fallon said, his hand still on Kenji's shoulder. "We're having troubles. Someone else has hacked into my system and disabled my cloaking and my DNA locking devices. Can we meet you? I need you to hack into a

104

DNA lock for me."

"Of course." Pete leaned over his control panel and started punching buttons. A set of numbers and letters appeared on another small screen on Fallon's control panel. "These are my coordinates. I'll wait here for you. Oh, and…" He punched more buttons and levers. "I accessed my remote cloaking capabilities. You're cloaked for the time being."

"Great. Thanks, Pete. You're the best. It should take me only a couple of hours to reach you. God willing, of course."

"See you soon. Out."

The screen went blank. Fallon pressed a few more buttons. "There, we're on auto-pilot for the time being. We're cloaked." Fallon turned to him and that large comforting hand squeezed his shoulder again. "You all right, Kenji?"

Kenji's skin tingled where Fallon's hand rested. Pete's revelation made him feel as if Fallon were already slipping away from him, before they'd even had a chance. World leaders didn't have boyfriends, did they? "Fallon, it can't be. I'm not…who Pete says I am. It's impossible."

The other man sighed. "It's possible, Kenji. It certainly explains why you were on a private space pod on Terran A. It explains the statue and your willingness to risk your life for it. The rumor about hiding in space could be true."

"But why would I leave my people when they're being relocated to another place in the world? It doesn't make sense. Wouldn't I need to be with them? What kind of leader would leave his people in the middle of such a big change?" He shook his head. "Not someone I'd want to be, that's for sure."

A touch of sadness sparked Fallon's blue eyes. "Those are good questions, Kenji," he said, "and I hope that a DNA lock to your mother will answer some of them. From what I know of you, though, you don't seem like the kind of leader who would willingly leave his people. Something else must have happened."

Kenji's shoulders sagged. So far what they'd found out was not good. He had a life, an entire life somewhere, which meant that Fallon would have to return him to his people and then leave. "I don't care, Fallon. I don't want to be a...world leader, or whatever it is. Did you hear what he was calling me? *Me*? Your Holiness. That's ridiculous."

"It's all right." Fallon pulled him close, burrowing a hand into his hair. "We'll work it out. I promise I'll do everything I can."

Kenji returned the embrace. "Please, Fallon, whatever you do, call me Kenji, all right?"

"You got it." Fallon squeezed him close.

Kenji rested his cheek against the large man's chest. The recurring vision flashed in his mind. *Plummeting toward Earth. The woman's screams. The ground rising. Strong arms closing around him, halting his deathly descent.* "I just don't want anything to happen to you." The mere thought filled him with dread. It would be his fault if Fallon got hurt or killed. The one person in the universe he felt completely safe with. The man who'd saved his life more than once. The only person he knew who bridged the life he didn't remember with this one.

"I'll do my best to prevent that too." Fallon ended the statement with the brush of his lips over Kenji's cheek. Fallon's hand slipped from his hair and caressed his bare back. Their chests rubbed together and the embrace shifted. Kenji's upset melted into awareness of Fallon's broad back under his hands and the tickle of Fallon's silky chest hair against his hairless skin.

Suddenly, Fallon stilled. Gently but firmly he pulled away, an inner battle showing on his rugged faced.

Kenji's heart thumped. "What is it?"

The other man pulled in a breath, obviously trying to control himself. "I was concerned before you might be married, but now…"

"Now what?" Fallon's hesitation touched off a sense of hysteria which he fought down.

Fallon gestured to him. "You might be celibate. Some of those leaders are."

"Celibate?"

"No sex."

Cold prickles invaded Kenji's skin. Could he have been celibate in the life he didn't remember? It certainly would explain why he was so resistant to every guy who flirted with him or propositioned him. Until Fallon. Fallon was…special. "But…we've already *had* sex," he said, the words slipping out. "Twice. Does it matter at this point?"

"Well, I…don't know."

Fallon's uncertainly left an odd imbalance, a void he needed to fill. Feeling suddenly bold, he stepped in close to Fallon and placed a hand on his chest. Nothing in the whole universe was better than being in Fallon's arms, that muscular body on top of his, inside of him. Holding Fallon's gaze he said, "Don't make me give you up before I have to."

He leaned in again, tentatively, then closer, when Fallon didn't pull away. He lifted his hand from Fallon's chest and caressed his cheek.

"Kenji...we shouldn't..." Fallon's breathing grew deeper.

"I know," Kenji whispered and pressed his lips to Fallon's jaw, the fingertips of one hand touching the other cheek. He brushed his lips back and forth, as if he were some master of seduction. Fallon smelled so good and his short dark stubble tickled his lips, sending sparks of want right down to his toes. Gingerly, yet with definite direction, he dropped soft kisses on the way to Fallon's lips.

"Dammit, Kenji." Fallon pulled him close and took his mouth in a searing kiss.

Kenji grasped Fallon's shoulders, the front of his body heating immediately from the full frontal press, chest to groin. He sighed into Fallon's mouth. Now that he'd had a taste of sex, he knew what he was missing. Not only that, but his body, his...male part, seemed to have taken on a mind of their own, beyond his control.

Fallon licked deep into his mouth, several passionate strokes of his tongue and pulled back. For a split second it seemed he might try to resist again, but instead, Fallon dropped a trail of equally impassioned kisses from his cheek, down the side of his neck while his hands rubbed circles over his back, dipping down to his ass, which he squeezed.

"Ohhh." Kenji released a sigh and moved his hips against Fallon's. Whatever was to come, they had this little time and space to explore, to pleasure each other. All those hours he'd spent working at Spike's, cheerfully fending off

Bud's and the other guys' advances…now he knew why, what it had meant. Even if he got his memory back and left this Kenji behind, he wouldn't forget Fallon.

The thought caused a pang in his chest. They had to make the most of this little bit of time.

Fallon kissed a trail back up Kenji's neck and tugged his earlobe between tongue and teeth. The sensuous scrape pulled another sigh from Kenji and he rubbed his cock against Fallon's harder.

"Damn," Fallon breathed in his ear. His hands tightened on Kenji's ass cheeks. He squeezed then let go, picking up Kenji's hand. "This way." Fallon led him back into the sleeping quarters then turned and worked open Kenji's pants. He pushed them all the way down and grinned, his hands going to his own trousers. He shucked them off and cocked his head toward the shower. "Time for a wash, you and me," he said and pressed a button.

Water shot out of two shower heads in a crisscross and steam immediately clouded the glass doors. Heat flaring through his body, Kenji stepped out of his trousers and followed Fallon into the small cubicle and crowded in with him under the deliciously hot water.

Fallon turned to him. Water beaded off his muscles and plastered down his chest hairs. His gaze swept down the length of Kenji's body and stopped at his cock, which already stood at attention. Kenji swallowed, as Fallon reached out and encircled it lightly with his warm hand. Fallon flattened his hand against him, pushing his cock upward against his pubic hair. The heel of Fallon's hand pressed against his balls, the tips of his large fingers at the tip of his cock.

Kenji's nipples felt rigid, his flat belly quivered and his ass ached to be penetrated again the way Fallon had done. Slowly, Fallon rubbed up and down the length of his cock. Kenji fell against the shower wall.

"You like that, eh?" Fallon's voice was low and seductive, his grin wicked. Kenji's mind went fuzzy.

"Yes," he breathed.

"Well, then why don't you open wider, give me more access."

"Whatever you say, Fallon."

Fallon quirked an eyebrow. "Whatever I say?"

Kenji nodded slowly. "Whatever."

Fallon pressed his cock more firmly against his lower belly, the tip of his index finger caressing the opening of his cock. Kenji could feel the moisture beginning to seep out of him. Fallon brought the tip of his finger to his lips and slowly licked it off with a swirl of his tongue.

Kenji swallowed, almost tasting it. As if reading his thoughts, Fallon brought the finger to Kenji's lips. "Here," he whispered hoarsely, "we can share." The next second, Fallon's hot fingertip was at his lips. He stuck his tongue out hesitantly and tasted a mixture of his own semen mixed with Fallon's saliva.

Fallon's smile deepened. "Just a preview." He then squeezed some soap onto his hands and ran them over his own chest. Kenji swallowed, captured by the man's large hands sliding over his pecs, working up a white lather over the dark chest hair. The hot spray beat down on him, flattening the hair and creating sudsy rivulets down his chest and belly into the thicker mass of hair at his groin.

Kenji stared at his thick, reddish cock impervious to the water pressure.

Fallon's hands began to soap up his pubic hair and then his cock and finally his balls. Kenji leaned against the slippery side of the cubicle, his gaze glued on Fallon's movements. With a wicked grin, Fallon put his hands behind him and scrubbed his ass.

Then he got some more soap from the dispenser and looked at Kenji. "Your turn now." His slick hands landed on Kenji's chest and made circles over his nipples. Kenji arched his back against the stall. "Like that?"

Kenji made a soft sound like an "Umm."

"I like it, too," he murmured, tweaking at Kenji's nipples and then roaming across his chest with his soapy hands.

Kenji exhaled and pushed his chest out. Wherever Fallon's hands slid, ecstasy followed. Fallon encircled Kenji's ribcage and finally came to rest his large hands on his buttocks, bringing Kenji's cock against his inner thigh. "I like this even better."

Kenji pushed himself up against Fallon's front and slid his hands around the man's broad back, fingertips grabbing at the muscles along Fallon's spine made slippery by the water. The heat of the shower made the clean scent of soap invade his senses, as did the feel of hard muscle filling his hands. But even without the steamy water, the cubicle would have been hot with just the feel of Fallon's body.

The large man released a small groan and his eyes went dusky. "Kenji," he said, voice tight, "Don't stop." Kenji rocked his hips, bringing his cock into the recess between Fallon's legs. Fallon's leg hairs created a pleasant friction against his sensitive skin. He could feel Fallon's hard cock against his belly.

Fallon groaned, at the same time half-lifting Kenji until their cocks slid against each other. "There, that's much better. Wouldn't you say?" he murmured against Kenji's face, bringing his lips to Kenji's and nuzzling them.

He pushed Kenji's shoulders further against the wall as his kiss grew deeper. Kenji's mind swirled. More hot energy moved through his body. The tingling spread through his chest, into his nipples, down his stomach and from his cock into his ass and thighs. The shower thundered around them, plastering their hair and making their mouths wet.

Kenji caressed Fallon's rear. Feeling bolder, he ran his fingers into the crack, feeling the rougher skin the deeper he got. He tried to copy what Fallon had done to him on the bed. He'd never imagined a man's opening there could feel so erotic.

"So...good," Fallon said against his lips.

What would it be like to penetrate him there the way Fallon had done to him? As he imagined it, he continued exploring the area. One hand sliding back across Fallon's hip, he reached as far down as he could and cupped Fallon's balls. He loved the feel of them — crinkly skin, yet heavy and full in his hand.

Fallon in the meantime, was doing his own exploration. Keeping Kenji suspended with Kenji's feet atop his so that their cocks were at the same level, Fallon pressed his own hands against Kenji's butt cheeks, massaging them and expanding them, each movement bringing their two cocks together.

Kenji pushed his hands against Fallon's chest a moment

until he loosened his hold. "Is something wrong?" he asked, his two eyebrows drawn together in puzzlement.

"Yes," said Kenji. Before Fallon could ask anything more, Kenji dropped down until his mouth was inches from the head of Fallon's cock. Placing his palms on Fallon's hips to steady himself, his mouth watered at the larger man's stiff member, with a glistening droplet seeping from the tiny opening. Kenji closed the gap and gave it a lick. "You're dripping and I've got to catch it before it falls." He pushed Fallon until the man stepped back and was trapped against the steel gray wall of the shower.

"Kenji…" Fallon whispered.

Closing his eyes, Kenji surrendered to the one thing that seemed to take his mind off his troubles, if even for a few moments. Fallon just tasted so good. The man's musky scent floated between them as did the heat from his body. Fallon's breathing blended with the roar of the shower and the silky skin of his cock glided against Kenji's tongue. Curling thumb and forefinger around the thick base, Kenji licked and sucked, as if he could pull Fallon's essence out through the head with each erotic tug.

Time blurred and Kenji felt his mind and body blend. The boundaries of his physical body seemed to lift and everything was pure existence, a flow of creation. He knew exactly how to lick Fallon, how to touch and tease and suck so that the large man's body sank against the opposite wall of the tiny cubicle. Tension ran out Fallon's body and he moaned softly. Even his breathing softened, fell into a gentle rhythm, as if he too, were experiencing this strange flow.

Whatever made Kenji lift his head, he didn't know. But when he looked up at Fallon's heavy-lidded gaze, he saw that Fallon was experiencing it. Fallon's lips were parted and his chest rose and fell evenly. "Kenji," he whispered. Droplets of water fell off his chin and hair, dropping onto Kenji's face.

"Shhh." Kenji leaned over again and ran his tongue over the smooth lobes of Fallon's cockhead. He rubbed the skin underneath it with the pad of his thumb. As if to accommodate him, Fallon shifted, spreading his legs farther apart. Kenji caressed the sensitive skin of Fallon's inner thighs, loving the feel of the curly hair growing there, so unlike his own legs. As he sucked at Fallon's cock, he continued stroking his balls and inner thighs and even drawing his fingers upward into the crack of his ass.

Fallon's seemed to flatten himself against the stall wall, completely submitted to whatever Kenji wanted to do to hm. It gave Kenji an odd feeling of power which he'd never had before.

It wouldn't take much longer, though Kenji didn't want it to end. Fallon's cock jumped against his lips. The shaft thickened between Kenji's fingers and from that ethereal place in his being, Kenji could practically envision Fallon's essence rising up, like lava in a volcano — an image he'd seen in a book not long ago — ready to spurt out from the pressure.

Kenji stroked the lower half of Fallon's cock while sucking the upper half. His hand and mouth found a rhythm, covering every delicious inch of the hard shaft, from base to head, in an erotic massage.

Fallon groaned. His hips jerked upward and the gush shot out. Kenji caught the warm essence in his mouth, swallowed a mouthful, then pulled back, eyes closed, and let it land on his skin, knowing somehow that would be a charge for Fallon. The milky cum coated his chin and chest.

Some of it even hit his forehead and cheeks before it washed away and Fallon's heavy breathing was the only other sound besides the ever-present spray of the water.

When Kenji opened his eyes, Fallon was staring down at him. Kenji's mind was still clear, as if the energy flowing through him and between him and Fallon had washed away his fear. "This is for you, too, Fallon," he said, his voice like a meeting place of the understanding and clarity in his mind and heart. He rose to his feet, keeping his gaze on Fallon's. Fallon turned off the water and slid open the door. Leaning over, he retrieved their towels from the floor and handed one to Kenji. "Let's dry off," he said softly.

Kenji obeyed. He ran the towel over his face and chest. When he moved the towel to his back, his gaze fell on the bed, rumpled with the evidence of two bodies having well used it. A pleasant shiver passed through him."

"I'll dry you off." Fallon's voice, still husky, sounded behind him. Before Kenji could answer, a towel was being wiped firmly yet gently across his upper back.

Eyes closing, Kenji succumbed to that pleasure too. His body moved under Fallon's hands wherever they rubbed the towel, over his hips, his bottom, his thighs. Fallon wiped the towel briskly yet sensually. "There, your back is dry." Fallon ended the sentence with the press of his lips into the small of Kenji's back. Then Fallon was turning Kenji and rubbing the towel over his chest.

Fallon's blue gaze simmered into his even as he wiped Kenji dry. Unspoken feeling seemed to float between them. A grin tugged at his lips. "Lift your arms."

Kenji obeyed and Fallon wiped there too. He giggled. "That tickles."

"Oh yeah? How about this?" Lowering the towel, Fallon pushed his lips into the sensitive area and nuzzled.

"Ahhh." Kenji's eyelids fluttered. Fallon lingered there then feathered a trail with his tongue down the outline of Kenji's pectoral muscle and over his nipple. When Fallon lifted his face, his eyes were hungry again. "Did that tickle?"

He shook his head. "No," he whispered.

Fallon grasped his upper arms and stepped into him. "I can't get enough of you, Kenji," he breathed and closed his lips over Kenji's.

Kenji's eyes closed. Nothing he'd ever experienced was like being with Fallon, the man who'd caught him when he was falling through the sky. The one person in the entire universe who bridged the gap between the life he'd forgotten and this one. Dropping his towel, he covered the man's strong shoulders and caressed them. It was the same for him. He couldn't get enough of Fallon, of his musky clean scent, his blue eyes, and broad, hard muscles.

One of Fallon's hands slid down his back and pulled Kenji closer. Their cocks rubbed together. Kenji caught his breath, his lips still against Fallon's. Without thinking he ran his hands down Fallon arms and slipped around to his back. Down further, sliding until Fallon's hard ass cheeks filled his seeking hands. The muscles flexed against his palms and he pulled, bringing Fallon's groin firmly against his.

Fallon's kiss grew hungrier. His tongue swirled madly against Kenji's and that feeling took over Kenji again, of being lost in a world of made only of Fallon, his scent, the heat shimmering off his muscles, the feel of him, his body and his essence...

The room felt like it was moving. No...Kenji was

116

moving, guided by Fallon. Then he was tilting backward, something soft meeting his back. The bed. They were back on the bed, Fallon above him. Kenji parted his legs instinctively and Fallon's large body fit right between them.

Yes. Sheer raw instinct took over and Kenji's clutched the rock hard ass as it flexed from the thrusting of Fallon's hips.

Fallon swooped down and captured his mouth, locking their tongues together in a never-ending kiss. As if their bodies were melting together, the boundaries between them seemed to melt, blending them into one body. One soul.

I love you. The phrase echoed in Kenji's mind. The emotions expressed in the passionate constant lick of his tongue against Fallon's. All those nights alone in his little rented room, his soul aching for something. Now it was here. With him. Fallon. It had always been Fallon…

"Ohhh." The pressure built so hard and fast, an orgasmic sneeze that rocked his entire body, followed by the splash of his own hot juices on his skin and Fallon's chest. He trembled, clinging to Fallon through the storm inside him. In the midst of it all, he felt the other man's body stiffen under his hands. Fallon's whole body clenched just before his climax added to the hot splash of cum between them, coating Kenji's stomach and chest with creamy thickness.

Droplets splashed onto his face, his lips and Kenji licked up whatever he could, taking Fallon's essence deep inside him.

"Kenji." The word was whispered hoarsely, thick with emotion and then Fallon's body wilted on top of his, trapping heat and moisture, fusing their naked torsos.

Fallon's weight sank Kenji into the mattress. He closed

his eyes enjoying the sensation of all that muscle-bound heat on top of him, shielding him, surrounding him.

Fallon caressed Kenji's hair. A while seemed to pass with only the hum of the pod's engines in the background. "I can't believe it," Fallon murmured close to his ear. "All these years I've wondered, what happened to that boy? Whatever became of him? And here you are." He levered up onto one elbow, gazing down. "How ever did you end up at Spike's?"

Kenji slid one hand lazily over Fallon's broad back. "There was this guy, Paul, who eats all the time at the Matsuotos' place. I waited on him and we used to chat."

Fallon's expression changed. "You just waited on him? That's all?"

"Yes, that's all." He touched Fallon's cheek. "Far as I know, you're the one and only."

A smile touched Fallon's lips. "Sorry. Go on."

"So one day we were chatting and he told me with my looks, I could make a good living just serving drinks at Spike's, enough to rent my own place. I wanted to do that because I felt uneasy staying with the Matsuotos. Since Mr. Matsuoto told me to hide my statue, I figured there was some kind of danger involved. I didn't want to put them at any risk."

"I see." Fallon stroked his cheek. "It's a miracle no one recognized you."

"I've wondered that myself."

Fallon studied Kenji's face a moment more. "Did you ever try to find out who you were?"

118

He shook his head. "No. Like I said, since Mr. Matsuoto was so cautious about my statue, I felt I shouldn't go asking around anywhere."

"That was wise."

He lay back and exhaled, his hand on Fallon's. "Truthfully, I'm not anxious to find out now. I just want to see that woman. What if she *is* my mother?" He turned his head on the pillow and looked up at Fallon. "What if she's in danger? I couldn't bear that."

Sadness tinged the blue of Fallon's eyes. "You're good-hearted, Kenji," he said softly, "and brave. Everything a good leader is. And even though you don't remember it all right now, you've suffered horribly. The ravages of war and oppression, disease." He brushed Kenji's cheek with his thumb. His emotions roiled in the air between them, but he didn't say anything more. Finally, he glanced up at the screen on the wall from which the time flashed. "We have fifteen minutes until we join Pete's craft." He started to roll away, pulling the covers off.

"Not yet," Kenji murmured and grasped Fallon's arm. His heart jumped. A few more minutes and this little bit of heaven would be gone. "We still have some time."

Fallon braced himself on one knee. He was staring down at Kenji from a face flushed with sexual exertion. He glanced at the screen on the wall, from which the time flashed. And then grinned. "You know? You're right. We can do a lot in fifteen minutes." He lowered himself back down onto Kenji.

* * * * *

"Have a seat, Kenji," Fallon said fifteen minutes later after they'd dressed and gone back to the cockpit. "I'm going to try reaching the Matsuotos again before we rendezvous with Pete."

Kenji sat in the co-pilot's chair a couple of feet away, his body still humming from their love-fest of the last couple of hours. A whining sound emanated from the corner and Mike unfolded his furry body from his sleeping mat and came over. While watching the screen, Kenji petted the dog's head and received grateful licks on his hand in response.

The Matsuotos place appeared again. Still no sign of movement. His worry returned. "They're still not there. Something's happened to them, Fallon. We've got to do something."

Fallon turned to him, his look sympathetic yet firm. "I know we do. Unfortunately, ISP is in on this, I'm nearly positive, and there's no one I can contact to help without taking the risk of their finding you." He squeezed Kenji's shoulder briefly. "I promise, as soon as I'm in a position to look for your friends, I will. Until then, your safety comes first. Which also means you need to take care of yourself. Are you hungry? I know I am."

"Not really." Kenji scratched Mike behind his fuzzy ears. Petting the dog gave him a small comfort, but not from the guilt clawing at his chest. "It's my fault they're in danger, Fallon. That brute must have seen Matsuoto-san trying to get me to leave the marketplace, even while he was busy wounding someone else."

"No. You're absolutely not at fault. Something else is going on here that you don't even know about. If we can unravel the mystery, we'll have a better chance of helping your friends." He sighed, manning the steering controls.

Kenji nodded. "Okay." He lowered himself back into Nicky's old seat.

Fallon's blue eyes searched his face for a few moments. "You have my word, Kenji," he said softly, then turned back to his controls.

Kenji watched the man's back muscles again, staring at him and alternately, through the windshield, until a small craft, about the size of Fallon's pod, its exterior covered with stickers that read, "Reunite Earth" and other such slogans, came into view on the screen.

Fallon chuckled. "There he is. That's Pete, all right." He pressed a button and Pete's face came onto the screen again, one fat cheek bulging with something he was chewing. "Glad to see your little space ship is the same, Pete. Says as much as you do."

Pete grinned. He mumbled something around his mouthful of food causing a spray of crumbs toward the screen.

Fallon laughed again. "Whatever you say. Get ready for a holding beam."

Pete nodded and pressed more controls on his end.

Fallon's pod began to rumble and vibrate and Kenji gripped the armrests.

"Don't worry, Kenji, it doesn't get rougher than this. I'm just locking Pete's craft onto ours so we can go in there without having to travel."

Kenji nodded. The process was all there, visible on the screen. Now Fallon's pod had a light beam on Pete's craft, pulling the two ships together.

Bump. Kenji lifted out of seat and fell back in. The movement stopped and Mike whined, pawing at the door of Fallon's pod. Fallon pressed a button and the door slid up. "Go ahead, see your friend Pete." He looked at Kenji. "Pete stuffs the dog as much as he stuffs himself."

"I see." He couldn't smile, though, for the pounding of his heart and the lump in his throat. A second door slid up, revealing the interior of Pete's craft.

"Come on." Kenji felt a gentle hand at his elbow. Fallon guided him forward, the pressure of his touch communicating he understood Kenji's reluctance.

"Hey, guys!" Pete's voice came from the doorway.

"Just a second, Pete," Fallon said over his shoulder and turned back to Kenji. Fallon's blue eyes looked sad. "Whatever we learn, Kenji, I just want you to know, I'm here for you." He touched Kenji's cheek, a whisper of touch that made a tingle of heat in Kenji's skin.

I'd rather stay here with you, he thought, looking into Fallon's blue eyes. Traveling through space, having sex, going on adventures to planets and galaxies he couldn't have dreamed of, as Fallon's sidekick. Then having more sex.

He sighed. It would be impossible anyway. If he really was the Sunyatan Jewel, then he very well couldn't abandon thousands of people who needed him just because he'd fallen in love. Could he? That wouldn't be right. Not at all. Slowly, he nodded. "All right. Let's go."

Chapter Seven

"Welcome to my pad, Your Holiness," Pete said, gesturing around his ship. He winked. "The place women can't resist."

"I wish you'd call me Kenji," he said. Pete's formal address caused such a chill.

Pete frowned. "Are you sure about that?"

"Yes." Kenji hovered in the doorway.

The inner battle went on in Pete's eyes, a brief window in which Kenji saw Pete as a child, being scolded by his mother for bad manners. Finally he saw his request of familiarity win out over propriety. Pete grinned. "I see you won't come in until I agree. All right. Please, Kenji, come in. I'm sorry I didn't have time to clean up before you got here, really."

"No problem." Kenji stepped in and held his breath, his nose immediately assaulted by the stench of dirty socks. The inside of Pete's pod looked like Spike's after an especially rowdy night. Food wrappers littered every surface, clothes were draped over computer screens and piles of outdated digital book and magazine readers. The place was a far cry from Fallon's clean, tidy space pod.

"I had several other jobs to do before we met," Pete said. "Otherwise I would have cleaned up." He yanked some socks and a t-shirt off a surface, revealing a machine and control panel vastly more button and lever-filled than Fallon's.

"Since when do you apologize, Pete?"

"I don't care if *you* see my mess, Fallon. But Kenji is a...guest. And a distinguished one, at that."

"I don't mind."

"You're doing us a great favor." Fallon stopped Pete's clean-up with a hand on his shoulder. "I can't go to Central with this. Someone on the inside may be involved."

Pete stopped, a wrinkled pair of undershorts in hand. He cleared his throat and Kenji saw a flash of something pass over his face, almost like guilt. He was hiding something from Fallon. In an almost imperceptible flash, Pete forced a grin. "No problema. I've always suspected some corrupt shitballs in that organization. Oh--excuse my language, Kenji."

"It's all right." Kenji's heart thumped. Should they be here? Maybe Pete was the insider.

But Fallon nodded, not seeming to suspect Pete in the least. "Yes, well, two crime scenes and no patrols answering the call. Kenji could have been killed both times."

Pete mulled this over a few seconds then tossed the underwear into a dark corner already piled with clothing. He rubbed his hands together. "Well, let's see what we can find out."

"Thanks, Pete. You're a good man."

He laughed. "Glad someone thinks so," he said, his secret tension seemingly forgotten in the banter. Kenji relaxed a tiny bit. If Fallon trusted Pete, maybe he needed to also. Certainly if Pete had a role in all of this, he wouldn't be helping Fallon to find answers, would he?

Pete stepped over to a weird-looking contraption on top of the control panel and began powering it up. "This is a slightly older model of the DNA receiving mechanism of the lock, but it should serve. This one will pick up the primary holder of your code first, that being a parent. The more sophisticated models can pick up all family members at once, like a conference call. I'm working on getting my sticky little hands on one of those." He winked at Kenji, then glanced about as if looking for something. "Ah, here it is." He leaned behind Kenji, who jumped out of his way.

Pete held out a strange helmet to him. "Put this on and have a seat. Whoever was looking for you besides that bastard McCray should be visible to us with this."

Kenji sat down, letting Pete lower the helmet onto him. It fit snugly, its foam padding protecting his skin from the scrape of the metal straps over his skull and forehead. Pete fastened the chin strap and connected a series of wires to the main mechanism then stood back, inspecting. "Okay. You're good to go."

"Pete," Fallon asked, "is there any reason that a DNA lock wouldn't work? What if Kenji's mother tried to contact him when he first went missing and couldn't connect with him?"

"Hmm. It's possible, if Kenji's DNA was somehow tampered with." Pete adjusted knobs on the DNA locking machine. The machine began to whine and squeak. "We're almost ready."

"What does it mean, *the one who sees*?'" Kenji asked as Pete worked some more on the contraption.

"From what I've read about the Sunyatan sect, *the one who sees* can look into people—not literally—but into their souls, like their thoughts and feelings. I think." He checked the helmet. "Okay. All set. Are you ready, Kenji?"

Kenji's insides jumped. Maybe that explained these weird feelings he got about people, like Pete's guilt a few moments ago. "Yes. Go ahead."

Pete flicked a switch and a beam of light shone from a small lens, creating a glow in the center of the room, right in front of where Kenji sat. Kenji stared into the glow while his heart beat against his chest so hard he grew slightly breathless.

"Don't worry, it won't hurt you. The electrodes in the helmet are recording your DNA code and running them through every tracked zone in the universe. Whoever shares your DNA code, the beam should lock onto them."

Seconds passed and the light began to shimmer in waves.

"Here! Something's happening." Pete pointed. "There, in the center. It's locked onto someone very far away."

Kenji felt as if he'd leaped across time and space. He closed his eyes and when he opened them, the ghostly shimmering of another place surrounded him. He was in a room. Timbers and whitewash made up the structure, and the floor on which he stood was dark polished wood.

"Kenji-chan!"

She was beautiful, a vision unlike no other. Seeing her for the second time, her beauty radiated outward, filling him with an instinctive recognition. Standing before him, she wore the same light robes as before, only with the hood hanging about her neck, he could see her face in full view. Her long black hair hung down her back and Kenji wanted only to run his hand down its smoothness, to feel it under his fingertips, to know she was real. "Kenji-chan?" she said. "Is that you?"

His heart lurched. "Are you…my mother?"

"Yes, Kenji-chan."

"Mother," he whispered. "I've wondered about you so many times. I just…don't remember anything."

Her eyes misted and she hurried toward him, arms outstretched. "Praise Kirei, you're safe!" She reached out to embrace him and he too, reached out, forgetting she was a projected image. Both their arms sliced through the air. Sorrow immediately flooded her delicate features. "Oh, Kenji-chan, I've missed you so much. We're trying to get you back. I'm sorry. We didn't mean for you to get so lost."

A pang squeezed his chest. "There was an accident, but I survived."

A tear pushed from her left eye. "I told them not to do it to you. Oh, Kenji, I'm so sorry."

"Do what to me?" His sight blurred and his breath came in tight gasps. "Where are you?"

"Amami Shoto. The island they're relocating us to."

So, what Pete had told him was true.

"The government of Japan is giving us asylum. All of us. That's why we want to bring you back, Kenji. Only, that hunter, that killer in the marketplace. He told me the danger of using that machine to find you. He said others could find you if I looked. But I couldn't help it. I've been desperate." A buzzing sound crackled around her and her image grew misty.

"Who, Mother? Who are you talking about?"

"Be careful, Kenji. Please." The light around her crackled and she faded.

"Wait! Don't go!" Kenji clawed at the air but his mother's image began to blur around the edges. "No, Mother!"

"Kenji!" His mother reached out her ghostly arms to him but to no avail. Her image grew more and more indistinct until she faded completely.

"No!" The word came out in a gasp. Kenji yanked off the helmet and fell to his knees, reaching for the spot his mother had been standing in. The room too, had disappeared and he was once again surrounded by the slovenly interior of Pete's space pod. "No." The empty space felt like a knife stabbed through his gut. To know he belonged to someone — and then to have it snatched away! The loneliness he'd felt for so long overwhelmed him and he covered his face with both hands, hunched over.

A second later a strong hand rubbed his back. No, he wasn't alone. Not anymore. Slowly, he uncovered his face. His body shook as if he were naked in the cold, while the image of his mother's face haunted his mind. Would he ever actually be with her? "I didn't even get a chance to talk to her," he choked out.

Fallon nodded, his blue eyes filled with understanding. "I'm sorry. The link was too weak out here to last." He moved his touch to Kenji's hair, caressing it back from his face. On his other side, Mike whined and licked Kenji's cheek.

He petted Mike's head, a thank you for the canine affection. "At least I know where she is." He looked at Fallon and then up at Pete. "Who was she talking about? Who told her it was dangerous to look for me?"

"I don't know." Darkness tinged Fallon's rugged face,

128

as if inwardly he was gathering his suspicions yet keeping them to himself. "I don't know."

"How will I get there, to this island she mentioned?"

Fallon raked a large hand through his hair, a gesture of frustration. "I can bring you there, Kenji," he said. "But with a bounty hunter and God knows who else after you, you're not safe. Since those are your people, that island is the first place they'll look for you."

"We need more information," Pete said before Kenji could answer. "We need to know who hired McCray and why."

Kenji looked at them both again. "You don't think the Sunyatan government would have hired McCray to find me, do you?"

"I can't imagine it, Kenji." Fallon shook his head. "I'd think they'd search for you through private channels, but not through a bounty hunter."

"Then if they didn't hire McCray, who would have? Why would someone be after me?"

"The People's Empire, for one," Fallon interjected. "They've been after your people for years. Perhaps they hired McCray to find you."

"Would they need to do that?" Pete asked then popped one of his crisps into his mouth. "I should think they have their own agents."

"They don't have jurisdiction outside of Earth's air and land space. If they went after Kenji themselves and got caught, the Intergalactic Council would be on them so hard, even they wouldn't have a chance. Technically, they'd need a third party to hire a bounty hunter for them so as not to leave a trail. Any proof that they did such a thing would come back to bite them."

Kenji shook his head. "The thing I don't understand is why I would have been sent away in the first place. My mother said something was done to me she hadn't wanted done. She apologized for having let them do it. Could that have something to do with it? And with my memory loss?"

Pete held up a curly crisp a few inches from his lips. "Maybe the thing your mother didn't want done to you was some sort of procedure, something that would suppress your memory while you were sent away in order to hide you. Seeing as there's been so much strife in the place you're from, perhaps you were sent away to keep you safe. But something went wrong and you were lost, along with your knowledge." Pete popped the crisp into his mouth then lumbered over to his control panel and set the bag down. Quickly wiping his fingers on his pants, he began furiously typing, then punched a key. The screen lit up. "Here's the report that came through the hacker channels." He pointed. "It says here *the one who sees* can look at someone and know his or her secrets." He cleared his throat and started looking around. "Speaking of which...where did I put my crisps?"

"Right here." Kenji picked them up off the console and handed the bag to him.

"Thanks, buddy." Pete studied his face again. The look on his face gave Kenji the feeling he wasn't saying something. "Didn't you mention you were a bartender in Spike's?"

Fallon's hand landed on Kenji's shoulder, giving Kenji a sense of protection and belonging. "Yes, he did. It's another long story."

Pete shook his head. "Wow, it must be."

"Why do you ask, Pete?" Fallon asked.

Pete shrugged. "I...I'm just glad you seem to have found a...friend, Fallon."

Kenji looked at him a moment. Pete was *definitely* hiding something.

"Me, too."

Kenji turned and caught Fallon gazing at him in that...*soft* kind of way. Comfort flooded him again, smoothing the edges of pain left by seeing his mother and having watched her fade. Fallon didn't seem to sense anything unusual about Pete. At least, if he was, he wasn't mentioning it.

Kenji sighed. Finding his mother had given them more questions that answer. Not only that, but now he'd actually seen her face, there was no going back. He had to get to the truth, even though it might mean losing Fallon. "If my memory was actually erased, how did they do it?"

"Probably a memory chip implanted somewhere on your body," Pete said. "It's so small you'd never even feel it but it would interfere with brain activity just enough to scramble your memory--suppress it, really. But it could have somehow scrambled your DNA code. At least temporarily. It must have returned to normal if your mom found you." Pete looked at him. "Kenji, put the helmet back on a minute, would you?"

Kenji obeyed, going back to sit in the chair. Pete pressed a couple more buttons. Another screen lit up, this one with an image of Kenji's insides glowing, like an X-ray. "This helmet has other capabilities aside from DNA locking.

I hooked it up myself." He continued pressing buttons and a light passed down the screen, highlighting Kenji's brain as it passed up and down. It fixed on one point and flashed, a reddish glow. "There's something there," he said, a note of excitement in his tone.

Kenji stared at the screen. "It's right where my eye is," he said.

Fallon leaned in closer and breathed. "Holy shite."

Kenji's suddenly sat up, looking back and forth between Fallon and Pete. Quickly he told them about the nightmare he'd had repeatedly in the years since the Matsuotos had found him.

Fallon nodded. "Chances are that's where the chip has been implanted."

"But you said my eye was damaged by disease."

"It was. But what better place to go digging than in an already damaged spot?"

Kenji raked both hands through his hair. "Oh no," he whispered. "It's true. I really am that leader." He looked between Fallon and Pete again. "It's like you said, isn't it? They sent me into hiding and put the memory chip in — "

"So that you wouldn't behave like *the one who sees*," Fallon finished for him. Silence settled over the three of them as the implications sank in.

Kenji pounded the top of the console lightly with his fist. "But *why*? It just doesn't make sense."

Pete tossed aside his empty crisps bag. "Hey, Fallon, I fixed your cloaking device. You *could* take Kenji back and speak to his mother. If you keep him hidden, no one else has to know until it's safe. Right?"

Kenji grasped Fallon's hand. "Would you do that? We can get answers and then figure out what to do. Please."

Fallon's gaze was sober. "I don't see how. Now they have your DNA, they can track you anywhere. We'll have to remain on the run, keeping out of reach."

"I can scramble Kenji's DNA," Pete interjected. "It'll last at least a while."

A heavy sigh. "All right. If that's the case, then we have a chance."

"Great." Pete's hands flew over his controls and keyboard. "Hold tight Kenji," he said. You'll feel a pinch."

Kenji's back tightened. A sensation like a million pin pricks skittered up and down his spine. Then it was gone.

"You're set. I'd say you have a few days before your DNA rights itself."

"Thanks, Pete. As usual. Now I have to unlock Pete's craft first and re-engage the cloak so we can get out of here."

"Sure thing," Pete said and went right to his control panel. "I'll have you disengaged faster than you can say —"

A faint whirring noise cut off his words. The noise grew louder, causing the joined space pods to vibrate.

Fallon grasped Kenji's arm with one hand and yanked the helmet off with the other. "Pete, take Mike and get the hell out of here, as far away as you can!"

Mike whined and barked, an obvious protest but Fallon glared at him and pointed while propelling Kenji toward the door. "Stay, Mike!"

Pete grasped Mike's collar and tugged him back. "Come on boy, it'll be all right."

The vibrations grew deafening. Kenji recognized the sound.

McCray. He'd locked onto them before Pete scrambled his DNA code. "Fallon, go with them! Save yourself!" he shouted over the din, struggling to loosen Fallon's hold on him.

"The hell I will!" Fallon shoved him through the door and bounded to the control panel. With a punch of a button, the door between them shut. Pete's little space ship was ejected and spun away until it was out of sight.

"Shite!" Fallon mumbled through his teeth as his hands flew over the control panel. The motors rose in pitch, matching the grinding of the approaching space pod. McCray's battered, patched-up piece of shite appeared through the windshield. "Hang on." He pulled back on the throttle and they shot forward.

McCray's scarred face materialized on the screen. "Stop now, or I'll blast you to kingdom come."

"Go to hell!" No way was that bastard getting his hands on Kenji. He pulled the throttle as far as it would go. "It's a bluff," he said to Kenji. "As long as you're in here, he won't shoot. He wants you alive." The pod catapulted forward and McCray's vehicle grew smaller. "Ah, that's better." He wiped his brows and heaved a breath.

A blinding light flooded the interior of ship and made the space around the pod glow as if they were nearing the sun. The next second, the pod halted, jolting Kenji against him. "Fallon, What's happening?"

Through the windshield, the belly of a larger ship came into sight and hovered above them, trapping the pod in its beam. "McCray's not the only one out there." He'd have ordered Kenji into the sleeping quarters and locked him in but it wouldn't have kept him safe. Not now. It was definitely a ship from ISP headquarters. All ISP agents' ships were programmed into their mainframe. Whoever was above them had complete control over his ship.

The pod lurched as the larger ISP ship locked onto the ramp, connecting the entryways.

Shite. He unsheathed his phazer and set it on kill. "Get behind me," he said, giving a hard look to Kenji. "And no heroics."

Defiance flashed in Kenji's eye but he gave a quick nod and obeyed.

Fallon gripped his phazer.

The door connecting the ships slid up.

McCray stood there, filling the space like a ragged giant. "I get the jewel now." He pointed his phazer rifle at Fallon, his eyes glittering at Kenji. "Drop your weapon."

"Like hell." Fallon moved in front of Kenji and aimed at McCray's chest. "Go now and I'll let you live."

McCray made a gurgling sound. His massive chest heaved and the hand holding his weapon shook with his laughter. "You're funny. Now, I count to three and if you don't hand him over, I shoot. One. Two. Thr—"

The sizzle of a laser shot through the air. McCray's smile faded and his huge body keeled over and hit the floor.

Kenji's hand closed around Fallon's upper arm and gripped. "You killed him," he breathed.

"I haven't fired," he said over his shoulder. "Stay there."

"Agent Fallon, are you all right?" The chief of ISP operations appeared in the space McCray had occupied seconds earlier, holding a mega-phazer. "You're safe from him now."

But Fallon held still, his phazer brandished. The sight of the chief should have been a relief, but it all made sense now. The lack of law enforcement back on Terran A. The deactivating of his cloaking device. He'd figured out that someone in ISP was in on this, but he hadn't stopped to consider the chief.

The chief frowned. "What is it, Fallon? You can stand down now." He peered around Fallon. "I see you have Kenji Shimizu. That's good. McCray would have hurt him and he needs to be returned to his people, alive." The older man gestured. "Come now, you and His Holiness get on board. We'll take him back to his people. He's an important man." The chief took a step toward them.

"Stay back." He raised the phazer. "No one touches Kenji. Not you, not anyone."

"It's all right, Fallon." The chief lowered his phazer. "You're safe now. McCray is dead."

"Why wasn't there ISP backup down on Terran A? Two incidents and no police assistance."

"The satellite link had gone on the fritz. We never received the distress calls."

"Or you didn't answer them."

136

"What are you saying, Fallon, that I had something to do with this?" The chief glanced at Kenji. "Come on. I have the same goal you do. To get this man back to his people."

"I'll take care of that." Every ounce of discipline he possessed kept him from firing his phazer at the corrupt piece of shite. "If you meant to take him home, then you'd let me go ahead. Lift the lock on my ship and I'll take him."

"I can't do that. I'm sorry, Fallon." The chief pointed his high-powered phazer at Fallon. "Throw me your phazer." At Fallon's hesitation, his cultivated voice hardened. "*Now.*"

Behind him stood what appeared a small private mercenary army, all huge men with automatic phazer rifles.

Fallon's heart pumped. Nicky used to tell him how naïve he was. Now he understood why. "You...hired McCray, didn't you?"

The chief's lip curled. "Yes, Agent Fallon, I hired him."

"Why?"

"A bounty hunter going after a man for profit is one thing. A cop, completely another. I procured the DNA from his mother when she first came to ISP for help. Then McCray did the searching and the dirty work. I get the prize. But I'm sure you're figuring this out as we stand here, without a bunch of time-wasting explanations. You were always one of our agents. Next to Agent Nichols."

A weird prickle of energy passed down Fallon's spine. Hearing Nicky's name on the chief's lips was...disturbing. "You put me on watch the other day so McCray would kill me."

The chief waved his phazer. "It's a shame you're so damned smart, Fallon. It's what will kill you. Now, hand over the jewel."

Fallon stood firmly in front of Kenji. "We don't have a jewel," he said. "There's been a mistake."

The chief scowled. "You think I'm an idiot? This man *is* the jewel. And I've paid a fortune to get him." He nodded at McCray's body. "Well, I *would* have paid a fortune. And you, Fallon, still haven't dropped your weapon."

"And won't—"

A push from behind cut off his words. In that flash of a second, the phazer was yanked from his hand.

He whirled and saw Kenji point the weapon at his own head. "If you hurt Fallon, I'll kill myself and then you'll have nothing."

"Hold off," the chief said to his men over his shoulder. "Let's be reasonable now, Your Holiness. Think of your people." He shook his head. "If I could explain everything, you'd understand." For the first time, strain splashed across the chief's flashy face.

Fallon felt time stand still, as if his whole universe were about to implode. Nothing had felt this hopeless since Nicky had died. "Kenji," he hissed, "Give me the bloody phazer." He held out his hand. He should have known Kenji's promise of no heroics had been an empty one.

Kenji stepped back. "No." He pointed to the farthest corner from the chief and his army. "Get over there. Now."

Fallon had never heard that note of authority in Kenji's voice. The guy who seemed so gentle and harmless sounded as if he'd like nothing better than blowing the chief's brains out if he didn't hop to it in the next second. "Kenji." His own voice came out a gravelly whisper, as pleading as Kenji's might have been in the past.

"Please, what?" Kenji pushed the barrel of the phazer to his temple. "Submit to these thieves so he can send me somewhere to get probed and brainwashed again? *After* he kills you?"

Kenji's good eye was wild, with a look Fallon had never seen in it before. Every nerve ending in his skin crackled with his fear for Kenji's life and the need to get them both out of there. Alive.

Instead of retreating to the corner Kenji had ordered him into, Fallon backed up a couple of steps so that he was near the control panel. "Kenji, please, I beg you, don't do anything stupid."

"Listen to Fallon, Your Holiness," the chief said, his voice tight, controlled. "And no one gets hurt."

"That's a lie," Kenji said. "You'll take me and then kill him anyway. If you think I won't pull this trigger on myself, you're dead wrong. If you kill Fallon, I have nothing to live for anyway."

Fallon's blood chilled. "Kenji, please."

"I'd think again if I were you," the chief said. He held up a small telescreen and flicked it on. "Recognize these people, Your Holiness?"

Fallon saw an elderly Japanese couple on a bench in a cell. They were huddled together, wrapped in coats. Both looked frightened and disheveled. The man had a bruise on one sharp cheekbone.

"Matsuoto-san!" Kenji called out as if the couple on the screen could hear him. He turned to the chief. "You have them!"

"Yes. My surveillance team caught you on telescreen in the marketplace, talking to them during McCray's attack. We figured they'd serve as leverage, if needed. So if you don't put down that phazer, you won't need to worry anymore about what will happen to them."

Kenji's harsh breathing filled the small space. Slowly, he lowered the phazer, his eyes misted. "My friends," he said under his breath.

Kenji's distracted horror gave Fallon the opening he needed. He took the phazer from Kenji's loosened hand and slid it across the floor. "There you are."

The chief knelt and picked it up, pointing it at Fallon. He then signaled over his shoulder. "Now!" he said and two gas pellets flew through the air and landed on the floor in sparks. In mere seconds, the cockpit filled with fumes.

Fallon's chest constricted. "Kenji," he rasped. Through the vapors, he heard the phazer hit the floor and saw Kenji double over in a fit of debilitating coughs. Pulling in a breath, Fallon lunged. One hand grabbed Kenji's shirt, pulling Kenji closer. But the world was dimming. All he could do was cough. Got to…get…Kenji…

Chapter Eight

Breathing. A gentle rise and fall of whisper-like sound. Then a burst of light. The breathing grew faster, harsher, as if air were being cut off…

Fallon jerked awake. Light flooded his eyes. His chest was heaving and pain made his temples throb. Typical side effect of having been gassed. As his consciousness trickled in, he became aware of his body. Naked, except for his briefs. Blinking again, he peered up. The room he was in was bare except for a small bed, toilet and sink. The walls and floor reflected an odd purplish light. He recognized the setting. The stark accommodations of an ISP holding ship brig.

He lifted his hands. Not bound, thank God. Pressure met his bottom and his back, as if he were sitting against a wall, yet the wall was warm and gave with the lift of his breathing, as if he were sitting back to back with someone.

Someone. Kenji? He stilled, listening for breath. Yes, it was a human being he sat against. The person was asleep, judging from the heavy way he rested against him. Fallon closed his eyes briefly, his heart pounding. *Please God,* he prayed silently, *let it be Kenji.*

He turned slightly, lest he dislodge the sleeping man and cause him to hit the cold floor. The warm skin of his cell mate brushed his back. Golden skin, he saw from the corner of his eye. He craned his neck a bit more and saw a slim, lightly muscled body, naked as his own, except for underwear.

Tears rushed his eyes. Thank God! Praise the Holy

Mother and whatever other deities were worshiped in the universe. Oh, Kenji. What would he have done if Kenji hadn't been here, with him? He remembered at the last second not to grab Kenji in his joy. After being gassed, that would deliver too much of a shock to his system. Impatiently, he waited for Kenji to awaken.

He didn't have long to wait. Kenji pulled in a sudden breath and sat up. "Wha..." he whispered and sat, staring straight ahead, unaware of Fallon's presence. It made sense, being physically smaller than Fallon, the gas from the pellet had hit his system much harder. He shivered slightly as the air of their cell passed over his bare body, then with growing awareness, hunched his bare shoulders and scrubbed both hands over his face.

Still suppressing the urge to pull Kenji to him, Fallon watched Kenji process the side effects of the gas while regaining consciousness. Kenji blinked heavy eyelids then rubbed his forehead, the way Fallon had moments ago. "Where am I?" he whispered. He froze, indicating the full return to consciousness and ensuing alarm. "Fallon? Fallon! Oh no!"

"I'm here, Kenji." He placed a hand on Kenji's arm.

Kenji whipped around. Relief immediately flooded his face. "Fallon, you're alive!" He reached out and Fallon caught him as Kenji launched his bare torso into his arms and squeezed him close. Ohhh, sweet relief. Kenji's touch, the warmth of their bare chests pressed together, he'd thought never to feel those things again. Ghastly images resurged—the chief shooting McCray dead, Kenji holding the deadly phazer to his own head, the explosion of gas pellets...

He pulled back just enough to get a look at Kenji. "They

didn't hurt you?"

"No. But I thought he'd killed — "

"Kenji, you scared the ever-living shite out of me. I thought you'd top yourself."

Kenji looked slightly sheepish. "I'm sorry about that. But I didn't want him to kill you — and it's the only thing I could think of."

Fallon didn't know whether to shake Kenji or hug him closer. Kenji's fine lips curled upward as if he knew what he was thinking. With a half-growl, half-laugh, he grabbed Kenji into his arms again. Kenji's hands pressed into his back. That small touch was the most reassuring thing in the whole damned universe. "It's all right. But promise me, *promise*, you'll never pull a stunt like that, ever again."

One of Kenji's hands slid over his back. "Don't ask me to make such a promise, Fallon," he whispered. "Not if it's all I can do to save your life."

He squeezed Kenji closer. "Kenji, don't do — "

"Isn't this touching?"

Fallon suppressed a growl. He released Kenji and pushed him behind him, feeling like a she-wolf protecting her pup. As if he could somehow still defend Kenji while naked in a bare cell. Were it not for the force field between him and the chief —

"You bloody bastard," he spat at the chief, "What the hell kind of game are you playing?"

"Before you go calling me names, Agent Fallon, you should thank me."

"What the hell for?"

"For giving you this one last night with your little friend here, before he goes where we're taking him. Truthfully, Fallon, it's good to see you have passion about someone again. You lost it when Nichols died. I spared your life so you could have this...chance." His eyes studied Fallon with a mixture of intensity and distraction, the way a man does when warring inwardly. "I know how much you've missed Nichols." He shrugged. "This was the least I could do."

Kenji stirred behind him and Fallon felt a hand on his shoulder. "You killed Nichols," Kenji breathed. "I saw it. It's on your conscience." His hand tightened on Fallon's shoulder.

The chief's fleshy face reddened and his very jowls appeared to sag. "Good work, Fallon," he muttered, "you really did find His Holiness, the Sunyatan Jewel, *the one who sees*. You know what that means? He sees into men's souls, did you know that?"

Fallon's blood chilled. Understanding bloomed inside him, shoved to the surface of his consciousness by Kenji's declaration. "That explosion in headquarters...it was planned." The light burned brighter with each word. It all fell into place. "Nicky was on to your corruption, wasn't he?" His eyes narrowed on the chief, a man who'd seemed above corruption. *And I never saw it.*

"Come on, Fallon, get off your high horse. We're all piss ants. I'm one rank above you. Thirty five years of service and what do I get? A sonar watch as a bonus. You know how it is. These bounty hunters are the scum of existence. What difference did it make if I skimmed off them a bit? Nicky was like you, some kind of moral compass. He thought he was above extortion. He threatened to expose me."

Pain squeezed Fallon's chest. Nicky hadn't said a word. He'd probably known what would happen to them both and hadn't wanted to implicate his lover. Kenji's hand pressed into his back, a comforting touch. "You piece of shite."

"Come on, Fallon, don't be as big an asshole as Nicky was. He thought he could stem the tide of corruption, but you've seen the state of the world, of every Terran outpost. We can colonize space but we can't stop oppression, murder and madness. Get what you can in this life, Fallon. Nicky was a fool, a damned fool."

"Why? Because he chose honor and integrity above your corruption?"

"No, actually." The chief's eyes flickered again to Kenji and back. "He was a fool for choosing honor and integrity above you."

The words were like a phazer shot. Fallon froze, stunned. Only Kenji's hand on his shoulder kept him rooted.

The chief shrugged. "I'm sorry, Fallon. I never meant to go this far, but now I have and it's too late. You and His Holiness have as long as it takes to get to Earth to enjoy each other. Make the most of it."

"Where are you taking us?" Kenji sounded regal.

A strange smile shadowed the chief's lips. "I suppose it makes no difference to keep it secret anymore. You're going to have your memory chip removed by the people who put out the bounty on you."

Kenji pressed in closer, chest pressing into Fallon's bare back. "Who is that?" he asked, a tremor in his voice. In spite of Kenji's show of anger, Fallon felt the slimmer man's torso trembling against him.

"The People's Empire."

The political entity that was swallowing up all the city-states along its border. An oppressive, murderous monster, and had been for centuries. *Shite*! "You're bluffing," Fallon said. "How could a government hire a cop to bring in a bounty?"

"Their government didn't hire me, Fallon. They hired McCray and then I hired McCray. You do the math on that one. Oh, I know about the Intergalactic Directives. But all I had to do was erase some records. You won't find a trail back to the Empire no matter how hard you look. Not even your hacker friend would be able to find it."

Fallon could only stare at the man he'd thought his superior all these years. The chief was nothing but a cold-blooded killer.

"Which is why," the chief continued when Fallon didn't speak, "you two should make the most of this short voyage to Earth. You have the equivalent of an Earth day. Say your goodbyes while you have the chance. I deprived you of that with Nicky. I'm giving it to you now."

Fallon released Kenji and lunged toward the chief.

"No, Fallon!" Kenji gripped his shoulders, pulling him back from electrocution by the force field. Cursing was now his only recourse. "You bastard! You piece of shite!"

"Good-bye, Fallon. You were one of the best agents I've ever worked with." With a small salute, the chief turned and left.

Fallon knelt, shivering, staring at the force field. His breath came in short gasps. His mind reeled. *The chief murdered Nicky. Kenji in the hands of the People's Empire—*

"I'm sorry, Fallon." Kenji's hand moved across his back. "I tried not to say it, but the words forced themselves out."

Kenji's voice pulled Fallon's gaze upward, to the other man's face. "What do you mean?"

Kenji's good eye was misted, ringed with lines from fear and the hangover effects of the gas. "About how the chief killed...Nicky. I tried not to say it, but the words forced themselves out."

Fallon's breath caught. "Kenji, you really saw into his soul?" With a trembling hand, he reached up and touched Kenji's cheek.

Kenji caught his hand and held it against his cheek. He nodded. "Yes. I didn't mean to. It just happened."

Fallon's sight blurred. The revelation about Nicky swirled in his mind and heart, melding with his horror. If there'd been any doubt before, it was gone. Kenji was the true leader of Sunyata. "That's why they put in the memory chip," he said. "So you wouldn't do this."

Kenji frowned. "But it happened now. Why?"

A chill shivered over Fallon's back. "Your DNA has apparently rearranged itself, bringing you closer to your memories."

He pulled Kenji against him, one hand burrowed into Kenji's hair. The chief had murdered Nicky and now he'd destroy Kenji. If Kenji disappeared somewhere in that mindless, bureaucratic realm, much of which was hidden away in the unreachable mountains of mid-Russia and Mongolia, there'd be no finding him again. Chances were he'd be tortured mercilessly until he succumbed to their psychological and ideological demands. The People's Empire sought to assimilate all cultures and religions into its generic melt of godless workers. Kenji's gentleness and innocence would be destroyed, as irrevocably as would his body and soul.

Kenji's fingers dug into his arm muscles and Fallon could no longer distinguish his own trembling from Kenji's. "Fallon, I'm so sorry about Nicky. So sorry." Kenji squeezed his arms and pushed back from him. His good eye was now red-rimmed, his usually smooth face creased in fear. "Why do they want me? Who are they? What will they do to me?"

Fallon let his gaze rove over Kenji's face, over the damaged eye, his spiky hair, his leanly muscled body, the white briefs covering his...

One of the most important religious leaders on Earth was sitting here in front of him, on the floor of a ship's brig, in his underwear. The jewel of an entire people had been working as a bartender, not knowing who the hell he was or what had happened to him. If that wasn't crazy enough, Kenji was going to be sent into the lion's den to be devoured, body and soul. "Kenji, you really know nothing of Earth, do you?"

Kenji shook his head. "Please, tell me."

Fallon raked a hand through his hair and looked down at the cold gray floor. The last thing he wanted was to tell Kenji about what awaited him, especially when there wasn't a hope in hell of getting him out of it, not without weapons, not locked in here behind a deadly force field. He drew in a deep breath, searching for a quick summary. "A couple of centuries ago, the Russian Empire joined forces politically with the People's Republic of China. They were both always communist...it'll take too long to explain all the history, but

148

both regimes had always relied on force to make certain that every citizen complied with their aims and beliefs. It wasn't always a matter of simple physical agreement, either, of living by their rules. They demanded complete psychological submission as well."

"Oh." Tortured understanding shadowed his features. "They'll take the memory chip out, make me remember who I really am and then torture me to make me do what they want." He sat up suddenly, his eye wide. "Fallon, you see it, don't you?" He grasped Fallon's arm. "They're going to use me to make my people, whoever they are, come under their control."

Fallon squeezed his hand. Kenji was so selfless. Figured he'd be thinking of his people in the face of his own demise. "I believe so," he said quietly.

Kenji's face tightened. His fear emanated from him, almost a physical force of its own.

Before Fallon knew what was happening, Kenji's arms were around him. Kenji's hard slim body was pressed to his and Kenji's lips brushed the side of his neck. Fallon tensed, his hands on Kenji's shoulders. He felt Kenji's lips part, followed by a tiny lick on his skin. Tingles radiated outward from Kenji's kiss, but Fallon resisted, his body stiffening, even before his mind understood why.

Kenji pulled back. His lids were heavy, the skin flushed under the harsh light of their prison cell. "Fallon," he whispered, "this may be our last chance." Kenji leaned toward him again but he held Kenji away from him.

"Kenji, we shouldn't."

"Why?" More worry saturated his face. As if things weren't bad enough. "Don't you want me? I know it's tense now, but you heard him, the journey to Earth is short—"

"Of course I want you, Kenji." Truth was, the chief had been right about his passion. Since Nicky, he hadn't thought to feel...passion for anyone ever again. Yet here he was, about to be annihilated and his cock burned for Kenji. There was just one problem.

"They're probably watching us, Kenji," he murmured, even as Kenji's touch made his skin tingle pleasantly.

"I don't care." He pressed his lips to Fallon's.

Fallon let himself surrender. Kenji's hand slipped down his cheek and cupped his neck possessively. Kenji pushed in closer, until they were once again chest to chest. Kenji was climbing onto his lap, his ass against Fallon's hardening cock, his sleek legs wrapped around Fallon's hips, arms around him as if to say, *I'll never let you go.* Which of course, he would be forced to do.

The evil thought slipped into Fallon's mind, like poison trying to destroy this bit of pleasure. Forcing the thought away, Fallon parted his lips, accepting the slide of Kenji's tongue against his. Even in this prison, his body and soul full of fear, Kenji smelled and tasted delicious. Innocent and masculine at the same time. Sort of the way Nicky used to taste and smell. Fallon slid his hands over Kenji's warm skin as their kisses heated. He nipped at Kenji's lips and swirled his tongue against Kenji's in wild turns, feeling Kenji's hands rub and clutch at his back. His own breath and Kenji's pulsed in his ears and the heat of their bodies filled the air close around them.

Fallon pulled one hand away long enough to grope for the nearby cot. His hand landed on something soft and he yanked the covers down. Pulling from their kiss, he got to his knees, tugging Kenji to his. "Come to bed, Kenji," he whispered and sat on the edge of the bed, intending to pull Kenji onto it with him, but before he could move, Kenji's fingers were sliding his briefs down, exposing his cock to the air just before he captured it between his soft, moist lips. "Ahhh." The prison cell and all it meant receded. His whole focus centered on the sensation of Kenji's wet mouth wrapped around his tight, hard cock. Fallon fell back on the bed.

Kenji grasped Fallon's hips, anchoring him in place as he continued to suck, drawing Fallon's cock deeper into his mouth. Fallon closed his eyes, feeling the build-up in his cock, determined to draw it out. His fingers burrowed into Kenji's thick, sleek hair, as if to anchor himself. Kenji's voluptuous lips slid up and down, causing him to groan. Each time, his skin was stretched taut then released again. Oh, dear God! He had already died and gone to heaven. How long could he stand the torture?

He had to have Kenji underneath him. "Kenji—" he ground out.

Kenji's response was to dip back down and take him in nearly to the root while palming his heavy sac. He was beautiful this way, but even more beautiful on his back, his legs wrapped around Fallon's hips. Besides, Fallon wanted them under the blanket. They could at least have that much privacy.

"Kenji," he groaned again and grasped the man's sleek upper arms.

This time Kenji paused, his tongue just touching the tip of Fallon's cock. It slipped from his mouth just as he looked up, his lids heavy, his lips swollen and gleaming, his cheeks flushed. "What is it? Am I hurting you?"

"Yes." Fallon grinned before Kenji could take him seriously. With one swift move, he slid back, pushing up the covers and making a space beside him on the narrow bed. "Get in here."

Kenji rose on his knees and started to climb in.

"Uh-uh." Fallon took hold of the waistband of his briefs and slid them down, careful of Kenji's rigid cock. He encircled it lightly with his hand as his other finished pushing down the briefs. In answer, Kenji pushed his body closer. Fallon gave the hard shift a few more quick strokes then tugged Kenji by the hand, down into the bed, Kenji's back to his front. Lying together under the thin blanket, Fallon tucked the cover more closely over their naked bodies. His cock slid into the warm crevice between Kenji's ass cheeks. Kenji's warm scent, male musk laced with sweat, invaded Fallon's senses and he closed his lips over a smooth spot on Kenji's nape.

"Ohhh." Kenji sank back against him.

The friction sent sparks through Fallon's cock, down into his balls. He slid a hand over Kenji's hip and caressed it. Closing his eyes, he savored the skin at the base of Kenji's neck. Tasting him slowly, he let his tongue linger in each spot he licked, as if his very taste buds could memorize Kenji's flavor and the texture of his skin.

A hand closed over his. Kenji was guiding his hand and the smooth curve of his hard cock pushed into his palm. Fallon moaned against Kenji's skin and stroked him. He had a great cock, slimmer than his own and with much less hair at the base, but long and rigid. A drop of cum seeped from the tip and Fallon caught it with his thumb pad, using it to make his palm glide more easily up and down the length of it.

Kenji sagged back against him, his ass cheeks rubbing Fallon's cock. A flash of heat shot through Fallon's groin and he stroked Kenji faster. The sooner Kenji came, the sooner Fallon would have something he could use as lubricant. All he wanted was to bury his cock deep inside Kenji, to join their bodies, the only way he knew to reassure Kenji he cared about him, that he wouldn't just hand Kenji over to his captors, that he...*loved* Kenji, even though it hurt too damn much to love a guy and lose him. He was powerless over his heart.

"Yes, Fallon, yes." Kenji's harsh whisper cut through Fallon's thoughts and brought him back to the hard, hot cock in his hand, the sleekly muscled body writhing against his, the hard, perfect ass cheeks sandwiching his own cock. Fallon stroked yet faster, light quick strokes that brought the nectar up, making Kenji's cock twitch. With a sudden groan, Kenji arched his back and the hot splash of cum covered Fallon's hand.

Perfect.

Covering the tip, Fallon captured the warm spurts in his palm. He pulled back and smoothed it over his own cock, coating it. "I want you, Kenji," he whispered and pushed his creamed fingertips against Kenji's hole.

"Yes!" Kenji opened his legs, pushing back against Fallon's seeking fingers. The bud of flesh was quite relaxed and open and Fallon's index finger slid in effortlessly. Fallon slid his finger in and out, earning a groan from Kenji each time.

Kenji's tilted his head back, panting, pushing his ass back as if he could swallow up Fallon's hand.

He was ready.

Fallon slid his finger out and pushed the head of his cock in. Kenji jumped slightly but moaned and wilted back against him. Resting a hand on Kenji's hip, Fallon pushed, just a bit. His cock slid in halfway. Sparks of heat invaded his cock, tightened his balls, made his entire body hard, alert, his senses full of Kenji scent, the feel of his hard, graceful body, the tiny whimpers of pleasure he made each time Fallon pushed his cock in a bit deeper. One more push and he slid in all the way. Their bodies met, cradled perfectly, skin to skin, their body heat releasing the feral scent of sex in the air around them.

Closing his eyes, Fallon rested his lips against Kenji's skin. He wanted to remember this feeling, the closeness, the powerful instinctive drive that made his heart meld itself to Kenji's heart, the way it had once with Nicky's. What a glorious feeling it had always been, to know that in the entire universe, no matter how difficult or sad or dangerous life was, there was this haven, this sweetness, this pleasure with someone special.

Kenji seemed to notice what was happening inside him. Kenji's hand covered his, lacing their fingers, pulling Fallon's arm around him. "Fallon," he whispered, turning his head as far as he could.

Fallon lifted his lips from Kenji's skin. Their gazes met.

The expression on Kenji's face seared him with its potent blend of faith and passion. Even the damaged eye seemed to radiate feeling. "Thank you."

Before Fallon could answer, Kenji had turned his head and thrust back, making Fallon's cock slide deep into Kenji's ass. The friction sent a jolt of heat through him. Anchoring himself on one elbow, he thrust again. In equal rhythm Kenji pushed back. Pleasure slammed through him, like a current traveling from Kenji's body into his. The energy cascaded through his cock, into his balls, his gut, thighs and up into his chest. Like one body, they moved in a flowing rhythm, the fingers of their joined hands clenching, anchoring them against the rocking of their bodies. Fallon had never felt anything like it, as if the ecstasy were spreading into his spirit, saturating the invisible part of him he'd wondered about but never knew for sure to exist.

He knew know. Because of Kenji.

How long they stayed like this, rocking against each other, Kenji's scent in his nostrils, the man's slim hard body pushing back against his brawn, he didn't know. Even the harsh light of their prison cell didn't seem so harsh, or the fact that the blanket had slid off them. His thoughts and his body were more pliant, his senses sharpened and relaxed at the same time. The intensity spread into his cock, the telltale pressure of climax. One long hard slide and he came. Squeezing Kenji's hand in his he moaned, lips pressed to Kenji's shoulder as his climax gushed in hot spurts, filling Kenji's tight, delicious passage.

When the last bit of pleasure had spiraled away, Fallon pulled Kenji to him, bringing the blanket back up to cover them. His breath rasped against Kenji's damp skin. Closing his eyes, he breathed in Kenji's scent. He'd loved to do that with Nicky. A pang shot through him. Nicky had been murdered, killed for uncovering corruption. And he'd never mentioned a word. No doubt he'd been protecting his lover, yet could it have been Nicky hadn't trusted him? No. He pushed that possibility away. Nicky had been his loyal friend. A lover and companion like no other.

Now there was Kenji. And Kenji would be ripped from him as well.

Fallon's gaze strayed to the force field which held them prisoner. He remembered the chief standing there, looking down at them, confessing to having murdered Nicky. Fallon screwed his eyes shut, the pain lancing him afresh. How had he missed the truth all this time? How had he not seen the chief's corruption? And how had he not noticed what Nicky was going through just before he died? Fallon thought of those times, searching his memory for any trace of clues to what had been going on. They'd been on their usual rounds together and never had Nicky seemed preoccupied or upset. It hadn't affected their sex life either. Nicky had been as robust and virile as always. Either Nicky had been a consummate actor, able to hide his stress, or he'd been confident that once he found the evidence he needed, he could expose the chief and end the problem. Nicky had been arrogant, cocky that way, for sure. And had gotten killed for it. Yet, it hurt that never once had Nicky confided in him.

You're naïve, Fallon. Echoes of Nicky's words. It was the only real criticism Nicky had had of him. He'd not been suspicious enough, not seen potential corruption lurking in every possible corner. Black and white thinking. In his world, bad guys were bad and the good guys were good. That's all there was to it.

How much time passed this way, Fallon didn't know. Only that his eyelids grew heavier. Kenji's breathing was steady and deep. He'd fallen asleep. Fighting sleep did no good, even though he wanted to savor the feel of Kenji in his arms. Finally, he succumbed...

The buzz of the force field lifting woke him. He peeked over the sleeping Kenji to see the guard slipping two trays of pink mush under the slightly raised force field then lowering the force field back down. Quietly he lay, listening to the hum of the ship's engines vibrating in the background.

156

Kenji's warm, sleekly muscled body still lay couched in his arms, the length of Kenji molded to his front.

Fallon pulled in a sigh. They'd probably been asleep a long time. They had little over half the day allotted before reaching Earth…

Kenji turned over in Fallon's arms so that they lay front to front under the cover. Sleepy sensuality flew from Kenji's demeanor, replaced by a piercing gaze.

"Kenji, are you all right?" Puzzled, Fallon reached out to touch Kenji's cheek.

In a flash, Kenji caught his wrist and held it still with surprising strength. His good eye narrowed. "Who are you?" he said, his voice almost a growl.

Fallon's blood chilled. "What?"

"You heard me," he said. "Who are you and where am I?"

Chapter Nine

Kenji held the large white man's wrist in place while he stared into the bluest eyes he'd ever seen. The look of hurt and shock passing through those eyes told him this man and he knew each other. The man had addressed him so familiarly and not as "Your Holiness." And...they were naked together in a bed...

"Kenji." The man's blue gaze flickered to a spot behind Kenji and back to his face. "Listen." He spoke in a low tone, barely moving his lips. "I'm Jake Fallon of the Intergalactic Safety Patrol. Whatever's going on with you, pretend you still know me. I promise I'll explain everything. We're in terrible danger. Lie back down with me and go along with whatever I do and say. You're safe with me, I promise."

That voice. He knew that voice. It whispered through him, teased at his memory. Like fingers it wound inside him, tugging. "Say that again."

"I'm Jake Fa—"

"No, that last thing."

"You're safe with me, I promise."

He pulled in a breath. "I've heard your voice before. I do know you, don't I?"

Jake Fallon was silent a moment then something passed through his eyes. "Yes," he said in a near whisper. "When you were twelve you fell from a space pod hovering high above the ground during a rescue of your people. I came wearing a jet pack and caught you."

Kenji's heart lurched. His grip tightened on Fallon's wrist. Could it really be him? The man he'd thought about endlessly? The hero who'd saved his life, caught him in strong arms and brought him to safety? An intense, long familiar ache pulled in Kenji's chest. During so many years of enforced celibacy he'd sought relief in that memory, fantasized about finding that strong, heroic man who'd saved him, wondering what the man's face looked like underneath his helmet and goggles. He searched the other man's gaze, penetrated it with his second sight. Then let out a breath. Yes, Jake Fallon was telling the truth. It really was him. "You," he whispered. "I can't believe it." He stared a few moments longer, tingles of warmth and joy spreading through his entire being. "I'd begun to think I imagined it all.

A shy look flitted across the other man's rugged face. "You didn't, Kenji. It's me."

How handsome he was. Kenji looked down quickly, at their nakedness. An unfamiliar scent permeated the warm air between them. Musk, like an animal's laced with sweat. *Sex*. It must be sex. All these years he'd imagined…doing…it with that man. Had they… He opened his mouth to ask the question.

The other man pressed a thick finger to his parted lips. "Shhh," he whispered. "I see you have questions. There's no time. Just lie back down with me and go along, all right?"

Wordlessly, he nodded and let Fallon ease him back onto the mattress, Fallon half-covering him. The heat and muscle of Fallon's torso invaded Kenji's skin. Fallon brushed Kenji's cheekbone with a thumb and lowered his mouth to Kenji's.

Kenji sighed at the touch of their lips. He couldn't help

it. For so long he'd yearned for that man's kiss, to know what he felt and tasted like. Fallon's lips were soft. His dark stubble tickled Kenji's chin. Without thinking, Kenji closed his eyes. He breathed in Fallon's musky scent. The aroma he'd smelled before. Now he knew. It *was* the smell of sex.

Fallon's lips lingered against his for what seemed a long time while the man's thumb brushed back and forth across his cheekbone. Kenji's heartbeat continued to pound, as it had since the starburst of intense light in his head that brought with it the return of his memory. He dared to part his lips just a bit, wanting a deeper kiss. With one hand, he reached up and gingerly brushed several fingertips across the dark stubble of Fallon's jaw. Mmm. Wonderful, the way it rasped his skin.

Instead of deepening the kiss, Fallon lifted his mouth. He remained hovering a few inches from Kenji's face. The look in Fallon's eyes sent a ripple of warmth through Kenji's chest. "Kenji," he whispered, "Have you completely forgotten me?"

Kenji gazed up at him. The shock had settled a bit now, replaced by the wonder of the kiss and the muscular body pressing down onto his. How could he ever forget the man who'd saved his life, who'd given him a brief but solid memory to comfort him through long lonely nights when the pleasure of passion and companionship could never be his? His people depended on his untarnished life force to give them strength. Sex, he was told since the priests had found him, would diminish his strength, harming his people's crops, fertility and everything else. Yet, all around him, they celebrated festivals, worshiping him and the statue of Kirei, the Beautiful One, by making love and bearing children while he'd been forced to sleep alone for their sakes. He'd never forgotten the nameless, faceless man. As

160

the years passed, he'd grown to love and treasure the man even from that brief encounter. The second sight that allowed him to see into men's souls, now allowed him to see his own. He adored this man like no other. And always would. "No, Fallon. I could never forget you."

Heart pounding, he let his touch slide down Fallon's cheek to his throat. The skin was smoother there, free of stubble. Fallon's male scent filled him. "Did I…wait for you? I mean, were you the one I chose even when I couldn't remember?"

A hopeful smile tugged at Fallon's lips. "Yes," he murmured, "I was the lucky one." But then, like a shadow passing over the sun, Fallon's rugged face grew solemn. He leaned in, his lips close to Kenji's ear. "Something must have happened when you and I were…together."

Kenji's cheeks burned again and he grew vividly aware of Fallon's naked brawn covering his body. Fallon was so big and hard. Everywhere.

"It must have shorted out your memory chip," Fallon went on. He touched Kenji's cheek again. He had a tender touch for such a large, rough-looking man. "Though truthfully, that's the least of our troubles now."

Kenji's languor evaporated. "What do you mean? Where are we?"

The larger man sighed, his face pained. The tormented expression remained through an explanation of corruption and bounty hunters, a flight through space and then their capture. Fallon caressed his hair, a gesture that gave Kenji comfort. "I tried to get you away, Kenji," he said softly, "but he caught up with us in mid-space. He gassed us and locked us in this brig. As soon as we reach Earth, he plans to turn you over to them."

He already knew he was wanted by the People's Empire but hearing it never failed to put fear into him. It was one thing to have training in the martial arts for self-defense such as he'd been given by the monks, quite another to fight an army of mega phazers and torture devices. "It's not your fault. They've been after me a long time. It's why my ministers decided to send me away during our relocation. They felt I was more vulnerable during a transition." A lifetime of duty and caring for the material and spiritual wellbeing of an entire population kicked in, like a light he could never turn off. "Fallon, how are they? My people, I mean. My mother, my ministers, my regent? Do you know?" He wanted to ask about his sister too, but she'd refused to be relocated, choosing to remain in the mountains with a rebel group whose life work was resistance of the People's Empire.

"We found your mother using a DNA lock just before we were caught. She seemed fine and wanted you to come home. She told you the relocation has been completed on that island off the coast of Japan."

"What a relief." Kenji heaved a sigh. Just before the memory chip was implanted, his concern for everyone's lives had weighed most heavily. And now…

He squeezed Fallon's arm. Briefly he wondered if Fallon could sense the fear in his clutch, the silent plea for protection. "The People's Empire wants to *re-educate* me. Their word for brainwash, of course. Their plan is for me to convince my followers to join the Empire. There, they can re-educate all of us, dilute us and destroy us." Just saying the words sent a shudder up his spine. He paused and set his jaw. "They can kill me if they want, but I'll not give them my soul or my people's souls." He stared into Fallon's blue eyes. No matter what there'd been between him and Fallon, the fate of thousands rested on him. If he succumbed to the People's Empire and their soul-killing ideology, he was effectively killing the others. Better that his body die. "I've got to get out of here," he said. "Even if I get killed trying. I won't let them inject me with their poison, or whatever it is they do to numb the mind and make a person pliant."

"I won't let you get killed," Fallon said, his voice near a growl.

Kenji looked into Fallon's eyes, and felt that movement through his heart again. "You're ISP," he said softly, "You must know how these ships work. There's got to be a way."

"Yes. I'm thinking." Fallon still half-covered Kenji, his head resting on one elbow while he caressed Kenji's cheek with the other hand. Even without Fallon's saying so, Kenji knew the man was making them appear to be cuddling, discussing intimate things that wouldn't matter to anyone else but the two of them. How wonderful it would be if that were indeed what was really happening. Kenji had always had his own rooms in the temple complex, a bed with nice pillows and soft blankets. He'd have given anything to be lying there with Fallon instead of here.

"We've been here in this cell I'm guessing for twelve hours. We have probably close to another twelve before reaching Earth's atmosphere. We can estimate the countdown of time by when they bring meals. When we get closer, I'll have to overpower the guard and steal his weapon." He leaned closer, his lips brushing Kenji's ear. "I don't dare explain more out loud," he whispered. "I need you to trust me."

"I trust you, Fallon. I *chose* you." He reached up and

brushed a hand through Fallon's hair. How soft it was, the way it sifted through his fingers. He'd never felt anything like it. The sensation on his skin sent a thrill up his arm, a gentle tingling energy that spread through his chest, down his stomach and into his...privates. "How did we meet?"

A sheepish look came into Fallon's eyes and he grinned, a strange, almost shy smile. "Not certain I should tell you."

Kenji's heart lurched. "Why not?"

"I don't think your followers would like it."

Kenji clenched his jaw. This kind of thing had always been an issue for him, ever since the priests had found him at the age of six, playing in his parents' front garden and had brought him back to their land with them. He'd always had to worry about setting an example. "I don't care what anyone thinks, Fallon." He levered up on an elbow and faced him. "I *need* to know."

Fallon chuckled. "All right then. You were working in a bar."

Now Kenji raised his eyebrows. "A bar? You mean a place that serves fermented grains?"

Another chuckle. "Yeah, alcohol."

"Did I drink to intoxication?" It would have been a terrible violation of one of the precepts against the abuse of intoxicants.

To his relief, Fallon shook his head. "I never saw you drink. You only drank fizzy water."

"But I served alcohol to others?"

Fallon laughed again, a low-throated rumble. "Yes, but let me tell it, all right? Without interruptions?"

Kenji looked down. "Sorry."

A gentle fingertip under his chin bade him look up. His stomach fluttered when he did. Fallon's blue eyes were probably more intoxicating than fermented grains anyhow. "I'm the one who's sorry, Kenji. I'm not being very understanding."

Kenji found himself staring back at Fallon who remained quiet instead of continuing. A gentle energy passed from the contact of Fallon's fingertip with his skin. He cleared his throat. "I won't interrupt again. I promise."

Fallon sighed and traced his jaw before lifting away. "You served drinks," he said quietly. "There were lots of blokes flirting with you all the time, propositioning you, but you refused them all. Until I came around. You'd decided to stay on at the bar that night you'd finished your work. I came in and sat down next to you." Fallon's eyes softened with that...look. "There seemed to be a...connection between us. We left together and got a room. It was a wonderful night. We couldn't wait to see each other again. We'd planned to meet again and that same night, the bounty hunter went after you and you came to me for help."

Kenji glanced away. The picture was clear now. If he and Fallon survived this nightmare, it seemed he would have destroyed his people now anyway by draining his life force.

Fallon hovered over him, his brow furrowed. "What is it, Kenji?"

He shook his head. "Did I have any idea of who I might be before we...?" He gestured between them.

The other man frowned. His eyes looked troubled, giving Kenji the sense he'd already considered something like this. "Not at first. But even when we began to uncover your identity, you...weren't concerned with celibacy. And I..." He paused, frowning, "I couldn't resist you. I'm sorry, Kenji," he said. "I truly am."

With a deep sigh, he avoided Fallon's gaze. For himself, he didn't care about that vow. Something about it had always seemed...strange. But if it helped his people, he was bound to it. Though he'd broken his it, it was best to honor it for whatever time he had left. Another sigh of frustration escaped him. His ministers and his regent had planned this all so poorly. They'd never provided for a contingency such as this. "It's not your fault," he murmured, still avoiding eye contact. "It's mine."

"Kenji, please, look at me."

The light pressure of fingertips bid him to obey. When he did, Fallon's gaze made a sensation travel through his chest, as if warm liquid were being poured through his body. Yet, there was something else in Fallon's look.

"The most important thing now is to escape," Fallon said. "I absolutely can't let you be delivered into the People's Empire. You understand?"

"Yes." The mere mention of the PE made his blood icy. The odds were highly against them. They were naked and unarmed on a ship full of armed guards. As strong and sure as Fallon seemed, what chance did they *really* have?

Fallon climbed over him and off the bed. His brawn flexed with his movements as he retrieved their underwear from the floor. "Here you go." He handed Kenji his underwear then took his own briefs and put them on. The gesture had a finality of its own, the understanding of which shone in Fallon's eyes. "I understand, Kenji," he said softly.

"I know you have a vow to honor." Without waiting for a response, he then picked up the two trays of food and brought them over, setting one of the trays on the bed in front of Kenji.

Then Fallon sat on the floor with his tray.

Wordlessly, Kenji pulled his tray closer, already mourning the loss of what he'd barely experienced. How incredible it had felt to have another human being so close. And that kiss they'd shared... more delicious than any food he'd ever tasted. With his memory suppressed, he'd made love with this man and yet, with his memory restored, could only imagine what it felt like. Now, he'd never know.

"Should I address you as Your Holiness? I don't want to be disrespectful. If I have been, I apologize deeply."

The question pulled him from his sad musing. Moved by the sorrow in Fallon's voice, Kenji touched his arm. "Only the people closest to me in the whole world call me Kenji."

"Oh." Fallon nodded. "I see." He looked down. "Forgive me."

"No. Call me Kenji, please. Nothing could give me greater comfort now."

The hurt lifted from Fallon's rugged face. Devotion burned in the larger man's eyes. Then he smiled. "Go on then, Kenji. Eat something. We need to keep our strength up." He leaned in a bit closer so that only Kenji could hear his voice. "And then I'll tell you my plan. Do you have any *kung fu*?"

Kung fu. The monks who'd trained him had used that term to encompass the whole of meditation and the martial arts forms, referring to any practice that encompassed the wholeness of being. He nodded. "Yes. I do. Karate, judo, jiu jutsu, praying mantis form, tai chi—"

"I'll take that as a yes."

"Yes."

Fallon nodded and picked up a piece of hardtack from his tray. He sniffed it and made a face before dipping it into the pile of mush. "Good," he said finally and pushed the food into his mouth. "You're going to need it."

Kenji's heart lurched again but he nodded. "I'm with you, Fallon," he said softly.

* * * * *

"It's almost time," Fallon whispered in his ear. They lay together under the covers where they'd been for their last hours, formulating their plan and resisting temptation with every ounce of discipline they possessed. Fallon pulled him close. "We can do this," he whispered, his breath warm in Kenji's ear. His gaze was a potent blend of determination and passion. Their unspoken feelings and needs swirled between them. Things that now would probably never be expressed. Survival came first.

"I'm with you," he said again. Heart pounding, cold sweat in his armpits, Kenji succumbed to Fallon's hold and closed his eyes, head against the larger man's chest, so as to appear peacefully asleep. Seconds later, he heard the buzz of the force field as the phazered guards lifted it enough to slide their food trays underneath then retreat. Fallon had said their food would be tainted, Kenji's with some sort of tranquilizer to make him easy to handle and Fallon's with poison.

When they'd gone and the force field was replaced, Fallon pulled back the covers. "Let's go," he said softly.

Kenji followed his lead over to the trays and pretended to eat, as he'd been instructed. He pushed the chunk of bread provided through the same pink oily stew of unknown substance, faking the act of biting, chewing and swallowing, as did Fallon, then pushing the mush around as best he could to make it appear mostly consumed. Fallon had told him his food would be laced with heavy tranquilizers while his own, most likely with poison. They waited the appropriate time before pretending to grow sleepy. Kenji yawned and fluttered his eyelids, then lay down on the floor and let his head fall to the side.

Nearby, he heard Fallon pretend to retch and gag before falling to the floor.

Some time passed and nothing happened. Kenji forced himself not to open his eyes and look at Fallon who seemed to be a master at breathing quietly enough so as to appear dead.

Then he heard the familiar buzzing sound of the force field being raised and the guards' voices. "All right, you know the chief's orders. Get the holy one dressed."

Once again, Kenji forced himself to make his limbs languid, as if he were asleep. One movement, one look at Fallon... His heart lurched. What were they doing to Fallon?

He forced himself not to steal a peek at Fallon while one of the guards worked a shirt over his head and then pushed one arm at a time into the sleeves. The guard buttoned up the shirt, then worked his legs into a pair of pants. He endured the rough hands on his body, relieved when the cretin finally got socks and boots onto him. "Hurry up, man," his guard said to the other.

"I'm working as fast as I can. You got the light one. This one's a damn bruiser." Kenji heard the sounds of clothing being worked onto Fallon. "Why are we dressing him anyway? He's just going to the vultures."

"Who knows? The chief said some crap about respect."

A guffaw. "Respect. Yeah, what about—"

The thud of a fist on flesh ended the sentence.

Kenji opened his eyes in time to see a guard fall to the floor and Fallon's fist swing round and land in the guard's gut. The man let out a breath of pain but whirled and elbowed Fallon's side hard. Fallon grimaced then recovered enough to punch the guard in the side of the head, causing him to fall unconscious. "Now, Kenji!" he yelled as the second guard lunged for him.

Coming to life, Kenji swung his body, letting the momentum propel him to his feet. He delivered a hard chop to the guard's back. The man left Fallon and turned to him. In a flash, he kneed the guard's groin. The man dropped to the floor, clutching his groin. Another flash and Kenji delivered a side-winding kick into the man's chest. The guard released his groin and staggered to his feet. "You little prick," he growled and lunged, only to be grabbed and punched by Fallon. The guard's head hit the steel sink and he blacked out. Kenji lunged and grabbed the phazer from his holster.

"Good job." Fallon was at his back, another phazer brandished. "Now, we get to the escape pod and take off."

They started for the door when the entire ship suddenly shook, as if caught in an earthquake. They both gripped the doorposts so as not to tumble around. Then, just as suddenly, it stopped.

"What was that?"

Fallon grimaced. "Shite! The ship's being locked onto another ship's tractor beam." He waited a moment, listening. "We'd better get to the pod. Follow me." Brandishing his phazer, Fallon looked in both directions and motioned for Kenji to follow when the corridor proved empty. He led Kenji through what appeared an endless maze of corridors and connecting vestibules.

A shudder of something ominous slithered down Kenji's arms. No other guards were anywhere, as if they'd all been diverted to one place. Something was seriously wrong. Did Fallon sense it too? "Fallon," he whispered and reached out, tapping the larger man's shoulder.

Fallon turned, a finger to his lips.

But Kenji ignored the warning. "Something's wrong," he said.

Fallon nodded and warned him again to be quiet. "We're almost to the bridge. Just past that is the escape pod."

That's when they heard it. Men's voices, shouting. What sounded like a blabber of different languages carried to Kenji's ears. He could make out a mixture of English, Russian and Mandarin Chinese. Understanding flooded him, made his heart claw in his chest. They were here. For him.

Fallon lunged, pushing Kenji ahead. "Fast, fast, fast!" he whispered fiercely. "We're almost there."

Kenji pumped his arms, breathing deeply as he

accelerated into a sprint. A dark uniformed guard appeared before him, phazer rifle brandished. "Stop, prisoners."

Fallon let out a yell and charged past Kenji, into the man. They both crashed to the floor, locked in a struggle. Before Kenji could find a way to help him, the men's voices grew louder. Soldiers poured into the corridor. Someone grabbed Kenji from behind and wrenched his arms back. Pain shot through his hand, forcing him to drop the phazer. The cold steel of cuffs closed around him. More soldiers were pulling Fallon off the guard he'd attacked and restraining him. The barrel of a hand phazer pressed into his temple. Then the chief appeared and stepped into the center.

"Get away from him," Kenji said and tried to lunge at the man, only to be yanked back hard.

The chief looked at him. The man's eyes were puffy, his skin red and chafed. In spite of what he was doing, his course of action was obviously causing him great strain. Kenji saw in the moment of looking into the man's watery blue eyes that he would not be alive too much longer. Yes, his second sight, the ability that had made him the leader of his people, now resurged fully, no longer suppressed by the memory chip. The chief was going to die before the day was finished.

"I appreciate the sentiment, Your Holiness," the chief said, "but Fallon is a troublemaker. And as such, will have to be dealt with." He gestured to the soldiers around him, the Russian and Chinese Kenji had heard in passing the bridge. "These gentlemen are representatives of the People's Empire. They came aboard a bit sooner than we'd agreed upon, but then, I know they're anxious to get on with your re-education."

"Chief, don't do this," Fallon said. His blue eyes shone

with a poignant mixture of anger and desperation.

"It's too late for that, Fallon."

Kenji's heart hammered. The cuffs bit into his skin. "I'll go with you. I know I have no choice at this point," he said to the chief, "but whatever you do, let Fallon go."

The chief gestured with his phazer. "Into the bridge. The Empire's ship will bring us in."

In the bridge, Kenji was pushed into a chair and strapped in, Fallon into a chair opposite him, equally restrained. There weren't enough seats but along the edge of the room, in between the control panels, were sections with small straps which the soldiers held onto.

"Match your coordinates to the Empire ship," the chief said to one of his men standing at a control panel in the center.

"Yes, sir."

Kenji watched the crew flip buttons and type into keyboards. The ship, which had been hovering, now began to move with a deep rumble. The engines hummed and ground with a deafening noise. Kenji felt the skin on his face tighten as the ship gained speed. Through the windshield, dark space gave way to orange light streaming in. The force of movement made him close his eyes. The shuddering continued until Kenji felt as if his internal organs were loosening inside him and his bones disconnecting from the joints. Only when the craft began to decelerate did the physical tension release.

Then it was over. The craft went still. The engines were powered down and the soldiers released their hand grips.

Kenji shot a look to Fallon. A sense of doom enveloped

him such as he'd never experienced in his life, not even when his father had died so many years ago. Fallon's rugged face was grim, mirroring his own sentiments.

A door opened. It floated down, slowly revealing the craggy landscape Kenji had known since the priests came for him in Japan twenty years ago. The small city-state his regent had prepared him to take over on his twenty-first birthday was probably quite close to where they'd landed, but they were far away now, safe. And he would never see them again.

A cold wind whistled across the opening. The sky above blazed a color the blue of Fallon's eyes. In spite of the altitude, the sun, though shining with brilliant light, gave off little warmth. Kenji took a deep breath. The only thing that mattered in this moment was that Fallon be allowed to live. Kenji pinned the chief with a look. "Let Fallon go," he said softly. "There's nothing he can do anyway." Before the chief could answer, one of the soldiers, a Chinese in a khaki military suit with the blazing red insignia of the People's Empire, a star suspended above the curve of a sickle, prodded Kenji forward, down the gang plank of the ship, to the ground. More soldiers surrounded Kenji, blocking most of his view of Fallon and of the chief.

The chief stepped forward and bowed to a Russian. This man was decorated the most, signifying his higher rank in the People's Army than the men who surrounded Kenji. "So, Captain Renkoff, I have fulfilled my part in our arrangement. All that's left is the payment."

The tall blond captain turned to one of his subordinates. The younger man, also Russian, stood at attention, his expression like a machine. "Lieutenant," Renkoff said, "Give this man what he is owed."

The lieutenant saluted Renkoff, clicked his heels and approached the chief. In an instant, the soldier raised his phazer and pointed it at the chief's chest.

The chief's face dropped. "What the hell's going on here? Renkoff? We had a de—"

"No!" Fallon yelled in unison with the crack of phazer fire. The chief froze. The shock of betrayal and coming of unexpected death showed in the wideness of his eyes. He fell to the ground, motionless.

Kenji closed his eyes. He uttered a quick silent prayer for the man's soul. Hopefully, the corrupt chief would burn off his bad karma in the next embodiment and have a chance at something better. A rude push from behind cut off his silent chant.

"Kenji!"

Kenji turned his head. One last look at Fallon would be all he had to take with him. Their gazes locked. *I love you, Fallon.* The man he'd dreamed about, thought about and wanted all these lonely years. Finding him had been a miracle, a precious moment he'd take with him no matter what happened.

Another phazer blast sizzled through the air and Fallon went down.

Chapter Ten

Kenji! Have…to…get…him. Fallon struggled to get up from where he'd fallen. Excruciating pain flooded him, pinning him to the ground. He lay still, gathering enough breath to try again. They'd taken Kenji. He couldn't afford to lie here, no matter how he felt.

He pushed again, struggling to rise from the ground but the pain made him fall back each time. *Kenji! Kenji!* He thrust forward again. Dear sweet mother of God —

A hand on his chest stayed him. "Don't move," a voice said. Feminine. Gentle. The pressure on his chest eased him back down. He grunted. Softness met him. Softness and warmth. A wave of pain passed through him, ending only when he became completely still. As long as he didn't move, there was no pain.

"There," she said, her voice soothing. "Rest now."

She sounded too kind for a doctor on the prison brig, so he probably hadn't been brought back to the ISP ship. Where the hell was he then? Not still on the ground where he'd gotten phazered, as he'd thought a moment ago. Not that it mattered. He had to get hell out of here. Kenji was in the hands of the People's Empire. Shite! There was no time to waste. "Let me up," he rasped.

A small light glowed near his eye and a careful thumb pulled down the skin below his eye. Then the other. The glow disappeared, replaced by darkness. The hand pressed across his forehead. "You were phazered with a deadly concentration of shock waves." She spoke like a physician, with the kind of a good practitioner. "It didn't break the skin but I want to make sure there's no internal bleeding. You mustn't move." She paused, her hand still resting on his forehead. "No fever, thank Kirei."

Fallon managed to open his eyes. His vision filled with shades of light and dark and blurry shapes. He blinked several times, slowly focusing.

A woman's face hovered over him. Almond-shaped eyes. High cheekbones, full soft lips. She looked so familiar. So much like Kenji as she pressed two fingertips to his wrist, along the tendon, by his pulse.

The next instant, his body went rigid with a memory of Kenji surrounded by soldiers of the People's Empire who marched him away, leaving Fallon with the chief dead on the ground, just as a People's Empire soldier shot a blast of searing, painful heat through his body, causing him to crumple to the ground. "Dammit," he ground out, "Let me up."

"Shhh. I must listen to your pulses." She moved her fingertips to the pulse on his neck and listened again. When she'd finished, she reached into a pocket and pulled out a small mechanism which she held several inches above his torso and ran it down the length of his body. A regulator. It blinked and clicked rapidly at some spots on Fallon's body, more slowly at others. "No internal bleeding. You'll heal up just fine with rest."

"Ken—"

"Don't speak yet, please." She clicked off the handheld scanner and slipped it into the unseen pocket of the heavy woolen coat she wore. Even the curve of her lips reminded him of Kenji. "It was your physical strength that saved you," she said then slipped one hand under his head inclining it slightly. She lifted a bottle carefully to his lips so he could take a sip. Water, cool and delicious slid down his parched throat.

He grasped her hand and held it fast so he could gulp.

"Easy now," she said, pulling the bottle away. "You're recovering from shock." She eased his head back down.

"How did I get here?"

"Some herders found you lying on the ground, unconscious. They feared for your life and brought you here for treatment."

"Who...are...you?" he panted, more easily now for having lubricated his mouth and throat.

She turned her head slightly. Fallon's rising consciousness allowed him to notice more about her, including long, shiny black hair pulled back off her face. Her clothing was heavy, a collection of woolen sweaters and overcoat that made her body appear shapeless. "My name is Mina."

"Where am I?"

"You're in a mountain cave just inside the Sunyatan border."

Fallon's insides jumped. How long had he been unconscious? For all he knew, he'd been transported more than fifty kilometers from where the chief's ship had landed. "Sunyata?" This woman was one of Kenji's citizens. She didn't know that her leader was in mortal danger. He tried to sit up again and she firmly stopped him again.

"You must rest. You're recovering from—"

"I can't rest," he said, his panic over Kenji supplanting

the pain. "Kenji is in danger. I need to find him."

Mina's hands tightened on his shoulders. She held him firmly and pinned his gaze. "You know where Kenji is?"

He stilled. *Only the people closest to me in the world call me Kenji.* The words rang in his memory. "Who are you?"

Her eyes narrowed. "I told you. I'm Mina."

"You know him," he rasped. "You're close to him."

She didn't answer but the air around her seemed to close down.

"He's been taken prisoner by the People's Empire," Fallon said in place of her silence. "They're going to *re-educate* him. I'm sure you know what that means."

"That's impossible! Kenji was sent—" She closed her mouth and pulled her hands back, then narrowed her eyes at him again. "Tinle!" she called over her shoulder.

A man hurried over. Like Mina, he had almond shaped eyes. But the resemblance ended there. His squashed features gave him the appearance of a human frog couched also in thick heavy woolen clothes. In his hands was a phazer rifle. "This man is claiming to know what's happened to His Holiness," Mina told him. "He could have been sent here by the Empire to ferret us out. Get the truth out of him."

Tinle scowled and pushed the barrel of the phazer to Fallon's head.

"I'm not Empire," he ground out. He held up his hands, causing a shot of pain through his body. "I'm Fallon. Jake Fallon of the Intergalactic Space Patrol. My badge was stripped from me. I was trying to protect Kenji. They shot me and took him away. If you kill me, you'll only put Kenji in worse danger than he's already in."

"That's a lie," Tinle growled. He cocked the phazer to the first level, the one that delivered a mild but uncomfortable current.

"Wait." Mina blocked the end of the barrel with her hand and pushed it away from Fallon's head. "Ken…His Holiness went missing months ago. How can I know you're telling me the truth? How do I know you're not trying to lure us out of the caves and mow us all down?"

"The ship he was riding in crashed on Terran A. Whoever else was with him was killed, but he had a memory chip implanted behind his damaged eye and didn't know how he got there. We met one night and became…friends." Best to omit the erotic details. "A bounty hunter was after him. Kenji came to me. I helped him escape but there were others after him. Corrupt ISP. They captured us and turned Kenji in to the People's Empire. Whoever brought me here found me inside the border of the People's Empire, outside one of their hidden facilities. I swear to you, it's true." Pain radiated through Fallon's body from the effort of speaking but his desperation drove him on. He fell back against the bedding, exhausted. Had they believed him? He waited several long seconds as they eyed him and then each other. Fear and horror saturated both their expressions.

"He's telling the truth," Mina finally said.

"How do you know?" Tinle's already wide mouth widened with the press of his lips. His eyes would have shot spikes the way they lit on Fallon. "His Holiness is the target of so much hatred."

"I don't hate Kenji. I love him," Fallon said. They had no idea how much. He heaved a breath. His body felt as if it had been dragged across rocks then set on fire. "I must get to him before they destroy his mind." Breathing past the pain, he struggled to sit up.

Mina's hands shot out. "You won't even get past the mouth of the cave in your condition. Rest now. The herders will look for him. They know where all the facilities are. They'll report to us." She looked over her shoulder, calling out in a language Fallon didn't recognize. In seconds, other figures emerged from shadowy corners of this place they were in, a cave of some sort. Men and women, dressed like Mina, crowded around him. An array of faces in all colors and apparent cultures surrounded him, looking at him with awed expressions.

Mina released him and instead of resting, he sat upright. "Ay!" Pain sliced through every muscle, sending him onto his back.

"I told you, you must rest," Mina said, though her voice held excitement now. "The sooner you recover, the sooner we can all search for Kenji. Several of the re-education centers are right here in these mountains."

Fallon panted from the effort of trying to rise. Pain still made his body clench. "Shite!" he breathed, fisting the bedding.

Mina waved the others away, speaking in that strange language. Then she turned back to Fallon. "Please," she said, "rest so that you'll recover. We don't have any technology in this cave, only our knowledge of the mountains and our willingness to risk our lives to help Kenji."

He managed to nod. As with the others, his physical

181

strength and willingness to risk his life for Kenji were all he had. Hopefully that would be enough. "All right, Mina," he said, his voice falling to a whisper. "I'll rest." No sooner had he said the words than exhaustion gripped him. His eyes drifted shut. The last thing he saw in his mind's eye before falling into a deep sleep was Kenji's sweet face…

* * * * *

Kenji closed his eyes against the relentless harsh lighting. How long would they keep him strapped in this narrow chair? He wouldn't treat even his own enemies this way, endless hours strapped in a chair, blaring a siren of some sort into the room whenever his eyelids began to flutter closed from his exhaustion. Every muscle in his body screamed for the sweet release of movement. The strap across his forehead, holding his head firmly in place, squeezed his head mercilessly.

"Hello, Comrade Shimizu."

The voice had a hushed, controlled quality that felt like oil slipping through his body. Unable to turn in the direction of the voice, Kenji gripped the armrests of his chair. He was powerless to do anything but wait for the source of the voice to reveal itself.

Not one man but two appeared before him and stood a few feet away, regarding him with machine-like expressions. Like all other Empire officials, they wore gray suits, button down jackets and plain slacks above black boots.

The shorter man, dark-haired, his eyes almond-shaped, skin light gold, stepped forward. His nondescript features made him blend with the myriad of Empire officials with whom Kenji had engaged in conference talks over the years in his efforts to co-exist peacefully with the People's Empire. "I am Comrade Commissioner Zong and this is Comrade Commissioner Maltov." He indicated his companion, taller and heavier, with blond hair and blue eyes. "We are your re-educators." His rat-like face creased into smiles. "Don't be afraid," he said, "in the end, we shall all be good friends."

Kenji remained silent though his heart pounded. The cool air in the room passed over his head, now more sensitive to cold after one of his captors had shaved his head, military style, short on the sides, leaving it just a bit longer on top, in the style of all the men he'd seen here.

Zong opened a small metal box on the table in front of Kenji while Maltov went to Kenji's side and rolled up the sleeve of the white shirt they'd dressed him in. "I hope you don't mind my not addressing you as Your Holiness, comrade," Zong said, lifting a syringe from the box. He proceeded to fill the syringe with a clear liquid. "But you see, we're all equal here, all comrades. There is no one man or woman who holds him or herself to be a god above the others and rule over them."

"I've never claimed to be a god," Kenji said, breaking his silence. "I'm not better or worse than anyone else."

Zong tapped on the needle then pushed on the syringe from which clear liquid spurted. Then the short, skinny man moved toward Kenji. "Oh? Then what *do* you claim, if not some sort of antiquated feudalism where one man is lord and there are ranks of others beneath him, and so on until one reaches the level of peasant and then, untouchable?"

"Mine is a path whereby any human being can discover his or her own true nature. We are all the Self. There is no hierarchy."

Zong chuckled. "That is a very selfish approach to existence for one who is called the Jewel of his people, comrade." He accepted a cotton ball soaked in alcohol from Maltov and rubbed it in the crook of Kenji's arm. "If you think I believe for one second that you see into men's souls, you are wrong. That is a sham."

The acrid scent of alcohol assaulted Kenji's nostrils, mocking him with its sterile coldness. He eyed the syringe, dreading the moment the stuff would be released into his veins. No need to show these lost souls his fear. They'd only use it to their wicked advantage. And anyway, he'd soon find out. "I see you," he said. "I see you the celebratory and hungry drive you harbor. You're a hunter who has trapped big game."

Zong's eyes narrowed. Anger slipped through them before he visibly schooled his features to keep the customary flat expression. "Very clever, comrade. It won't work."

"And as for your accusation of selfishness, our way is not selfish, Comrade Commissioner Zong. A realized human being does not enter bliss until all sentient beings have reached the same enlightenment. There could be nothing less selfish."

Zong's eyes grew steely and he frowned. "The people are all that matter. They sing and dance and procreate while you hold yourself apart, remaining chaste so that they can feed on your life force." He shook his head. "You're deluded, comrade. Which is why we're here to help you. You will understand the truth about the good of all and that will liberate you." He pushed the needle into the spot he'd just cleaned.

Kenji suppressed a flinch. He watched the clear liquid empty from the syringe into his arm.

The liquid injected into his body spread through his veins. Its creeping warmth traveled up each arm, across his back, down into his groin and legs, all the way to his toes, as if metal were cooling and solidifying throughout his entire being. It made him so sleepy, yet his mind was wide awake.

"There, Comrade Shimizu. In moments, you will begin to have clarity." Zong held the cotton ball to the needle and slipped it from Kenji's skin, holding the cotton ball in place. "You are exactly the kind of strong personality the People's Empire needs. Once you see the truth, your people will join us, and then the world will begin to enter a new age, a glorious age. Where our predecessors failed centuries ago, we will succeed."

Zong's words elongated. His wide face contorted, stretching and retracting, growing shapeless as if he were made of rubber. Kenji blinked hard, but the distortion of the men in front of him remained. The entire room tilted and shifted. He closed his eyes, but the eerie floating sensation only intensified.

"You can't begin to understand, Comrade, the crucial role you will play in the future of the People's Empire." He kept himself in Kenji's view, forcing Kenji to watch him speak. Each word Zong spoke sank into Kenji's mind as if injected with the same needle that had pierced his arm. Kenji felt as if his head weighed hundreds of pounds. Had his forehead not been strapped, his head would have lolled forward.

"Use your intelligence, comrade…"

With Zong's voice droning in the background, images from Kenji's life rose and passed across his memory like a film. Playing in his front yard when the priests approached him. Crying because he wanted to go back to Sunyata with them. Sitting with them in meditation from the earliest age, and sometimes crying in his bed at night because he missed his mother.

The images shifted to the trouble with Mina years later. She'd been as upset as his mother about the plan the Council had to hide him in space. Mina had objected so vocally the Council had pushed for her resignation. Rather than produce more friction, she had voluntarily resigned her post as his personal physician and gone to tend to the Sunyatan citizens who resided in the mountains, far from the main population.

His memory shifted again, to the tool descending toward his eye, the dread, the horror of what his own ministers felt was best for him — to forget who he was while in hiding lest he bring attention to himself and get captured. He'd argued against leaving his people but they were so concerned a transition made him vulnerable to attack, it was best he be somewhere safe. They'd told him a doctor on Terran A would repair his eye so that he wouldn't be so easily recognized. But something had obviously happened to prevent the repair. The rest of it was time out of his life he'd never get back.

His only other memory was waking up in that small bed next to Fallon. In moments, Fallon had gone from being a stranger to the mysterious ISP agent he'd fantasized about nearly a lifetime, to being his first kiss. Fallon had saved his life again at great risk to his own and had helped him learn who he was, to fill the void of memory. Fallon was the one who looked at him the way he'd always yearned to be looked at, as a lover, a friend, a fellow human being, and not only as some revered figure who was somehow less human than everyone else.

A sharp pang squeezed Kenji's chest. Fallon had been a crucial part of his life even though their time together had been woefully short. Deep down, he'd had understood something that went against the very tenets of his people's path. There was a middle way, which included the acceptance of his physical body and its needs, passions that should neither be ignored nor indulged. Fallon had filled those needs and Kenji's life now included his memory of that man.

And now Fallon was dead. The image of the large man crumpling to the ground at the phazer shot had burned itself into his memory, undulled in the slightest by the drug invading his body.

With Fallon gone and Mina lost somewhere in the mountains, forsaken by her own community, there was little reason to go on. It would be so easy to succumb. All he had to do was say the words Zong wanted to hear and they would stop this process. They'd provide for all his needs, give him prestige and power within their ranks in exchange for the manipulation of his own people. And many would listen to him.

"I see, comrade," Zong said, his voice penetrating the haze of reflections, "you are seriously considering all I'm telling you. Very wise of you. Very wise."

Kenji's mind felt as if someone had wrapped his brain in wool. His thoughts now formulated at the pace a snail took to cross the floor of a cave, struggling against the tide of the mind-altering drug. Yet, something else was there, another voice, one of sanity that whispered like a good friend, in his ear. *"Don't listen to them, Kenji."* It was Fallon's voice. He could see the man's rugged face in his mind, the cleft in his chin, the sparkle of his blue eyes. *"They're full of shite.*"

Fallon would have pulled him out of here had he lived. Fallon would have been willing to die to get him out of here. He needed to hang on to that thought.

Every cell of his body and mind fought Zong's voice.

Closing his eyes, he heard his mantra rise from deep inside him and repeat. He listened to the holy words which blended with the outside noises yet was not absorbed. The habit of giving his attention to meditation since the age of six now served him in the throes of the psychological torture to which he was being subjected. His sense of time, long dissipated from being kept in a harshly lighted room with no clock, no longer mattered. Zong and his comrades could keep him here for a day or a hundred years. He was timeless. That was the truth.

Kenji's breathing evened. He felt deep calm even though Zong's bee-like voice buzzed around him, penetrating his very brains cells.

Whether he lost this battle or not no longer mattered. He was one with eternity…

* * * * *

The entry into Earth's atmosphere went smoothly enough. Pete powered down the controls and took a deep breath. He tossed a chocolate chip cookie to Mike who snapped it out of mid-air. Pretty good feat for a dog strapped into his seat.

"Good boy, Mike," he said and grabbed a cookie for himself. There were only a couple left of the supply he'd found stashed in the small galley of Fallon's space pod, but when they got to Earth, Fallon's mom would no doubt have a mountainous plate of them fresh out of the oven. It was a wonder Fallon didn't have as big a gut as he did, growing up with Super Cook for a mother.

Turning to the Matsuotos, he held the plate out. After all they'd been through, it was only fair not to glom all the cookies for himself. They both shook their heads, declining with their usual politeness. "Well, help yourselves whenever you get hungry," Pete said and bowed, the show of courtesy they had given him since he'd sprung them from that horrible chief's cell at ISP. The poor people, having been snatched from their little home on Terran A, bound and roughed up, barely given enough food and water. They were no spring chickens, maybe even in their fifties. A miracle they'd survived.

It hadn't been too hard to get them out of Headquarters. After saving Fallon's space buggy and updating all the software, he'd gotten the thing back online and had access to all of Fallon's security codes. It had been a cinch then, to saunter into ISP with the digital codes of Fallon's hands and eye impressions to flash at security scans. His little laser pointer did the rest as far as dismantling the shields on the cell in which the Matsuotos were being held prisoner. Once he'd told the poor huddled couple of his connection to Kenji, they'd gone with him willingly. Every security guard there bought the fake uniform and his story of the chief's orders to transport the prisoners to the floating brig for deportation. No wonder ISP was so corrupt, with a bunch of dickheads like that running the place.

Pete leaned into the control panel and flicked switches here and there. Fallon's space buggy was far less complex than his own and had been even easier to learn to fly. So after hovering in space a safe enough distance from Fallon's space pod, Pete had watched the larger craft lock itself on. He'd recognized the markings on the side to be an ISP craft. Locking onto the signal, he'd hacked in and found out what was going on, including the chief's confession to having murdered Nicky. Guilt gripped his chest. He never meant to have such a secret from Fallon, the best friend he'd ever had. But Fallon would have been utterly devastated to know that Nicky had hired him to do the hacking that had led to Nicky's confirmation of the chief's corruption. No doubt, the information that had gotten Nicky killed.

How I'm going to live that down is beyond me, he thought and glanced at Mike. What a relief Kenji hadn't guessed what was going on, him being *the one who sees* and all that. "We're going to get your master back as soon as we can," he said to the dog.

Mike barked.

Pete pulled the throttle, setting a course for Manchester, England. He'd been there before with Fallon on a visit to Fallon's folks, though he didn't relish the task of telling them now the danger their son was in--if he was even alive. Which was why he needed Fallon's mother or father to do the DNA lock. Getting Fallon out of whatever danger he was in was the least Pete could do, the only way he could make up for his role in Nicky's death. Besides, Fallon was his best friend. No way was he going to let anyone kill the guy, if he could prevent it. Maybe then, they could even save Kenji.

Manchester came into sight in less than a half hour. In spite of their terrible lack of technology, these ISP buggies could really move. Pete pushed down on the throttle and searched for the nearest parking lot to Fallon's house in which to land. No one would question an ISP vehicle in their midst. ISP were legitimate cops, always landing here and there in search of renegade bounty hunters and other missing persons.

After landing, Pete packed up his portable DNA locking device into a backpack, unstrapped Mike and opened the pod door. Once outside, the moist warm summer air struck his face. The sun shone on his skin and into his eyes, nearly blinding him. He shielded his eyes, letting them adjust to Earth's brilliant light. When he was ready, he started walking. He ushered the Matsuotos out and to the ground, keeping them close to him. "C'mon, Mike. Lead us to the Fallon residence."

Mike barked and trotted ahead of him. While walking, Pete pulled out his mobile, the one that could be used on Earth. Best to make sure Fallon's parents were home.

"Hello?" A woman's voice answered on the third ring.

"Mrs. Fallon?"

"Yes?"

"It's Pete, Jake's friend."

Mrs. Fallon paused. "Oh, yes! How are you, dear? How's Jake?"

"Well, I haven't spoken to him recently. I was in the neighborhood and wanted to stop in. Are you available?" Best not to alarm her just yet.

"Yes, Peter. It would be lovely to see you. I just baked some cookies. How soon will you be here?"

The Fallons' block came into view. Their red brick flat was the third in the row, a street of brick and row houses dotted only by the occasional spindly tree. "I'm almost there. And I have a couple of friends with me who need help. If that's all right."

"Of course, Peter. See you soon, dear."

Mrs. Fallon was waiting on the stoop, the door open. A big woman with dark hair and blue eyes, Fallon looked just like her, including his large size. She was like a quarterback dressed as someone's grandmother, with the blouse, skirt and cardigan sweater.

Mike bounded up the steps and went up on his hind legs, licking the woman's face.

She laughed. "Oh, Mike, good to see you, too. Down, boy." Mike obeyed and loped into the house. Mrs. Fallon turned with a smile. "Peter, what a pleasure." After a quick introduction, she ushered him and the Matsuotos into the front hallway. In the background, Pete heard the telescreen blaring what sounded like a football game from another room. Mr. Fallon was a freak for Manchester United.

"Come into the kitchen," Mrs. Fallon said. "I just made a pot of—" She stopped when their gazes met and her blue eyes searched his. Pete saw her mother's intuition kick in immediately. "Peter, you didn't tell me the truth before, did you? You wouldn't have come here without Jake. Why is the dog here without Jake? What's happened?"

"Well, Mrs. Fallon, yeah, I didn't want to alarm you at first, but Jake is in some trouble."

The large woman grasped his forearm, her wide face lined with upset. "Where is he?"

"That's just it. I don't know. Somewhere on Earth, but I don't know exactly. I have a…machine. I mean, something that can help us find him, but I need you…or Mr. Fallon."

Mrs. Fallon looked over her shoulder. "Ben! Turn off

that bloody telly and get in here!"

The telescreen went silent. "What are you going on about, you damned—" Mr. Fallon halted when he saw the Matsuotos standing there. "Oh—I--" He turned to his wife in confusion then noticed Pete in the hall, Mike standing by them, panting. "What's this? You're Jake's hacker friend, Pete, isn't it? Where's Jakie?"

Pete slid the backpack off and held out his hand to Jake's father. "Hey, Mr. F. That's what I'm here to find out. Well, that and to see if someone can give these folks shelter for a while. The same threat to Fallon is a threat to them."

"Threat? What threat?" Mr. Fallon asked as his wife ushered the Matsuotos toward the kitchen.

"Please," she said, "let's all go into the kitchen. Can we use that thing of yours in there?"

"Yes." Pete explained to them the principles of the DNA lock while Mrs. Fallon pulled out chairs for the Matsuotos.

"You've come such a long way," Fallon's mother said. "At least have a cup of tea."

The Matsuotos, quiet as usual, politely sat with their tea off to the side.

Pete chose to stand while he explained the situation, all the while unpacking his equipment to set up the DNA lock on the table.

"Oh my God." Mrs. Fallon's hand trembled around the teapot. Mr. Fallon took it from her and set it down. "Sit down, Gwen. It'll be all right. Our Jakie's a survivor. Always has been." He patted his wife's hand and turned to the DNA lock machine. "Bloody hell," he breathed. "What in the devil is that thing?"

Pete explained the concept of the DNA lock and how to use it.

"Go on," Mr. Fallon said, "hook me up. I want to find our son."

* * * * *

"Jakie? Jakie? Are you there?"

Fallon blinked. His father's voice filtered through the heaviness of sleep, a healing slumber he'd drifted in and out of after waking up and finding Mina hovering over him. According to the passage of light and darkness at the mouth of the cave, he'd been resting for about two days. Mina had been correct. Deep rest had sped his recovery. Most of the pain was gone from his limbs and he felt almost ready to look for Kenji.

"Jakie, it's your dad. I see you now." The large man's pasty brow furrowed. *"Are you all right, laddie? What's been done to you?"*

His father stood at the foot of his sleeping pallet, looking down at him, his button-down sweater and baggy trousers, his belly pushing against his plaid shirt, a memory of all those mornings his dad used to wake him up for school.

"Dad." Fallon's voice came out a croak from lack of use. Scrubbing a hand over his face, he tried to sit up. Mina, who was usually at his bedside when he awoke, wasn't there. "Am I hallucinating now on top of it all?"

Ben Fallon grinned. "You're not hallucinating, laddie. I'm doing one of those, oh, what's the bloody thing called

194

again?" He addressed the question to someone Fallon couldn't see. Then he nodded and turned back to Fallon. "A DNA lock. That's what it is. Can't you hear the others? Your mum, and Pete?"

Wide awake, Fallon sat bolt upright despite the residual twinges of pain. Thankfully he was fully clothed against the chilly air of the cave. "No. It doesn't work that way. And Dad, where did you get a DNA lock? Pete's there with you?"

"Yes. Pete, the hacker. He's come looking for you. Mike's with him and he brought this little Japanese couple." His father looked away again, as if speaking to someone else. "Yeah, the Matsuotos. Pete said to tell you he sprung them out of ISP headquarters. They're going to stay here with us for a bit. Your mum is thrilled. She's always wanted to make that bloody sushi crap."

Relief cascaded through Fallon's chest. That was his dad, always ready to try new things. Thank God for Pete. "Please thank Pete for me, Dad. Tell him I owe him a big one."

Ben Fallon repeated the message and then listened to the response. He chuckled. "Pete said to tell you if that did it for him, he'd have just won the Universal Lotto." Before Fallon could ask after Mum, his father frowned again. "Now, that's just like you, Jakie, to be concerned with everyone else. What about *you*? Are you all right?"

Compared to how he'd *been*, it was a million times improved. Perhaps today he could actually get up and take a piss without assistance. "I'm okay, Dad. Don't worry." He explained the situation to his father who repeated the information to Pete.

His father listened to Pete's response then nodded.

"Pete says he's locking onto your coordinates. When he leaves here, he's setting a course straight for your location. He's going to help you find Kenji and get him out."

Unshed tears stung Fallon's eyes. He'd known Pete was a good guy, but nothing like this. "Please tell him I'm grateful."

His father repeated the message and then looked at him. "Pete says, no problem, dude. That's what he's here for."

Fallon nodded, struck with a sudden pang for his folks. They'd always been close, and he loved them even though at times they could be overbearing. "How's Mum?"

"She's just fine. Can't wait to see you." His father's blue eyes looked watery then. "Be careful, Jakie. We love you."

"I love you too, Dad. I'll be careful. I promise."

Ben Fallon nodded just before fading from sight.

Fallon sighed and raked both hands through his hair. Time to get up, relieve himself, walk around and pull himself together. Pete would be here in a few hours. The only problem, however, was finding Kenji. Without a DNA lock, it could take days, weeks, time they didn't have, unless they could somehow get one of his parents to lock onto him from where they were on that Japanese island.

"How are you today, Fallon?"

Mina's gentle voice beside him made him look up. The lantern light glowed on her smooth oval face. The urge to pull her to him and kiss her seized him. These last few days, her resemblance to Kenji teased at his consciousness, almost causing him several times to imagine Kenji knelt by him each time she came around. She looked concerned now, her smooth brow furrowed. "Tinle heard you speaking to someone, but when he looked over, there was no one there. Were you using a DNA lock?"

"Yes! My father was communicating with me."

She nodded. "I see." Then suddenly, her face brightened. She touched his arm. "Do you have one with you? I didn't see one in your clothing, but maybe you have a very small one." Excitement made Mina's face glow. "We could use it to find Kenji!"

Kenji. There she was again, referring to him by name. "Mina, who are you?" he asked softly. Now that she trusted him, he felt he could ask the question. "Only a few people call Kenji by his first name."

Mina's eyes misted over and her fingertips pressed more firmly into his skin. "I'm his…sister."

He raked a hand through his hair and looked up at the shadowy ceiling of the cave. "Damn, I've been bloody out of it, haven't I? The first thing I noticed when I saw your face was how much you looked like Kenji." He gave a small rueful laugh. "I'm getting too old for this." Nicky would have picked up on the resemblance immediately, tired or not.

"No, you're not, Fallon. You've been asleep all this time except for our brief conversation. I'm sure you would have realized it sooner."

"Perhaps. Well then, we have what we need." Fallon's heart lurched. *Please God, don't let it be too late.* "Pete will be here soon. We'll find Kenji."

Chapter Eleven

"Kenji never mentioned he had a sister." Fallon addressed Mina from behind the privacy curtain of animal skins hung by his sleeping pallet. He'd given himself a quick wash with a rag and a small bucket of water Tinle had provided for him from melted ice and now dressed.

"He never mentioned me probably because he feels so painfully guilty toward me."

He closed a belt over the thick woolen sweaters Mina had left on his pallet then stepped to the other side of the curtain to face her, one eyebrow quirked. "Guilty? Why?"

"Because of what happened before the memory chip was implanted." Mina frowned and her eyes clouded in the same way Kenji's did in certain moments. "I was very opposed to the idea of erasing Kenji's memory. When I argued vehemently against the operation to put the memory chip behind Kenji's bad eye, Kenji's ministers wanted to remove me from my post as his personal physician. Kenji objected of course, but I didn't want to cause more trouble for him. I resigned voluntarily, but he blames himself."

Fallon took a step toward her, wishing he could offer her some comfort. "Wow, I'm sorry."

Mina's delicate face darkened. "When it comes to survival, the Great Jewel followers are as unmovable as the rocks that make up these caves. Kenji only agreed to his ministers' plan because he'd do anything to help his people."

"Apparently. Is that why you stayed here?"

She nodded. "Yes. As much as I love Kenji, and I do, I felt I could be of much more service here, for these people who have no one else to give them medical care."

Just then, Fallon heard a familiar bark at the mouth of the cave. The sight before him drained the residual stiffness right out of his limbs. "Mike!" He knelt down as the dog bounded up to him, covering his face with slobbery licks. "Hey, there, I'm glad to see you, too." He scratched behind the mutt's ears and buried his fingers into the dog's thick black fur. He'd thought never to see Mike again.

Or Pete, for that matter.

"Hey Fallon!"

Fallon looked up from Mike. "Hey." He rose to his feet and wrapped Pete in a bear hug. "Pete, thank God." Of course, Fallon smelled his mum's cookies on the bloke. Not that it mattered. Because of Pete, there was hope of finding Kenji again. When he pulled away, Pete was grinning.

"You look like shit as usual, my friend."

Fallon laughed. "And here I went and took a bath just for you!" He eyed his Pete up and down. "Well, I won't say anything about you, Pete, not after everything you've done for me."

"Geez, Fallon, you don't have to slobber over me. It's what I'm here—" Pete's lips clamped shut and his fat cheeks bloomed with reddish spots beneath the golden stubble. "Please, tell me I didn't just curse in front of…"

Fallon followed Pete's gaze to the source of his embarrassment.

Mina stood before them, smiling. "Hello," she said softly.

An awkward, adolescent-like silence filled the space. He'd never seen Pete like this before. "Pete, this is Mina. Kenji's sister."

Pete blinked, not taking his eyes off Mina. Suddenly, Fallon's statement registered and he jerked his gaze to Fallon. "Sister? Kenji has a sister?" He looked back at Mina and seemed to forget his tongue as quickly as he'd found it again.

"Long story," Fallon said. "I'll tell you all about it after we find Kenji."

That knocked Pete out of his trance. "Right." He shifted the pack off his shoulder and dug out the machine. His hands moved swiftly, setting it on the table Fallon had indicated. With flicks of his fingers, the metal box powered up, blinking lights everywhere. Quickly, he attached the helmet and turned to Mina. "You put...this on," he said to her, obviously struggling to put aside his shyness in the urgency of helping Kenji. Then to Fallon, "I managed to find a way to adjust it so that anyone with Kenji's DNA code can find him, not just a parent."

"Good job, Pete."

Mina approached the box, taking a stool that someone else set down for her.

Fallon stepped forward. "Now, Mina, this device will send an image of you to wherever Kenji is. Your shared genetic code is the magnet that will transmit your image. If you can, try to stay out of Kenji's sight. If he's under his captors' control and lets on that you're there, it could be bad."

Mina nodded, her dark almond-shaped eyes darting between the machine and Fallon. "I understand." She pulled the helmet down onto her head while Pete tested the controls.

"Now," Fallon went on, "I'll need you to describe to me what you're seeing while Pete works on locking the coordinates of Kenji's location."

"Got it."

"All set, Fallon," Pete said.

Fallon looked at him. "Do it." He sat, every muscle in his newly-healed body tense as if pulled with many pounds of pressure. In a few seconds, he saw Mina's expression shift. Her eyes were distant, as if she were physically in a different place, seeing unseen people, hearing unheard things. "I see him," she whispered. "He's in a room, a cold-looking room. An interrogation room. Bright lights are shining into his face." Her brow creased. "He's strapped into a chair and…" She shifted forward on her seat, as if moving closer to Kenji, then let out a tiny gasp. "He's been drugged. I see it in his pupil."

Fallon's heart lurched. "Mina, if you can, look around the room, look at the ceiling. Tell me what else you see."

"Everything looks metallic and glass. We must hurry to him! They're torturing him with psychotropic injections. Every neuron in his body is being tampered with. If we don't give him an antidote in time, he'll be permanently damaged."

"Shite. Pete, you flew the space bug here?"

"I did," Pete said, his eyes not leaving the controls of the DNA lock.

"I don't have the technology necessary for a rescue mission of this sort."

Pete glanced at him, a sideways grin like a pink slash folding one cheek. "You do now."

"Oh no!" Mina's outburst pulled his and Pete's attention. Her eyes were wide with a terrified look. "He saw me! He's calling my name." Her finger went to her lips. "Shhh, Kenji. No. Please, be quiet."

Icy prickles skittered over every surface of Fallon's skin. "Pete, do you have the coordinates yet?"

Pete's fingers flew over the controls and the attached keyboard. "Not yet. There seems to be some security device that scrambles the radar.

Fallon dropped to his knees beside Mina. "Mina, tell him he's hallucinating from the drugs. Don't let him think you're real." To Pete, "Pete, please, hurry!"

"Kenji, you're seeing things," Mina said. Her voice quavered with what to Fallon's ears was a mixture of terror for her brother and distress at lying to him. "It's not really me," she went on. "It's the drugs."

"Pete, dammit, what's going on?"

"I'm sorry, Fallon. I'm having to try and hack into their system. That's the only way I can dismantle their scrambling device."

Fallon shoved a hand through his hair. Sweat beaded on his forehead. Poor Kenji, alone in that place, bound and drugged and God only knew what else had been done to him in the days they'd had him prisoner. Given his way, he'd have gone in with phazer rifles strapped to both hands.

"Got it!" Pete glanced up. "Their cloaking device is dismantled. I'm almost there, Fallon."

"Hang on, Kenji," Fallon muttered under his breath. "If it's the last thing I do in this life, I'll get you out of there. Alive."

"Yes!" Pete pumped his fist in the air. "Got the coordinates! He's thirty kilometers east-southeast of here."

Fallon lifted the helmet off of Mina lest in her excitement she forget herself and let Kenji know what was happening. To inform Kenji was to run the deadly risk of informing his captors as well. "All right, let's go." He started for the mouth of the cave.

"I'm coming with you."

The determination in Mina's voice stopped him and he turned. "I can't let you. It's too dangerous."

"He'll need me, Fallon," she said and ran to a corner where jumbles of equipment and boxes were piled in an attempt at organization in a cave. She grabbed a medical bag and started throwing stuff in it. "Do *you* know how to reverse the effects of the drugs in him?" she asked, her hands flying over the shelves dropping bottles and small boxes of things into the bag."

Fallon let out a breath. She was right, of course. "All right, let's go."

* * * * *

"Mina," Kenji whispered again. His beautiful sister. He kept his gaze rooted to the spot where she'd stood and then vanished. Had it been her ghost? Had she died out in the mountains? Through the haze of drugs, his heart ached so hard he thought the grief alone would kill him.

203

"Why do you keep saying your physician's name?" Zong's rat-like face peered at Kenji from the stool where he perched. There was barely a moment Zong wasn't there, droning on, tapping a riding crop again one palm as he paced in front of Kenji's seat. Kenji's eyelids fluttered.

"Comrade? You haven't answered my question. She isn't here. You must be hallucinating. Or..." He turned to the guard at the door. "Scan the room for excess DNA radiation." Then to Kenji, "Perhaps you've been visited."

Kenji's heart lurched. A DNA lock! He hadn't thought of it. Then Mina *had* really been here! If that was so, Zong would search her down and capture her too. He needed to protect her. "No," he whispered with all the strength he could muster. "Hallucinating."

Tap tap went the crop on his cheek, lightly enough not to hurt but firmly enough to serve as a warning—he wasn't responding well to re-education and if this lack continued, stronger measures would be employed. "I understand, comrade, you must be homesick for your family and friends, for those who are familiar to you. But this approach is all wrong." Zong's arm rose in a grand gesture. The riding crop stood straight up like a flag to emphasize the glory he was about to expound. "We are all friends and family. The People's Empire has done away with grades and distinctions." He lowered his arms and pointed to Kenji. "However, it won't hurt to check. Your sister needs to join us. We'll find her in any case. It will be as beneficial for her to serve the People's Empire outside of your selfish little realm."

Zong resumed a slow pace. Back and forth, back and forth while the drug made Zong appear to be many. With each step the man took, he seemed to multiply. Without warning, he whirled and pinned Kenji with a scowl. "You are arrogant, you realize? You presume to know what's better for your people! Meanwhile, some of them are scattered among these mountains, living like animals in caves, while a few of you now live in luxury, protected by the Japanese government. How can you live with yourself knowing that, Comrade? Don't you wish to bring them all peace and security? Only *you* have that power. You're abusing your power. Is this what you want?"

Kenji's heart felt as if it would sink into the pit of his gut. Hot tears welled in his eyes. If it had been Mina he'd seen and she was alive, then the People's Empire would kill her spirit. That was almost as horrifying, or maybe as horrifying, as the death of her body. The thought forced a whimper from him.

A smile spread on Zong's face. "There, comrade. A twinge of conscience. Very good. One of the most important things a good leader has. A *good* leader does not subject his people to more suffering, starvation and alienation. A *good* leader does what is best for them. I can see you wish to do what is best for them."

"Yes," he whispered. Mina's ghostly image remained in his mind. That beautiful sweet woman, his sister, his confidante, his physician, was in terrible danger. And it was his own fault.

There was only one way to end this. He had only to say the words. "Comrade Zong," he said softly.

Wild glee spread through Zong's compact, lined features. "Yes, comrade?"

"Kill me…"

"What? Comrade, that is not the answer."

"Kill me —"

A sudden crash swallowed Kenji's words. Before him, chunks of stone rained down, knocking Zong to the floor. The very world seemed to shake, yet Kenji couldn't move, strapped as he was, arms, legs and head, to the chair. Loud whirring noises filled the space and it seemed as if existence itself was being destroyed. Guards poured in, phazer rifles brandished, though the chunks of rock piling up between Kenji and the entrance of the room impeded them from reaching Kenji or Zong. He squeezed his eyes shut from the assault of spraying pebbles.

"Kenji!"

At the sound of his name shouted over the din, Kenji's eyes flew open. It sounded so much like Fallon. Someone floated in front of him as if he'd been lowered from the heavens. The face came into focus. Rugged cheeks. Blazing blue eyes. It was Fallon!

Phazer shots crackled in the air around them and Fallon turned, firing a barrage of answering lasers. Holding the assault back for a few seconds, he gestured. "Hold on, Kenji," he yelled and aimed a strange device in his other hand at Kenji. A blue shaft of light shot out of the smaller tool and Kenji felt his bonds snapping open. "Let's go." Two iron-hard arms enclosed him and scooped him out of the chair. The next thing he knew, they were gliding up through a gigantic ragged hole in the roof. The blue sky shone through like a glorious beacon. The arms around Kenji pulled him close. Against the man's chest, which smelled of wool and something clean and manly, Kenji tried to hold on though his arms were weak from the drugs.

Cool air hit his face as they passed through the hole. Phazer rifles made zinging sounds below them and men's shouts rang in the air, but they continued sailing upward.

"I've got you, Kenji," Fallon said in his ear. "You're safe with me."

Fallon. Kenji sagged against him in relief.

The other man's lips turned in a smile. "Yes, it's me, Kenji. You're free now."

Kenji tried to nod but his body felt as if it had been filled with sludge. Shadows seemed to engulf him and hands covered his arms and legs, lifting him. Just before his body landed on something firm.

"Kenji," a female voice said close by, "don't stop fighting the drugs. I'm giving you an antidote."

Mina! He saw her face through a blurred haze and tried to say her name but his lips felt frozen. He was sinking ands sinking. They were too late. Unable to keep his eyes open a second longer, he succumbed. The light faded as his eyelids lowered. He heard the buzz of another machine, felt the warmth of light pass over his face. The exhaustion was too great and he closed his eyes, sinking into darkness.

Chapter Twelve

When Kenji opened his eyes, he saw daylight. The light and heat were intense, as if the sun's rays poured directly through the window. Blinking until his good eye adjusted, he focused. Blue sky in a patch above a darker strip of blue that moved like…waves. The ocean. Such as he remembered when he was small, playing on the sand with Mina. Was he back in Japan?

Yes, he was, judging by the half-timbered interior of the room in which he found himself. Yellow curtains framed the picture of the outside. Inside, he saw walls, whitewashed, divided in sections by heavy dark wood beams.

Slowly he became aware of his other surroundings. A soft bed underneath him. The ceiling, also whitewashed and lined with dark beams. A steady beeping sounded close to his head. He glanced up and saw a monitor with jagged green lines. A hospital? Was Fallon here? He tried to say Fallon's name, but it stuck in his throat as if his mouth had been glued shut.

Mina's face appeared above him. She was smiling down at him, her long dark hair pulled back, the way she'd always worn it since they were children.

Kenji's heart thumped. Was she really here or was it another DNA lock? Memories crowded in his mind, fuzzy edges blending so he couldn't tell what was vision, what was reality. A strange noise, like a cough traveled up his windpipe and forced its way out. *I'm sorry, Mina.* The words coursed through his mind. His throat was thick, too parched to talk. More of those forceful coughs pushed their way from his body.

Mina's smile faded. "Kenji, shhh." She reached up and passed her hand over his brow. How comforting her touch was. "The drugs are still in your system. You had much more than any human being should ever be given."

Fallon's face appeared next to Mina's. Worry darkened his blue eyes and made deep lines in his brow. "Kenji, it's all right. You're safe now."

Hot tears pooled in his good eye. They were really here. No DNA lock.

"He's crying," Fallon said. He reached for something Kenji couldn't see and then a gentle hand slipped under his head. Fallon slipped a tube between his lips. "Drink some water, Kenji. You'll be better in no time."

On pure instinct, Kenji pulled at the straw. Cool liquid pooled in his mouth. He swallowed greedily.

"Easy, Kenji," Mina said gently. She adjusted the tubes hanging from a sack of clear liquid. Then a light tug on his inner arm where small needles burrowed into his skin, enabling the tubes to drip the content of the bag into him.

When the dryness was gone, he released the straw and lay back, breathing heavily. Fallon and Mina were still there. A small light sparked within him. "Alive," he whispered, speech possible now for the moisture in his mouth.

Fallon caressed his brow. "Yes, thank God. We're all alive and together."

Kenji's forceful coughing resumed. His eyes felt hot and tears slipped onto his cheeks. Fallon's hand never stopped its caress on his hair. The light friction of the man's palm against his skin calmed him. Praise Kirei! Had he the strength, he would have sat up and grabbed them both into an embrace. He managed to grasp Fallon's hand and hold it to his damp cheek. "Fallon." Through his tears, he saw Fallon's blue eyes mist. "I thought you'd died that day."

A smile played on his lips. "I was pretty hurt, but Mina and some of the others found me in time. Mina fixed me up."

Kenji looked at her, not releasing Fallon's hand, as if Fallon would slip away if he let go. "Mina. I've missed you so."

Mina stood next to Fallon, her smooth cheeks also damp. She reached out and touched his face. "Same here, my sweet brother."

Kenji's heart swelled with a rush of emotion. "I'm so sorry." He reached up, groping for her hand.

She caught it and pressed it to her cheek. "I'm so happy that memory chip has been removed from your head."

"Actually," Fallon said, "the chip was never removed." A sheepish look slipped into his face. "It...shorted out."

Mina looked at him. "Shorted out? You mean it's still inside him?"

Fallon exchanged a quick glance with him. His eyes showed he remembered Kenji's distress about having broken his chastity.

"It doesn't hurt, Mina," Kenji assured her, suppressing the rising memory of lying naked in that bed with Fallon. He didn't want to crave more of that. He needed to regain his vows. His people's survival depended on it. "Where are we?"

"A health clinic on Amami Shoto," Fallon said. "We flew here in the space bug after pulling you out of that place. There was such chaos at the re-education center from having busted in to get you, we were able to escape without any dogfights with Empire craft."

"You saved my life yet again," he breathed. "Thank you."

"You're most welcome."

"Thanks to you I can see my mother and the rest of my people again." Then to Mina, he asked, "Where's Mother? I want to see her."

"I sent word to Mother just a few moments ago that you're here. I was going to inform the ministers of your presence as soon as you were stabilized. There just hasn't been a moment."

"Is she all right?"

"Yes, Kenji. She's well. Don't worry."

"And Regent Nobu. I've missed him so much. Please, fetch him for me."

"Okay, Kenji. I will." Mina's forehead creased and distress slipped into her eyes. Kenji's heart did a small flip. "What is it, Mina? What aren't you telling me?"

Fallon didn't like the distress in Kenji's face. He was too young to carry such burdens. "Please rest, Kenji." He brushed his thumb back and forth across Kenji's smooth forehead. His skin was pale and lines ringed his eyes. The only other person he'd been able to read so clearly had been Nicky.

"Listen to Fallon." Mina pressed a kiss to his hand then set it gently on the bed.

"Mina, where is Regent Nobu?"

Mina frowned. "I don't know, Kenji-chan. I've only been here as long as you have and tending to you the whole time."

Kenji gave them both a look, pleading and demanding at once. "Before the memory chip was implanted, my ministers and I outlined the complete provisional government for our exile. I signed off on it and agreed to that blasted chip only when I knew that I would be immediately apprised of the entire situation. I must know."

"Kenji-chan." A woman's soft voice came from the doorway.

Kenji turned his head on the pillow. "Mother!"

Fallon moved aside and watched Kenji's mother, a petite woman with Kenji's refined features and soft dark eyes cross the room. Her pale robes whispered around her as she rushed to the bed and picked up Kenji's hand.

"Kenji-chan, you're home, finally." She kissed Kenji's hand and looked down at him, tears on her pale golden cheeks. "I've prayed every day for this moment since you left. I thought that horrible man…oh," she shook her head, tears falling. "I'm so sorry, Kenji-chan. I should never have allowed this."

"It's not your fault, Mother. Please, don't cry." Kenji pulled his hand from her grasp and reached up, cupping her cheek. "I'm back now. Be at rest."

Kenji's mother nodded in an obedient way, though her tears continued to fall and her narrow frame shook with

212

sobs.

"Mother, please, bring my ministers, and Regent Nobu. I must see them. The condition of my body doesn't matter. My heart and spirit ache to know the situation."

She bowed her head. "Of course, Kenji. I'll go right now and bring them, but only if you promise to rest afterward."

"I promise I'll *try*."

Kenji's mother looked at him a moment longer then slowly turned, the deliberate yet slow movements of a woman who'd long ago resigned herself to the reality that her son was no ordinary man and was never to be hers the way she wished him to be.

Fallon suppressed a frustrated sigh. The Kenji he'd known at Spike's had been just as stubborn, he thought, remembering the way Kenji had stolen his wallet and forced him into pursuit. All because Kenji wouldn't leave his statue. Some personality traits had certainly carried over.

"Fallon."

Kenji's voice pulled him from his musing.

Kenji's gaze was on him and in it, Fallon could see the true fire that made him the jewel of his people. "I need you here with me."

Fallon's annoyance dissipated with the word "need." He'd do anything for Kenji. He'd stay by Kenji's side, protect him every minute of every day, attend to his every need, even if it meant not having sex with him. Just to be near him. If Kenji needed to keep a vow of celibacy, so be it. He nodded. "Of course, Kenji," he said softly. He'd already decided he wasn't letting Kenji out of his sight.

Gratitude flooded Kenji's expression. He looked at Fallon a moment longer then turned. "Mina," he said.

In an instant she was at the bedside. "Yes, Kenji-chan." She bowed her head. "Your Holiness."

"I'm reinstating you as my primary personal physician. I will not let anyone pull you from that post again." He took a deep breath. "I was wrong to let myself be talked into leaving. I will not ignore my instincts again either. You understand?"

Mina's eyes misted again and she bowed. "Yes, Kenji-chan. Thank you." When she straightened, a tear drop rolled down her cheek. "I don't suppose you will heed my advice to rest, since you are not inclined to listen to others."

Kenji smiled. "You know as well as I do, that only tending to my duties will heal me."

Mina bowed again. "Yes, Your Holiness. But for now, you must remain in the bed."

Kenji nodded. "I will concede that much."

She turned to Fallon. "Kenji will need you to help him prepare for his ministers. I will not be present for this meeting so you must ensure that his IV remains secure and doesn't pull at his skin."

Fallon nodded. "Of course I will."

"Good." Mina pressed a button on the side of the bed and slowly raised it so that Kenji was sitting almost upright. "He'll need a sponge bath. I'll go and get some hot water." She bowed to Kenji and went out.

"You don't have to do that, Fallon," Kenji said softly. "I'm certain I can arrange for a personal attendant. You shouldn't have to bathe me. I'd understand if you—"

"Hush, Kenji." Fallon spoke gently. "I don't mind at all." The guilt in Kenji's expression told Fallon he was referring to his celibacy. But Fallon didn't want anyone else touching Kenji anyway.

Kenji breathed what sounded like a sigh of relief. "Thank you."

Just then Mina returned with a small plastic tub of water. Steam rose from its surface. Smiling, she set it down on a table with wheels and pushed it close to the bed. From a cabinet, she retrieved a pile of towels and a small washcloth and set them down. "If you need anything else, Your Holiness," she said, "there's a button here. It will call me."

"Thank you, Mina." Kenji smiled at her again.

She bowed, hands clasped, then left.

Fallon's stomach did a small flip. Taking care not to bump the tube connected to Kenji's I.V., he leaned over and gently opened Kenji's robe, averting his gaze from Kenji's leanly muscled torso and dark brown nipples. Thankfully, the covers remained pulled up to Kenji's waist, hiding the man's delicious organ. Terrible to feel a whiplash of lust through his body at a moment like this, but he couldn't help it.

"Fallon—"

"It's all right, Kenji." Fallon wheeled the mobile table over to the other side of the bed so as to avoid the I.V. altogether. He took up the washcloth and dipped it into the warm water. Remembering the way Mina had bathed him when he was injured, he wrung the excess water from the cloth and touched it to Kenji's chest.

Kenji's eyelids fluttered and he sighed. "That feels nice," he said.

Fallon grinned. "I've barely begun." He wiped the cloth in a slow circle over Kenji's chest then up around his neck, and behind each ear. The water darkened Kenji's golden tan skin and his nipples shrank the tiniest bit. "Not too cold?"

"No."

Fallon swallowed and dipped the cloth back into the water. In the motion of wringing out, his gaze met Kenji's.

"What was I like, Fallon? When the memory chip was in? Was I…different?"

The lump in Fallon's throat felt as if it had just grown a bit bigger. "Um, a bit different, I suppose."

"I mean, aside from being a…bartender."

Disturbed by the self-criticism in Kenji's tone, Fallon put his attention on Kenji's bath. The topic at hand helped drain a bit of his arousal at seeing Kenji's bare chest and abdomen. He perched on the edge of the bed and helped Kenji lean forward d so he could slide the robe down and sponge off Kenji's back.

"So, was I nicer?"

Fallon chuckled. Kenji's hands rested on his arm as Kenji balanced himself. He wiped the back of Kenji's neck, just under the hairline. "No, you weren't *nicer*. You were the sweetest person I've ever met." He finished his sentence by sliding the warm cloth down Kenji's spine.

Kenji's hands tightened perceptibly on his arm. Fallon paused, sensing his words sink into Kenji's consciousness. "Really?"

Resisting the urge to lean in and kiss the man's lips, Fallon nodded. "Yes. I wouldn't just say that. You were sweet and gentle. You still are."

Kenji gave a small laugh. "Yes, so gentle I sent my mother right out to do my bidding when we hadn't seen each other in months." He leaned back and pinned Fallon with his earnest gaze. "I'm demanding."

Fallon smiled down at him. "I know. But you were then, in your own way. Even with a bounty hunter on your tail, you wouldn't go anywhere without your statue." He pointed to the statue on a side table across from the bed. Pete had brought it in earlier from the pod, while Kenji was still unconscious. "You had it with you the whole time. I tried to get you to leave without it and you stole my wallet right out of my pocket so I'd follow you back to your place to get the statue."

Kenji fell back against the pillows, staring up at him. "Did I really do that? Did I really violate so many precepts?"

He dipped and wrung the cloth again and then lifted Kenji's left arm so he could wash his arm pit. "I don't know about these precepts, Kenji, but you're also the same man who threw yourself between me and a man with a gun. And you tried to save a bloke who was being beaten to death in the Terran marketplace when no one else was helping him."

Kenji bowed his head. "Oh." He sighed. "Forgive me for being so self-concerned. I've always had difficulty with humility. Perhaps that one will take many more embodiments to learn."

"You seem pretty humble to me." He dropped the cloth into the bowl and unfolded a towel. Then he thought of something. "Do you need the lower part washed?"

Color bloomed Kenji's smooth cheeks. "Perhaps later," he murmured. "I feel clean now. Thank you."

An awkward moment passed which he used to wipe the towel over Kenji's chest and under his arms. "No problem."

"I don't just mean for the bath. For your words also. They helped me."

He resisted the urge to touch Kenji's cheek. Probably best to minimize physical contact. Instead, he pulled up Kenji's robe and helped him get his arms back through. Closing the robe, he tied the sash and set the washing things aside. He noticed then that Kenji didn't ask for an eye patch. In his simple white robe, face pale and drawn against the pillows, he made a sharp contrast to the hip, fashionably dressed bartender in Spike's. Instead of the spiked up hair, he wore the short para-military haircut of the People's Empire. They'd also been passionate lovers and now, would never even kiss again. A few days could make all the difference.

"What are you thinking, Fallon?"

His heart jumped. The man was perceptive too, in spite of his weakened state. "I was thinking of how quickly things can change."

Kenji nodded. Empathy showed in his expression. "Yes. In an instant. That was one of the first lessons Regent Nobu taught me when I was only six."

Before Fallon could say more, Mina announced herself. At Kenji's response, she stepped inside the room and bowed to him. "Your ministers are here, Your Holiness," she said.

"Thank you, Mina. Please let them in. But apologize to

them on my behalf for my being in the bed."

She bowed again. "I've no doubt they'll understand." Then she was gone.

"Fallon, please stay."

He nodded. "I wasn't planning to leave," he said and positioned himself at the side of the bed, just as Kenji's ministers filed into the room.

There were four of them, heads shaved, dark robes tied at the waist with a wide sash. One by one they approached him, their faces twisting in emotion as each received a blessing from Kenji.

Fallon tried not to stare, moved as he was by his first real glimpse into the life Kenji had left behind, the life his memory chip had suppressed. These men, decades older than Kenji, their faces etched with lines and a toughness their lives had given them, were bowing to him, eager for the touch of Kenji's forehead to theirs, his fingertips on their cheeks. The interaction was some kind of blending of traditions from their own religion and the paths of their neighboring states, a mixture that history of the last few centuries had made crucial to the survival of this spiritual path. The languages Fallon heard in breathy and emotion-filled tones were Japanese and Tibetan, neither of which he spoke. When human existence had spread into outer space, English had been adopted as the common universal language and most people spoke the language as well as their own native tongue.

In spite of Kenji's weakened state, the strength and calm of authority he emanated was unmistakable. Even back at Spike's he'd been unmistakably drawn to Kenji and had felt comfortable with him in a way he hadn't with any other human being. Not even Nicky.

The greetings were over. The four ministers stood side by side at the foot of Kenji's bed, so that he could speak with them and not need to turn his head or strain in any way.

However, Kenji's brow furrowed. "Where is Nobu-sama?" he asked. "Where's my regent?"

All four faces went still. One man even shifted his stance slightly. Sudden tension radiated from them, replacing the emotions of moments earlier.

"Dawa." Kenji looked at the first man, a shorter, stocky man with thick eyebrows. "Where is Regent Nobu? He is my prime minister now. Is he unwell?"

The man called Dawa bowed. "He is not unwell, Your Holiness. He is…occupied. We have been working tirelessly to make sure the provisional government was all in place for your arrival."

"Yes, Your Holiness." A taller, thinner man next to Dawa spoke now. His voice quavered. "Everything is in place now, all seven councils, including the Community Affairs to oversee the absorption of our numbers into this society. Regent Nobu was most helpful, as always."

Fallon's back tightened. These men were lying to Kenji. Fallon bit back the urge to blurt this out. He wanted to protect Kenji, yet he was a stranger, not knowing what effect his interference could have. These ministers had already manipulated their leader in ways that had hurt him, emotionally and physically. They were probably capable of just about anything.

Kenji stared between them for several moments, then pulled in a breath. "He's in a prison cell, isn't he? Did you think I'd not see it?"

A third man cleared his throat. "Yes, Your Holiness. He is in prison."

Chapter Thirteen

Kenji's already pale skin blanched. One of his hands gripped the bedding. "Prison! Why?"

"This is not for you to worry about, Your Holiness," Dawa said softly.

Kenji's features tightened. It was the closest to rage Fallon had ever seen in him. "Nobu has been a father to me since I was six years old. He has protected me and raised me to this position. If you feel I'm at all a good man and a compassionate leader, then it is because of Nobu. Tell me what he has done that is so terrible he should be in prison."

The four robed men were now shifting their stances, the way Fallon had seen cows standing hunched together before an electric fence, back in the days before the cattle were all destroyed.

Kenji motioned with his hand in a regal gesture. "One of you, speak."

Finally Dawa stepped forward and bowed. "Since our arrival here, Regent Nobu has been given to excesses. He has spent his stipend on drink and prostitutes from the town." When Kenji said nothing, but continued to stare at him, Dawa's heavy brow creased. "You must understand, Your Holiness, what does such behavior say to our hosts about us? The Japanese government has taken us in at great expense to its own people. Nearly three thousand people have been airlifted to this island, the population of which must now change its entire existence to adjust to our presence here. We have nowhere else in the world to go. I beg you to understand our position."

Kenji sagged against the pillows, as if the last of his strength were draining rapidly. Fallon leaned toward him. "Perhaps you'd better—"

Kenji silenced him with a gesture. "Wait…please." He brooded for several moments while his ministers stood, heads bowed. Time seemed frozen for a long time before Kenji spoke again. "I've always known Nobu to be a fair and gentle human being," he said at last, his voice still tight and controlled. "Has he physically harmed anyone? Raped? Murdered or beaten?"

"Not that we know of, Your Holiness," Dawa said, head bowed.

"He carries the greatest burden of everyone here," Kenji went on, "more than any single one of us can imagine. Perhaps he needs comfort and doesn't have anywhere else to turn. He's always come to me for counsel when he's troubled. We haven't been apart since I was six. For all he knew I could have been dead in the time I was missing. How would *that* have weighed on his heart and conscience? I would not presume to judge him and neither are any of you in a position to do so either."

"But Your Holiness," Dawa said, a plea in his voice, "What about our tenuous position with our hosts? We need to fit in here. Our survival as a people depends upon their good will."

"I will concern myself with that. The rest of you concern yourself with your duties. I wish to see Nobu. *Now*."

Dawa bowed deeply and the other three ministers did the same, the deep, slow movement of officials who realized they would get no further with their leader. Fallon watched the ministers straighten and file silently out of the room. In

223

their wake, Kenji sighed and closed his eyes. "Fallon," he said softly, reaching out a hand.

Fallon grasped it. "I'm here."

Kenji turned on the pillow, his refined beauty pinched with sadness. "Perhaps I should have listened to you and Mina and rested first. But I need to see him. He's been a father to me when I didn't have anyone else." He sighed again. "I can't allow him to be punished for taking comfort. Even if I hadn't served alcohol and broken my vow, I would not have allowed him to be punished."

"I know that, Kenji."

Kenji sighed again, this time sounding exhausted.

"Do you need some water?"

Kenji shook his head. "No," he whispered. His fingers curled within Fallon's, like a child seeking warmth. "Just you."

Icy shivers traveled down Fallon's arms. No doubt, Kenji's thoughts, at least in part, mirrored his own. If the ministers had imprisoned their regent for having sex, what would they do to Kenji? He squeezed Kenji's hand. There really was nothing he could say.

A weak smile came to the man's lips. "Thank you."

Fallon closed his hand around Kenji's. If his touch brought Kenji comfort, then so be it. He remained silent, letting Kenji rest until his regent was brought to him. He looked down at Kenji's hand in his while he listened to the rise and fall of Kenji's breathing, a sound full of troubled emotions. What could it possibly have been like for a young man to be shouldered with such responsibilities? He tried to envision the boy Kenji had been, finding himself such an important figure all of a sudden, wrapped in robes, bowed to, and given the responsibility for the spiritual and temporal wellbeing of several thousand people.

He sighed. In so many centuries mankind had changed barely at all. The reach into space had only served to accommodate the spilling over of beleaguered populations rather than act as a positive sign that human beings had learned to cooperate and explore the universe in the spirit of adventure.

Voices murmured outside Kenji's room. Kenji's hand slipped from his and he opened his eyes, roused from the sleep he'd fallen into. The ministers filed in, each man bowing as he entered. The formation in which they stood, a sort of shallow half-circle seemed to make a silent space for someone else to enter.

A fifth man shuffled quietly in, his demeanor utterly servile, his shaved head bowed.

Kenji sat up, as if jolted by an electric current. "Nobu-sama," he whispered.

Nobu looked up. Watery eyes ringed with grief met Kenji's. Though he stood about Kenji's height, his tunic and baggy pants hung on his slim frame in the way Fallon had seen on many prisoners. Barefoot, he stepped a bit closer and dropped to his knees, his torso imbalanced by his hands cuffed behind him. "Your Holiness," he said in a hushed voice and prostrated, his forehead touching the wooden floor. The man's back and shoulders trembled with sobs he was obviously trying, and failing, to suppress.

"Why is he cuffed?" Kenji's voice had dropped low, thick with emotion, not the least of which was anger. "Release him immediately. How dare you insult him this way!"

"Yes, Your Holiness." Dawa signaled to someone Fallon couldn't see. A man in what appeared a local policeman's uniform came in and unlocked the cuffs.

The regent remained prostrated and when his hands were free, lowered them, palms down, to the floor on either side of his head. "Forgive me, Your Holiness," Nobu sobbed.

Fallon saw a tear roll from Kenji's good eye.

"Nobu-sama," Kenji said softly, "Please, come here for your blessing."

The regent looked up, his face red and tear-stained. Obediently, he rose and approached the bed.

Kenji reached out to him, fingertips landing on Nobu's cheeks. With his thumbs, Kenji wiped away the man's tears, then pressed his forehead to the crying man's and held him there.

Fallon looked down. A warm hum of energy crackled in the room. He felt the tingle of it in his hands. The quiet of the room was broken only by the regent's sobbing.

"I can't survive without you, Nobu-sama," Kenji said.

"I have shamed you, Your Holiness."

"No. Shhh." Kenji pulled the man into an embrace and held him. The air filled with Kenji's whispers, words of comfort meant only for Nobu's ears.

Fallon glanced at the ministers. Their faces showed a mixture of upset and censure. They clearly did not agree with Kenji's amnesty.

Finally, Kenji held Nobu away from him, his gaze

serious. "You are once again my prime minister, Nobu-sama," he said. "I do not feel you've done anything to damage our position here. Perhaps you need to take a wife or some such companion for comfort."

Small gasps came from the ministers.

Kenji looked up at them. "What is it? Nobu is not a monk. He's taken no vow of celibacy. I'm the only one out of all of you who has such a responsibility." His hands rested on Nobu's shoulders as he spoke.

"We understand that, Your Holiness," Lobsang said and bowed. "It is simply that we have never...you have never discussed such matters before."

Kenji squared his shoulders, one hand continuing to rest on Nobu. "Do you know what I did during the time I was missing?"

Fallon's gut lurched. He glanced at the ministers who all looked suddenly as if they were seated on spikes.

"No, Your Holiness," Dawa said softly, apprehension clear in his tone.

"I worked in a bar, for men. I served intoxicants to them. *And* I...broke my vow. I've reinstated it, but it happened."

Fallon had never been in a room more silent. Then, someone cleared his throat. It was Nobu.

The man turned to Kenji and knelt down, bowing. "Your Holiness, I'll never forgive myself for letting you go. I should have opposed the idea."

"It's all right, Nobu-sama. All is forgiven. My main concern is that what I've done will hurt our people."

"I believe they will be fine, Your Holiness," Nobu said. "You're human."

"Nobu!" Deep lines furrowed Dawa's forehead and his deep-set eyes glared at the man.

"You will not scold him, Dawa," Kenji said. "Nobu-sama, thank you for the reassurance. If you're in need of human comfort, do not fight it. You have my blessing, if that's what you need."

Nobu picked up Kenji's hand from his shoulder and pressed it to his lips. The older man's eyes misted. "My little heart," he whispered, then rose and bowed quickly, as if remembering decorum for the sake of the ministers watching him.

"Be at peace, Nobu-sama." Suddenly he sighed and lay back against his pillow. "I apologize for my rudeness." He lifted his other hand and indicated Fallon. "This is Jake Fallon. He saved my life several times at risk to his own. He's my dear friend and protector. When it comes to my safety, Fallon has the last word. Is that understood?" Kenji's tone showed it wasn't a question for debate.

Left no other choice, the ministers all bowed and murmured their agreement.

"We will let you rest, Your Holiness," Nobu said, gently setting Kenji's hand on the bed. "I will take care of everything until you're well."

Kenji nodded. "I know you will, thank you. Forgive me for not seeing you out."

The five men bowed deeply before filing out.

Fallon went immediately to Kenji's side and knelt down.

228

Though Kenji's face was drawn, a tiny smile came to his lips. "Fallon, I'm grateful you're here. It makes me feel stronger." He lifted his hand and Fallon captured it.

Fallon pressed Kenji's hand to his lips. When he lifted his face, Kenji's gaze still rested on him, though the man was obviously succumbing to exhaustion. "You bring out the best in me, Kenji," he said. "Now rest."

Kenji nodded faintly. His eyes closed and his breathing steadied.

With a sigh, he placed Kenji's hand on the bed the way Nobu had done moments earlier and then paced to the window. Kenji's room faced out onto the ocean. A two-lane road ran in front of the clinic which seemed to be one building in a cluster making its way up the hillside. Whitecaps in the ocean tipped the swells of the dark blue waves which reflected the brilliance of the sky even in the darkening sunset. It sure as hell was good to be looking at Earth again, breathing in its atmosphere. Though he'd always enjoyed the vastness of space, its mind-blowing dimensions and adventure-laden atmosphere, he was always glad to get back to Earth.

He stood at the window until night had fallen. The roll of the waves carried through the window, invisible sounds rising from the inky blackness of the sea. Stars dotted the night sky. Strange to think that for a little while, he and Kenji had been so much closer to those stars, just the two of them in the little space pod. No ministers, no warring states, no rules or regulations. Just the two of them, together in his bed, naked bodies entwined.

Fallon's groin tightened. Kenji's soft breathing in the background reminded him of the beautiful man sleeping there, so close and yet now separated from him in a more distant way than if he'd been standing on the other side of Earth. With a sigh, he crossed the room and looked at Kenji one more time before lowering the lights.

Kenji's lashes rested on his cheeks. His skin, though pale, was still clear and smooth. And his lips...

Best not to think about Kenji's luscious body parts. Fallon went to the cot that had been set up for him nearby and lowered himself down heavily. Lying back, he clasped his hands behind his head and stared up at the shadowy rafters. Outside the room, soft voices spoke in hushed tones, machinery beeped. Occasionally, someone in another room coughed. The air had that clean, clinical kind of smell that hospitals had.

Heaving a deep breath, he listened to Kenji's even breathing nearby, syncopated with the occasional beep on the monitor of his I.V. drip. The urge to get up and slide in next to Kenji, pulling the slim man close to him seized him. He closed his eyes and willed it away. He'd been so cocksure of being able to stay close to Kenji and not be his lover. But could he really do that? Even if Kenji weren't hot and sensuous, everything they'd been through together had bonded them. Fallon felt it deep inside and it seemed Kenji did as well, the way he'd basically begged Fallon to stay close to him at all times and told him how he felt stronger when Fallon was around. No way in hell he could abandon Kenji when the man felt that way.

Perhaps it sounded crazy, but really, there was no life he could want or even imagine wanting that didn't have Kenji in it. Even this way...without sex...the mere thought of leaving and not seeing Kenji again filled him with despair.

There'd only been one other person he'd felt this way with.

Nicky.

* * * *

Three weeks later…

Fallon stood on the platform, as always never more than a few feet from Kenji who was seated on cushions, his dais above the others. The cheers of his people, assembled in what had once been a playing field, drowned out the chanting of the priests and clash of cymbals and other instruments marking the procession of Kenji and the ministers.

Kenji held up his hands. Music and people all went silent except for the echoes of joyous sobbing in various parts of the field. "My beautiful friends," Kenji began into the microphone set in front of him, "words cannot express my joy at being with you all once again. It's truly a miracle what has happened. We are here together in a safe place, a place in which we can coexist with our neighbors and welcome a new chapter in our lives together."

His words were met with cheers and sobs and thousands of pairs of hands reaching toward him, each person obviously hungry for a blessing from him.

Which he gave, after finishing his speech in which he thanked and praised Fallon and Pete publicly, telling the assembled crowd of how these two men had saved his life and made it possible for them all to be together again. He stayed close behind Kenji as Kenji rose from his cushions and proceeded to give blessings. As he'd done with his ministers and with Nobu, Kenji pressed his forehead to every man, woman and child.

One by one, the people proceeded, each one smiling and bowing to Fallon as well receiving a blessing. In spite of the warm acceptance, however, he couldn't help longing for those few quiet days of Kenji's recovery, before everyone else beside the ministers knew that Kenji had returned. Strolls in the hospital garden, sitting by a fountain, just conversing about the lives they'd had before they met. Kenji also spent many hours sitting with his mother or with Mina and Pete, observing the budding romance between the two people. Fallon often wished time could freeze them in that peaceful bubble, especially after everything that had happened. Those days had been sweet and fulfilling, even without being able to make love to Kenji.

Their lives had fallen into a pattern in the weeks that followed. Fallon marveled at Kenji's energy with the schedule they kept. With the exception of the quiet period for meditation and contemplation, Kenji's days were filled with meetings with his ministers and with the various committees of the provisional government. When Kenji wasn't in meetings he was visiting with his people, with the school children, the elderly, attending one function after the next in between trips down to Tokyo to meet with the Japanese government, both to pay his respects and to maintain a diplomatic relationship. With each day completely filled, Fallon didn't have time to consider the lack of physical contact with Kenji, except in the evenings before sleep.

Each night, Fallon was glad finally to reach the refuge of Kenji's rooms in the back of the main temple. There too, they had their routine. Fallon went into his own little room off of Kenji's to shower and change for bed while Kenji's attendants looked after him. After drying off, he put on a pair of baggy pants and sat down on the edge of his bed.

Through the doorway, he saw Kenji pass by, dressed in one of those long kimonos they called a *yukata*, worn before and after bathing.

As he did each night, Kenji sat on the edge of his own bed, a black futon on a low platform, where he could stare out the window at the neatly manicured temple garden with its stone Kirei in the center of the courtyard. Even when it was dark, Kenji gazed outside, as if he could see everything perfectly. How the man didn't simply collapse from exhaustion, Fallon didn't begin to know. But with each moment that passed, each action Kenji took and each word he said, Fallon had begun to understand what made Kenji the leader he was and why Kenji held fast to his vow of celibacy. It was the belief of these people that Kenji's purity brought them strength and fortune. Business ventures would prosper, children would be born healthy; the list of blessings gleaned from Kenji's abstinence was nearly endless. Truthfully, Fallon didn't believe it for a second. With or without Kenji's celibacy, Sunyatans would still bear children, some of whom wouldn't be completely healthy. What did Kenji's sexuality have to do with someone else's fertility? But the tradition had been practiced for centuries apparently, and they felt it worked.

Releasing a deep sigh, Fallon raked both hands through his hair, shoulders slumped. Though he was tired, his mind and spirit felt agitated, wired as it did practically every night. He needed to rest and felt he couldn't.

"Fallon?"

He looked up.

Kenji stood in the doorway, looking hesitant.

He grabbed the T-shirt on the bed beside him, slipped it

233

on then stood up. "Are you all right, Kenji?"

Kenji nodded. "May I come in?"

Fallon's heart sped up a bit. Kenji didn't usually visit his room as part of their routine. "Of course."

Kenji walked over and perched on the edge of the bed. "Please, sit with me?"

Nodding, he sat down, as safe a distance from Kenji as he could.

Kenji smiled, though up close, Fallon saw the tiredness he hadn't noticed before. "I just wanted to see how you are," he said softly. "It's too easy to forget about the person closest to me."

Fallon squelched the urge to reach out and touch Kenji's hand. "You've been busy, I understand that. I'm fine. Don't worry about me. You need to rest. The drugs may be out of your system but they were powerful."

"I promise I will." Kenji's smile faded. "When I asked how you are I also meant, how you are with...this change. It's been a few weeks now and I worry about how it's affecting you." He indicated himself and then Fallon.

"Oh." Even this tiny reminder made a tickle in Fallon's groin. He pulled his gaze away from Kenji's voluptuous lips. Although, scanning downward didn't exactly relieve the ache. Even though Kenji wore a heavy robe, Fallon was well familiar with the hard planes and smooth muscles hidden beneath. To his dismay, his mouth watered. "I admit it's a big adjustment, but I'm not changing my mind, if that's what you're worried about. I'll do anything if it means being with you."

He saw his words register. Kenji's finely chiseled

features softened. His lips parted slightly. He tilted his face down. "I'm honored, Fallon. You can't imagine what you've come to mean to me. Just knowing you're here."

Fallon smiled. He dared to reach out and brush his fingertips across Kenji's cheek. Kenji's eyelids closed and he sighed, obviously savoring the light touch. "It's mutual," he said softly. Kenji's skin was creamy smooth, incredible. He lifted away before he lost control.

Kenji opened his eyes. His shoulders slumped a bit and he heaved a sigh. "It's difficult for me too, Fallon," he said softly. "I was thinking the other day about the Buddhist tradition. Did you know, the Buddha once admitted that the sexual drive was the most difficult attachment to overcome? He admitted that if there had been anything more difficult, he wouldn't have achieved nirvana."

Fallon chuckled and sat back. "I can believe that."

Kenji's cheeks colored a bit. "I'm supposed to have wisdom, but I think it wasn't so wise to come in here."

Fallon cleared his throat. "Perhaps not." He thought Kenji would leave immediately, but the other man hesitated, not breaking his gaze.

"I keep worrying that you'll get fed up and leave, Fallon."

Unable to resist, Fallon reached out and took Kenji's hand. Thankfully, Kenji didn't pull away and let Fallon brush his lips over the tops of his knuckles before releasing him. "Don't worry about that, Kenji. Like I said, I'm not going anywhere."

Kenji's eyes misted over. He gave a brief nod. "Thank you."

"Get some rest. As the one responsible for your safety and wellbeing, I'm ordering you."

Kenji smiled. "Good night."

"Good night." He watched Kenji leave the room. Kenji removed his robe and Fallon swallowed nervously. But Kenji was well aware of the possible temptations and kept his body covered in baggy pants and a loose tunic. Kenji slid into his bed and turned off the bedside lamp.

It didn't matter. Just watching Kenji lie back in the bed was enough to get him going, to dredge up not so distant memories...

In the darkness, Fallon lay back, again staring up at the ceiling. The feel of Kenji's skin remained on his lips. All he'd wanted to do was pull Kenji to him, lay the slim man underneath him and make passionate love to him. He'd done his best to hide the hard-on in his pants, but even now his cock strained, engorged, desperate for release.

He glanced in the direction of Kenji's room. Dark and quiet. If Kenji was lying in his own bed with an erection, Fallon didn't know. But the thought only fueled the pressure in his cock.

With a sigh, he pushed his hand under the waist of the pants and palmed his cock. His breath caught with the first friction. Quickly, softly, he stroked himself, remembering that time in the space pod when Kenji asked to be penetrated. Kenji's sweet body underneath his, the way the other man had surrendered so joyfully to sex, the tiny moans and whimpers he made, the tight hotness of his ass, all of it incredible.

Fallon suppressed a groan. The pleasure of his own strokes echoed through his body, down his thighs, in his ass, through his balls. Even his nipples tingled. Each memory of Kenji's lips on his cock, sucking up and down only intensified the sensations. Even the way Kenji had run up to him in Spike's and grabbed him into a wild kiss in front of the whole bar had been hot, in spite of the urgent situation.

Kenji was wild, a sex god underneath his celibate exterior. Of all the people who'd ever come into contact with Kenji, only he knew the truth.

He bit his lower lip to stifle a groan. The pressure built and exploded, leaving a hot puddle of cum on his stomach and chest. He stopped stroking and lay quietly, catching his breath before cleaning up and pulling the covers over himself.

Kenji's room was still dark but Fallon swore he could hear Kenji breathing. The sound was comforting. He wouldn't want Kenji to be anywhere else.

Finally, after listening to Kenji for what felt a long time, his eyelids began to close and he surrendered to sleep.

* * * * *

"Fallon!"

Fallon's eyes popped open. Hints of dawn showed through his window.

"Fallon, where are you?"

Kenji's distressed call pierced his consciousness. He sat bolt upright. "Kenji," he called, "I'm here."

"Please, I can't see you! Where are you?"

Throwing back the covers, Fallon jumped from the bed and bolted into Kenji's room.

Kenji's head whipped in his direction, his face frantic. "Fallon, they're drugging me!" Kenji's chest was heaving and he slapped at his arm, where the I.V. had been weeks earlier.

"Kenji, it's all right. I'm here." Fallon rushed over to Kenji, knelt by his bed and gripped Kenji's upper arms.

Recognition flooded Kenji's good eye. He calmed immediately. "Fallon," he breathed then fell forward, grasping him in a desperate embrace. "I didn't know where you were. I thought the chief had grabbed me away from you again."

Fallon stilled, one palm down on Kenji's back. "The chief," he whispered. "He's dead."

Kenji's hands tightened on Fallon's back. "Dead? But we just saw him moments ago. He came to our cell on his ship. He has the Matsuotos."

Fallon's blood went cold. Dear sweet mother of God, Kenji had lost his memory again.

Chapter Fourteen

"Look up, Kenji-chan."

Kenji stared at Mina. "I still can't believe it. I have a sister. A beautiful sister.

She smiled. "I'm happy to see you too," she said softly. "Now, please look up."

He obeyed and Mina pointed a small light into his good eye. He struggled not to blink. Bad enough he'd caused such a commotion in the middle of the night. If he'd understood what was happening and that Fallon was sleeping nearby, he might have waited. As it was he'd disturbed a temple full of priests, a clinic full of doctors and Fallon, his constant companion and bodyguard, who had been getting much-needed rest when he'd all but carried Kenji here to the hospital.

The other man remained nearby through Mina's examination, hovering worriedly.

Another wave of gratitude rushed over him. He'd thought never to see Fallon again after their last moments together in that prison cell.

With her thumb pad, she gently pulled down on the flesh beneath his eye and shone the light on it. "Your eye is normal," she said and lifted her hand away. "Thankfully, you're fine." But Kenji still read worry in her gaze.

"What's happening to me?"

She pushed her hands into the pockets of the white coat she wore. "Well, the scan of your brain shows that the

239

memory chip activates and deactivates due to physiological activity in your body."

"You can remove it, right?"

Mina glanced away then turned back, frowning. "No, Kenji-chan," she said softly. "Somehow the chip melded to your very brain structure. There's no way to remove it without causing permanent damage. Blindness being the very least of it. I'm sorry."

His blood chilled. He glanced at Fallon whose brow was deeply creased. "Do you mean I'm stuck going back and forth between these two…people that I am?"

"It's possible," Mina said. "If the chip doesn't burn out permanently. Your brain waves deliver enough energy to keep it active."

He looked between Mina and Fallon. This was almost as bad as being pursued by the bounty hunter. Was he to live in perpetual uncertainty? Any moment he could black out and wake up the "other" Kenji. There was no stability in that. "Regardless of the personal discomfort of this…condition," he said, "there's no way I can have a nation full of people depending on me. I'm not the same person they believe to be their leader."

"Mina," Fallon interjected, "Couldn't Kenji bridge the gap enough in his memory to carry out his duties?"

Before Mina could answer, Kenji cut in, "Only if I told the people the truth. I can't deceive anyone, not knowingly."

Fallon began to pace, something Kenji recognized as his pensive mode. Then he stopped and swiveled back to look at him. He had that look Kenji had seen on his face before, as if a light were going on. "That's just it, Kenji," he said softly.

"You speak of yourself as two different people. You do the same thing with your memory restored, as if you really see yourself as two separate entities."

Kenji frowned, trying to grasp what he was saying. "Maybe I really *am* two separate people," he began slowly, as if seeing himself for the very first time. "Think about it. Why was I missing for so long? With the DNA lock, I should have been found long ago. You and Pete even said that the chip probably did something to scramble my genetic code so that a DNA lock couldn't work. Then, at some point, when the memory chip began to fritz, my DNA code was able to come through."

Fallon gestured. "Look at it this way, even with the memory chip active, you remembered me, didn't you? You remembered falling through the air and being caught. You just didn't know it was me. That proves there's crossover. That you're not completely separated inside."

"You?" Mina's eyes were wide as she stared at Fallon. "You're the one who saved Kenji that day, all those years ago?"

Fallon nodded. "Yes."

Gratitude shone from Mina's eyes. "Thank you."

"You're welcome. But you don't need to keep thanking me. Really."

Kenji smiled at him. "Yes, we do."

"Kenji," Mina said softly, turning to him, "that's a sign, isn't it? A cross-over between your worlds."

"Mina's right, Kenji," Fallon said, "It does serve to solve that mystery. But even so, you're not really two separate people. You're Kenji with your memory intact and you're

241

Kenji with your memory suppressed. *That's* the reality."

Kenji nodded. "Yes. It makes sense." Fallon and Mina had both crossed over in his memory. However, he wasn't fully convinced. "But I feel so separate from...him." He waved a hand. "He's some high being who has a country to run. And I'm a...bartender."

"That's not true." Fallon sounded suddenly angry. "You're him and he's you. I didn't differentiate between the two of you when we...well, you know. Nor did I differentiate between you when I tried to save you."

Kenji bowed his head. "I'm sorry," he murmured.

Fallon sighed. Suddenly he was there, at Kenji's side, an arm across his shoulders. "I'm sorry. I shouldn't have snapped at you." He was quiet a moment, then noticed Mina, staring at them, her eyes wide. It had to be shocking to hear anyone address Kenji with anger. "I think it's that differentiation you're making that's causing a worse division." He looked up at Mina. "Mina, is that possible? Is it possible that the chip is only exaggerating something that was already in Kenji's mind?"

She nodded. "Yes. It's possible." A shy look flitted through her eyes. "Kenji, you probably don't remember right now, but you and I used to talk about psychology a lot, back when I was in school. You used to say that people became divided because they hated and judged parts of themselves they believed were wrong or bad and that compassion and forgiveness would be the way to heal."

"I said that? Sounds pretty intelligent."

Mina laughed. "Yes. You say intelligent things most of the time."

He looked at her. "I grew up with you my entire life, didn't?"

Her laughter faded and she looked down, obviously avoiding his gaze. She didn't answer. Which really, was an answer. "Yes, Kenji-chan," she said softly.

He shook his head, the heaviness of guilt on his chest. "A lifetime we've spent together and when I'm this Kenji, you're a stranger."

When she looked up again, her eyes glistened. "No you're not. Don't worry. You're my brother no matter what."

With her words, the reality of his situation slammed in on him. "Will I always be divided this way for the rest of my life? What about all the people who depend on me? The problem with my memory being suppressed is I don't remember whatever wisdom I'm supposed to have, either. And I can't fake it. I wouldn't do that to people. How could I? That would be cruel." He looked at Fallon. "And what about you, Fallon?"

Fallon touched his cheek. "What about me?"

In spite of everything going on, the tiny brush of the man's fingertip melted Kenji's insides. Which was just the point. Kenji's cheeks heated and he glanced down. "I mean, what about you and me? We have…feelings between us. More than feelings. I'm supposed to be celibate, right? What about us then? Are you supposed to just go without…sex? That wouldn't be fair, either." He became aware of Mina then. "I'm sorry, Mina. This is probably embarrassing for you."

"Not at all. I'm a doctor."

"I told you this before, Kenji, when you had your memory, that it doesn't matter," Fallon said. "I'm here for you regardless."

"But you'd be...deprived. You'll need...you know..." The thought of Fallon going to other guys made an ache in Kenji's chest so bad he couldn't even finish the sentence.

"I'm a one-man kind of bloke. Don't worry about it."

"Your Holiness, are you all right?"

Kenji turned at the unfamiliar male voice.

The man bowed before taking a step into the room. "Your Holiness, I came as soon as my attendant informed me you'd been rushed to the clinic." His loosely-belted robe gaped open at the top, indicating the haste with which he'd gotten out of bed to come running.

Kenji stared at the older man. Here was yet another person, obviously important to him, who was a stranger to him. "I — I'm — "

The man approached the examining table on which he sat and bowed again, this time deeply. When he straightened, his eyes reflected deep worry and compassion. "Kenji-chan, my little heart, you look at me as if you don't know who I am. It's me, Nobu, your regent, your prime minister."

Kenji heart squeezed at the man's respectful, compassionate demeanor. "I'm sorry, I've lost my memory again," he said, his voice laced with frustration. The regent drew closer, so close, Kenji could see the unshed tears in his dark eyes. "I assure you, Your Holiness, we are the dearest of friends." He continued to study Kenji's face with a penetrating gaze. Then sorrow lined his forehead. "This is entirely my fault. I will never forgive myself for allowing that memory-destroying chip to be inserted in your head. It was disgusting." He reached up and cupped Kenji's cheek.

The touch was so kind, so gentle, Kenji felt a wave of warmth. He knew somehow he could trust this man, that the Kenji he usually was, did trust him deeply. "As my regent, you take care of my duties when I'm unable to, correct?"

"Yes, Kenji-chan," Nobu said. "That's what I'm here for. To help you."

He sighed. "I don't want to lie to anyone about who I am. Everyone involved needs to know what's happened. I don't know when I'll get my memory back again or if this will continue to happen. Or, even if there's a cure." He gestured toward Mina. "My sister tells me it's impossible to remove the chip."

"There is one thing, perhaps, that could help heal the rift in your brain," Mina's voice cut softly in.

Kenji's gaze flashed to the woman who looked so much like him, a glimmer of hope rising in him. "What is it? I need to heal my brain. I can't just go back and forth between these two...Kenjis."

She nodded and her delicate cheeks colored. "It was something else we used to talk about when we discussed this chapter in the text book I was studying." She paused, her lips pressed together. It was obvious she was about to propose something...delicate. A look of resolve crossed her features. "One theory holds that a person so divided must heal the rift by engaging in the activities of one personality while in the other personality. For example, when you have your memory, you know you're supposed to practice celibacy. You have a certain code of conduct to maintain. But this Kenji…" she gestured to him, "has a different code. You need to bridge the gap between the two sides. The most tangible way to do this is in the physical realm. The physical acts will impact themselves on the emotional and spiritual realms, too. Then, perhaps, you'll be more unified. Does that make sense?"

Kenji's heart lurched. "It makes sense, but what about our people? Won't they be affected by this? They're used to a certain way. It could cause rifts in the population. It's…revolutionary. And I could never keep something like that secret. It wouldn't be right." He turned to Fallon. "Even if I did, it would be obvious. I look at you and I…melt inside." Fallon was silent in the wake of his admission and Kenji avoided his gaze. He remembered that first night at Spike's. The night that had changed his life.

"It is revolutionary," Nobu said, "but if you were to ask me, I would say anything that could heal you, Kenji-chan, and make you whole again, is something that should be tried." He looked between Kenji and Fallon. "If I'm not mistaken, Your Holiness, this is the man with whom you broke your vow?" He indicated Fallon.

Kenji's cheeks heated. "Yes," he said softly."

"And he is the one person whom you remember at all times, correct?"

"Yes. I remembered that he saved my life when I was twelve."

Nobu's gaze whipped up to Fallon. "You're the hero who saved our Jewel," he breathed, his voice holding the same reverence as Mina's had earlier. He turned back to Kenji. "This changes everything."

Kenji stared at him, his heart skidding. "How — "

Fallon's Jewel   Sedonia Guillone

"Well, Agent Fallon saved your life, more than once. We are indebted to him. Without his courage and selflessness, we would have been deprived of our precious jewel. So truly, because of Agent Fallon's service to our people, the law of celibacy is, in a sense, cancelled out." He shook his head. "I've never agreed with it myself, anyway. Nobu patted his hand and sighed. "I have long had contentions with your other ministers over this issue. I've always felt it unwise to impose celibacy on you without letting you have your choice. You always speak to me about our Buddhist neighbors and compare yourself to their figurehead. But in all fairness to you, when the Buddha overcame his attachment to sex, he'd already been with many beautiful women. He'd had a wife for years and fathered a child with her. He'd had the opportunity he needed to burn out those seeds in his nature. You haven't had that chance."

Nobu shook his head, sadness making his features look heavy again. "Your Holiness, perhaps if we'd not allowed this memory chip to be implanted in you and hadn't sent you away, you would not have met Fallon-san and this door would not have been opened. However, we can't take any of it back and this is the way things are. Even if he hadn't been the one to cancel out the law, the compassionate thing to do would be not to force you apart if your natures draw you together."

"Prime Minister," Fallon said, "I understand Kenji's hesitation. Don't you fear that this issue would divide your people? How would they feel about Kenji having a…partner?"

Nobu reflected for several moments. "Of course I cannot say for sure what would happen. Where there are people, there are hosts of opinions and viewpoints, but I also

247

know that survival most often depends on adaptability. We have entered a new chapter of our existence. Much has changed in a very brief time, drastic changes that might put an end to a less resilient culture. But…" He leaned forward as if to tell a secret, "Before the Religious Wars three centuries ago, Kenji's predecessors did not practice celibacy. That was put into practice in the hopes that the conservation of life force would give our people strength to survive in the worse conditions." He put a hand on Kenji's shoulder. "Those conditions no longer apply, Kenji-chan. When they learn of Fallon's service to us, not even the council will be able to object." He paused. "If I may advise you."

"Yes, of course."

"You've been through a great deal and have not had a chance to rest. Perhaps it's the stress alone that's causing your memory chip to activate and deactivate. I want you to take at least several days just to rest. I will take care of everything and then debrief you when you're ready to return to your duties. Are you willing to do that?"

Without thinking, he nodded. "Yes, I'd like that." He glanced at Fallon and felt his cheeks heat up.

Nobu patted his shoulder. "Good. Now, I'm ordering you back to your quarters to rest. Any further testing on your brain and body your physician wishes to do can wait until you've rested."

"Yes, Prime Minister," Mina said, bowing to the regent.

"Thank you, Nobu-sama," Kenji said, hoping he was addressing the older man correctly.

Apparently he was, for Nobu smiled and bowed to him. "Enjoy your time off, Kenji-chan," he said softly, then turned to leave, ushering Mina out of the room with him.

248

Kenji's heart jumped. He looked up at Fallon. The heat in his cheeks spread like a small fire down his neck into his chest.

Fallon was gazing at him in a way that made him feel naked. He held out his hand to Kenji. "So, Kenji, are you ready to begin your…vacation?"

Kenji took his hand and let Fallon tug him so that he slid off the examining table to his feet. When Fallon released him, he gathered the folds of his kimono and quickly wound the sash. "Yes," he murmured. "Let's go."

Fallon offered his arm and Kenji slipped his hand into the crook of Fallon's elbow. Outside the examining room, the monks who acted as Kenji's guards fell into step around them, their constant companions through the corridors of the clinic and onto the graveled pathway that went through the clinic gardens onto the temple grounds.

Reaching Kenji's room, Kenji dismissed the guards to take their regular places in the hall so he could be alone with Fallon. Inside, a tray awaited them with a pot of steaming tea and vegetable dumplings that Kenji favored, when he had his memory. Quietly, they sat together on opposite sides of the tray and shared the meal.

Kenji sipped his tea and set the cup down, finally able to ask Fallon the question that weighed on him since Nobu had ordered him to rest. "Fallon, are you all right with this change? I mean, whether I'm celibate or not is one matter, but you're involved. It's your life too. I don't want you to feel like a ball being batted back and forth between a cat's paws."

Fallon chuckled. "I like your analogy," he said, his large fingers around his own small porcelain cup. "Of course I don't feel that way at all. We can be together now, the way we truly want. I'm thrilled." His grin faded and his blue eyes took on the look that made Kenji's insides feel like mush and made his toes curl inside his socks. He reached out with his free hand and smoothed a hand over Kenji's brow. "You've changed my life, Kenji Shimizu."

Kenji set his cup down before the trembling in his hand made him spill the contents. "You didn't only change my life, Fallon, you saved it. More than once." He sighed and glanced over to the bed. The sight of the soft coverlet and pillows made a pleasant shiver through his body. That was *their* bed now. Then he thought of something. "Last time I got my memory back," he said, "you and I were in bed together, in that prison cell."

"I remember very well."

Kenji smiled briefly. "Well, I'm just concerned that it could happen again while we're...you know, in bed. Will I freak and jump out? Will I accuse you of helping me break my vow? I won't know about Nobu's policy change."

Fallon cleared his throat and set down his cup. He was silent several moments. Obviously, the questions had given him pause. "I'm sure you'll be a bit surprised," he said finally. "But I have faith you'll believe what I explain to you." His eyes softened. "Kenji, even with your memory intact, you knew me. You recognized my voice and you trusted me immediately without reserve."

Kenji shifted quickly around so that he was beside Fallon. "Did I really?"

"Yes."

He smiled, feeling a burden lift. "That's wonderful."

"It is."

Unbidden, the heaviness descended again. "I just hope I won't insist that Nobu is wrong. I have no idea how committed to celibacy I am."

"You're pretty committed to it." Fallon leaned in closer to him and cupped the back of his neck. "We'll have to wait and see what happens. We don't even know when your memory could come back." His thumb brushed across Kenji's jaw, a tender movement Kenji loved. "I'm not certain it's important to me, Kenji, whether you remember who you are or not. I...love you, either way."

Kenji pulled in a breath. He stared back at Fallon. Time seemed to slow down. It filled his mind with images passing across it, all of them Fallon. Fallon in Spike's, drinking, laughing with him and then in the love hotel, kissing, stroking, sucking, Fallon chasing him through Terran City when he stole Fallon's wallet, Fallon shooting the bounty hunter down and pulling him onto the bus, being in the space pod in Fallon's bed, facing Fallon's corrupt chief and soldiers, being locked in the prison cell together, in bed again. And now, in his private apartments of a temple in Japan, kneeling on the tatami mat, with Fallon's tender gaze on him.

And all because he'd waited on a barstool that night. Something inside him had known, had sensed a different destiny. His soul calling to him through the confines of the memory chip, guiding him to the one man who wanted to be his constant companion through life, for whatever time they had together.

There was only one response to Fallon's simple, beautiful statement.

"I love you too, Fallon," he said softly. He reached up and touched the other man's cheek. The dark stubble was rough-smooth under his fingertips. The contact sent a thrill up his arm, a warm tingle that traveled invisibly throughout the rest of his body.

The larger man let out a harsh breath, as if Kenji's mere touch had aroused him to a pitch. Fallon leaned in closer. His familiar scent invaded Kenji's senses, heightening the warmth already coursing through his body.

"How long's it been since we last did it, Fallon?"

"Too damn long," Fallon whispered and closed the small space between their mouths.

A sigh escaped Kenji. Fallon's fingers were warm and strong on the back of his neck as he pulled their faces closer together. It felt like so long since they'd kissed, even though for him, it had been moments.

Fallon pushed between Kenji's lips, a moist warm invasion of his tongue. The room filled with the soft wet sound of their mouths chafing together. Kenji sighed again and pulled Fallon closer. He yanked at Fallon's shirt and pushed his hands underneath. He loved Fallon's skin, warm and masculine, his chest hair silky, nipples smooth and flat.

Fallon groaned into his mouth. His hand slipped from Kenji's neck and tugged wildly at the sash. Kenji felt his robe fall open and then Fallon's large hands were under his tunic, sliding over his chest, over his waist and back. He yanked up Fallon's t-shirt, breaking their kiss long enough to pull it up, over his head. He tossed it aside and let Fallon lift off his tunic. Both breathing heavily, they knelt, staring at each other, as if unsure what to do next.

Kenji's erection pushed mercilessly at his baggy pants.

"Do we have something slippery?" he breathed.

Fallon's eyes widened a second then he grinned. "We do actually." Leaning over, he took the cover off one of the dishes on the nearby tray. "Butter," he said. "That will do."

Kenji remembered the synthetic vegetable butter he used to have sometimes on Terran A. It supposedly tasted just like cow's butter. He frowned. "Is that why it's on the tray? For…us?"

Fallon chuckled. "No. It was for your dumplings. You like butter on your dumplings."

"That's weird. Am I really so strange?"

Fallon reached up and rubbed his hands over Kenji's shoulders and over his back. He pushed in closer so that their chests almost touched. "You have a few quirks, Kenji, but nothing that's not endearing."

Fallon's body heat bounced off Kenji's skin, an almost palpable force. Suddenly inspired, Kenji dipped several fingers into the small pot. The butter was nice and soft and a small scoop came up in his hand. Inspired, he dabbed butter on Fallon's left nipple. The man pulled in a breath. Kenji leaned forward and licked the butter off. Fallon's nipple tightened under his tongue. Fallon's hands squeezed Kenji's upper arms. Fallon tasted so good, salty sweet and buttery.

"Damn, Kenji," he whispered.

Kenji grinned. Feeling wicked, he smoothed more butter over Fallon's other nipple and licked it off. "You're right," he breathed, "the butter will do nicely."

Fallon grasped his wrist and brought Kenji's hand to his mouth. He pulled Kenji's index finger between his lips.

Kenji sighed. The light roughness of Fallon's tongue against the pad of his fingertip made his whole body feel melty and soft. He breathed heavily while Fallon took each finger and sucked the butter off, one by one.

"My turn now," Fallon said, his voice husky. He scooped up some of the butter and smeared it across Kenji's chest, over the muscles and over his nipples.

"Ooohhh." Kenji tilted his head back under the delicious invasion. The butter made Fallon's hand slide easily over his skin and made the heat sink into his skin, a layer of sparks that traveled right into his cock.

"I didn't know you had a food fetish, Kenji," Fallon whispered and licked Kenji's nipples. Around and around in hot swirls he teased the sensitive disk until icy heat made it tingle madly.

Kenji groaned and clasped Fallon's head, following the man's path over his chest to his other nipple. "I...didn't know...either," he panted and burrowed his fingers into Fallon's short hair.

Fallon's hands yanked hungrily at Kenji's pants. "Take these off and lie down," Kenji," he murmured against Kenji's chest.

The husky order sent a thrill right to Kenji's toes, but he wasn't finished with the butter for his own purposes. Not yet. Grasping Fallon's shoulders, he pushed back and dipped his fingers into the butter. "You first, Fallon. Pants off."

Fallon's pale skin was flushed red. He was panting and his lids were heavy over his blue eyes. Wordlessly, he obeyed Kenji's order.

Kenji watched Fallon slide his pants down. His mouth watered at the thick hard cock that sprang up, free of its confines. Without hesitation he reached out and smeared the butter up and down the length of that delicious cock. The melting butter glistened over the reddish silky skin and veins.

"Damn, Kenji," Fallon ground out then groaned when Kenji leaned over and licked the butter off his cock with hungry strokes of his tongue. Kenji smoothed more butter over the man's plump balls and licked that off too with long, careful licks.

"I can't wait now." Fallon grasped Kenji's shoulders and pushed. Kenji found himself on his back, his discarded tunic and robe underneath him.

Fallon towered above him, kneeling, then grasped the waist of Kenji's pants and slid them off. He didn't stop until he'd pulled them over Kenji's feet and tossed them away. He scooped out more butter and slathered it on his straining cock. Reaching down, he pushed his slippery fingers against Kenji's opening.

"Ohhh."

"Like that, Kenji?" Fallon grinned and pushed a buttery finger right in. He wiggled it about.

"Wow, yes!" Kenji panted and pushed against Fallon's hand. One finger went in deeper, stretched him in the most incredible way. Then a second finger. Kenji stared up, mesmerized by the thrilling pressure in his ass and Fallon's blue eyes staring down at him.

"Good," Fallon whispered. "I want you to feel good."

"I do."

Fallon slipped his fingers out and settled between Kenji's legs. In the next second, the head of Fallon's cock bumped his opening. The buttery head slipped in.

Kenji pulled in a breath. His eyelids fluttered and his good eye rolled back in his head. He clutched Fallon's hips and pulled. In one hard slide, Fallon's cock filled him. The butter on Kenji's chest made Fallon's torso slide against his.

"Holy shite, Kenji," Fallon ground out, his words mixed with the rhythm of his hips.

Kenji's hands rested there, feeling each powerful, commanding movement. Every upward thrust hit a magic spot inside him. His body relaxed, opened, completely surrendered to the overwhelming experience. That's what a guy like Jake Fallon was. An experience. A wonder. The best in the universe. He felt his lips curving up in an ecstatic smile. The world seemed to shatter into a million pinpoints of light...

Wow. Kenji lay still, frozen in place by the incredible sensations covering his body. His back passage was full, something rubbing against a special spot inside him that made his head feel as if it would spin off. Another solid entity rubbed his male stem. Each slide against it took his breath away. This was some dream he was having. Not like the sexual dreams he usually had, which never gave such intense physical feelings.

The tiny lights dancing in his vision faded. The mist before his eyes evaporated. Fallon's face replaced it. Those blue eyes staring down at him, yet moving up and down. Fallon was sweating, supporting his upper body on his elbows. Fallon's chest brushed his.

Then it hit him. He was remembering! The way he had in the prison cell and woken up naked in the bed with Fallon. Only this time they were actually…

"Fallon," he whispered, unable to say more than the man's name. Then he became aware of his hands on Fallon's hips, moving languidly with Fallon's thrusts into his passage. His knees were bent. The soles of his feet rested on Fallon's hard ass cheeks.

Sex. They were having sex.

"Fallon," he whispered again, trapped by the overwhelming pleasure. "Fallon…you…nnnnhh—"

Fallon's lips cut off his attempt to speak. Mmm, Fallon's lips were soft yet firm. Moist from kissing. The stubble on Fallon's jaw brushed Kenji's chin. Fallon's tongue was hot and moist and stroked his tongue. The scent of kissing was so new, so incredible. So…beautiful, as if their souls were speaking to each other in this quiet yet hot way. Kenji parted his lips and Fallon slid his tongue in deeper. Fallon's skin was warm and damp with sweat. The man's breath was ragged in his ears, mixing with the moist suction of their kisses and the rustle of the clothing underneath his back. This passion involved everything, every sense, every organ, every inch of his soul. As well as his heart.

How could he live without this incredible form of love?

Fallon groaned into Kenji's mouth. He thrust faster, deeper, harder. The quick movements rubbed Kenji's cock sandwiched between their torsos. His lips fell open, tongue resting against Fallon's as the pressure built and built. Kenji had dared to bring himself relief with his hand many times in his life, but the solitary act was nothing compared to a living breathing human being whose naked body was joined with his.

His climax hit. Kenji dug his fingertips into Fallon's hips, as if to anchor himself against the bliss pulling at his body. Wave after wave hit him and in his haze, he heard Fallon moan, his large body trembling, followed by warm gushes into his passage.

Fallon pulled from their kiss and exhaled, his damp forehead on Kenji's shoulder, his back heaving. "That was incredible, Kenji," he breathed.

"Yes...incredible." Kenji rested like that, his hands not moving from Fallon's hips. Whispers of blissful pleasure ghosted through him, threatening to tangle with the pangs of guilt he felt building in his chest.

Suddenly Fallon raised his head and peered into Kenji's face. "Kenji, you got your memory back, didn't you?"

Kenji nodded. "How did you know?"

"I sensed it. Before you say anything, I promise you this was consensual. Your prime minister, Nobu, practically ordered you to do it. He's changing the policy on celibacy. It's no longer mandatory. He thinks being with me...letting you have your desires met, will heal you. Well, there's even more to it than that. I'll explain everything, I promise." Panic tinged Fallon's voice. He was obviously afraid Kenji would think he'd been manipulated and that Kenji would insist on opposing Nobu's action.

"Don't worry, Fallon. It's all right." He slid his hands up Fallon's back. Contrary to what he thought he'd feel, a burden lifted, rising off his chest, leaving lightness and joy in its place. Nobu's support this way was everything. "I'm not upset. Words can't describe how I feel in this moment."

Relief splashed through Fallon's rugged features. "As long as *good* can describe how you feel, I'm all right with that."

"Good is an understatement." His smile faded and he touched Fallon's cheek. "I can't find the words to tell you what you mean to me. Whatever happens because of this, as long as I can be with you, I'll face it."

Fallon's eyes misted. "That's how I feel about you, Kenji."

"I know." It was more than obvious how much the man cared about him. And now they were mates, partners, hopefully for the rest of their lives. "Thank you, Fallon. For everything."

Fallon's grin returned. "Nothing to thank me for," he said, then dropped a kiss on Kenji's lips. "That's what friends do."

Kenji smiled back at him. "Yes," he said softly. "Friends."

About the Author

Award-winning, multi-published author of erotic romance, Sedonia Guillone spends her days writing deliciously naughty romances—when she's not cuddling with the man she loves or watching kung fu and samurai films and eating chocolate.

Sedonia welcomes comments from readers. You can find her website and email address on her author bio page at www.sedoniaguillone.com.

Tell Us What You Think

We appreciate hearing reader opinions about our books. You can email us at Sedonia@sedoniaguillone.com.

Now Available at Ai Press

Aki's Love Song

Taming Kate